THE HUNDRED LIES OF LIZZIE LOVETT

THE HUNDRED LIES OF LIZZIE LOVETT

CHELSEA SEDOTI

sourcebooks
fire

Copyright © 2017 by Chelsea Sedoti
Cover and internal design © 2017 by Sourcebooks, Inc.
Cover design by Connie Gabbert
Cover photography by Tiffany Lausen

Sourcebooks and the colophon are registered trademarks of Sourcebooks, Inc.

Published by Sourcebooks Fire, an imprint of Sourcebooks, Inc.
P.O. Box 4410, Naperville, Illinois 60567-4410
(630) 961-3900
Fax: (630) 961-2168
www.sourcebooks.com

Library of Congress Cataloging-in-Publication data is on file with the publisher.

Printed and bound in the United States of America.
WOZ 10 9 8 7 6 5 4 3 2 1

FOR JOANNA BRUZZESE

CHAPTER 1

THE FIRST THING

❈ ❈

The first thing that happened was Lizzie Lovett disappeared, and everyone was all, "How can someone like Lizzie be missing?" and I was like, "Who cares?" A few days later, there was talk about Lizzie maybe being dead, and it was still kinda boring, but not totally boring, because I'd never known a dead person before.

After that, I started to get fascinated by the whole situation, mostly because I noticed a bunch of weird stuff. Which was how I figured out Lizzie Lovett's secret.

But I'm probably doing that thing again where I get ahead of myself and skip all over the place, which I'm trying to stop doing.

So the beginning, or the beginning for me at least, was when I found out Lizzie Lovett was missing. It happened like this:

It was Monday morning, and I needed an excuse to stay home. I was dreading school even more than usual, because the Welcome Back dance had been on Saturday, and I was probably the only senior at Griffin Mills High School who hadn't gone, and everyone would be talking about it while I sat there thinking, *Wow, I'm a loser.*

I figured I could pretend to be sick and stay home, and by Tuesday, all the dance story swapping would've died down. Then no one would ask why I hadn't gone, and I wouldn't have to roll my eyes and say, "High school events are so stupid and pointless." And no one would have to nod like they believed me, even though we all knew it was really because I hadn't been asked.

But maybe I wouldn't have to pretend to be sick, because my breakfast seemed more like silly putty than oatmeal and was quite possibly going to make me throw up.

"I don't think I can digest this," I said, using my spoon to make peaks and valleys.

My mom was washing dishes on the other side of the kitchen and didn't bother to look up.

I tried again. "What's wrong with pancakes? You could make them organic or vegan or whatever."

"I'm not having this discussion right now, Hawthorn."

"Or even better, we could drop being vegan completely, since it's clearly never going to stick."

Mom frowned, and I supposed I should shut up if I wanted to get out of school. So I sighed and shoveled a heaping spoonful of oatmeal putty into my mouth.

I immediately regretted it, because it was too much food and way too thick, and I wasn't going to be able to swallow. Or maybe I *would*, but the food would get stuck on the way down, and I'd choke and die right there at the kitchen table. Which would be a super unpleasant way to go. Food I could barely identify would be my last meal, and at my funeral, my mom would cry and say, "If only I'd made pancakes like Hawthorn wanted."

On the plus side, I wouldn't have to go to school.

But then everyone would be like, "Oh, poor Hawthorn, she was the only girl who wasn't asked to the Welcome Back dance, and now she's dead," and they'd think I was even *more* pathetic.

I forced myself to swallow. It was maybe, probably, the right thing to do. I glanced at my mom, but she hadn't even noticed my near-death experience. She was looking dreamily out the window as if there was something fascinating outside and not just the same boring view of the woods.

It was almost time to leave, so I started preparing my speech about it not being in my best interest to attend school that day. But before I could begin, Rush shuffled awkwardly down the hallway toward the kitchen. This immediately got my attention, because usually I'm the awkward one in the family.

Even on mornings when Rush was hungover, he managed to come across as an energetic superjock. The pale face and unfocused eyes and lumbering around were completely abnormal for him. I took a moment to assess the situation. Maybe he was sick. He certainly looked like he had a cold or a virus.

Rush opened his mouth, but no words came out. He seemed unsteady on his feet. Suddenly, I had this thought that maybe the virus was deadly—or worse than deadly. Maybe my brother had been turned into a zombie.

I glanced at my mom to see how she was taking this new development, but she was still lost in whatever world she goes to when she's ignoring me.

Rush hesitated in the doorway, giving me time to evaluate my options. Obviously, it was up to me to save both me and my mom, which I found slightly unfair. If I was smart, I'd leave her to fend for herself. But considering that she gave birth to me, it wouldn't be very nice to run off and let her be devoured by her only son. On the other hand, if I tried to save us both, there was a good chance I'd get bitten in the process, and then I'd have roughly twenty-four hours before I became a zombie too. And from what I've read, the process of turning into a zombie is totally painful.

Before I could take any kind of action, like trying to chop off Rush's head, he cleared his throat. I was taken aback. Generally, the undead aren't big communicators. Or so I've heard.

My mom looked over, and I could tell she knew something was up. She put down the plate she was washing. "Rush, what is it?"

I opened my mouth to tell her to keep her distance, but Rush started talking. I could accept a zombie clearing his throat, but talking was entirely out of character. Which meant I'd jumped the gun, and Rush probably wasn't undead after all.

What Rush said, while my mind was still filled with thoughts of zombieism, was, "Lizzie Lovett is missing."

I was disappointed. My zombie fantasy was ripped away for Lizzie Lovett of all people. I'd never been a member of the Lizzie Lovett fan club and didn't have much interest in her whereabouts. Not to mention, if my brother really *had* turned into a zombie, my boring life would've become way more exciting. Also, it would have probably gotten me out of school.

My mom said, "She's missing?"

Rush looked like he might cry. I couldn't remember the last time that had happened. He sighed and slumped into the seat across from me. My mom left the sink and joined us at the table. We were almost like a normal family having a normal breakfast. Almost.

"Are you really having an episode over a girl you haven't talked to in years?" I asked.

My mom gave me an unamused look, then turned to my brother with concern. "What happened, Rush?"

I could feel my chances of skipping school diminishing. But seriously, I was pretty sure Rush and Lizzie hadn't seen each other since their graduation.

"Whatever happened, I'm sure she's fine," I said. "This is Lizzie Lovett we're talking about."

Rush ignored me. He pulled his phone from his pocket and read my mom the texts he'd gotten from one of the guys who'd been on the football team with him, Kyle something-or-other.

Kyle something-or-other used to date Lizzie, which he figured was why Lizzie's mom called him, even though they'd broken up three years ago, right after their senior year. But Kyle guessed Lizzie's mom must be calling everyone she'd been close to, just in case. So she called and asked if he'd randomly heard from Lizzie, and of course, Kyle hadn't, because that would be weird, and she said to let her know if he did, and Kyle said OK and blah, blah, blah.

And that's how I found out Lizzie Lovett disappeared before it was even on the news.

"But missing from *where*, Rush?" my mom asked.

While Rush was taking eight million years to answer the question, my mind wandered back to zombies. I *enjoyed* the thought of my brother as a zombie. I quite frankly found it preferable to his actual personality. That probably meant something was very wrong with our sibling bond.

Rush was scrolling through his text messages and still hadn't answered the question, which was kind of annoying, because I was actually a little curious, which was even more annoying. I kicked him under the table. "Seriously. Are you going to tell us what happened or not?"

Rush put his phone down and glared at me. "I don't know details, OK? Lizzie and her boyfriend were camping, and this morning, he woke up, and she was gone."

Silence descended on the kitchen. I decided to say what all of us were certainly thinking. "Probably the most incredible part of the story is that Lizzie Lovett went *camping*."

My mom and Rush looked at me like I'd just admitted to bombing a kindergarten, and I realized, possibly, we *hadn't* all been thinking that same thing.

My mom reached across the table and took my hand. "Hawthorn, I really wish you'd find more compassionate ways to express yourself."

I was going to explain that I wasn't trying to be a jerk. I just didn't believe anything bad could really happen to a girl like Lizzie. That's not how her life worked.

But before I could respond, Rush asked, "Shouldn't you be in school?"

Traitor.

"About that." I smiled sweetly at my mom. "I was thinking I should probably stay home today."

"Were you?"

Lizzie going missing had given me a much better excuse than just being sick. "Yeah. To, you know, comfort Rush."

"Hawthorn, go to school."

"Seriously?"

Mom's expression told me she was quite serious. Like she might try to murder me if I made any attempt to resist. Which doesn't mean I didn't consider resisting, because I did. I knew it was pointless though.

I stood up but didn't move toward the door. Rush was staring at his phone like he was willing it to ring. As dumb as it seemed to me, he was really worried.

I sort of felt like I should hug him. Maybe tell him I was only messing around, and I was sorry Lizzie was missing, and I was sorry it made him sad.

But then I imagined Rush rolling his eyes and pushing me away and me slinking off to school, feeling like the biggest idiot in the world.

So instead, I grabbed my backpack and left my mom and brother sitting at the kitchen table talking quietly. About poor Lizzie Lovett, no doubt.

CHAPTER 2

DAY ONE

* *

The thing is, Lizzie Lovett's disappearance turned out to be a totally big deal, which I *almost* realized in my first period algebra II class but didn't *all the way* realize like I should have.

What happened was, I waited in the second floor bathroom until the bell rang. I figured if I showed up late to class, I could avoid the dance talk. And it totally worked, except for Mr. Bennett being all, "Is there a reason you're late, Miss Creely?" which was annoying but not as annoying as having to deal with my peers.

I hesitated, then decided to be honest. And by honest, I mean semihonest, since saying you were hiding in the bathroom to avoid ridicule is generally the kind of thing that opens you up to *more* ridicule.

"Yeah, there's a reason. Lizzie Lovett disappeared this morning, and my brother is totally freaked out about it, so I was trying to comfort him."

The classroom, which a second ago had been filled with normal classroom sounds, was suddenly completely silent. And everyone was staring at me like I'd run in screaming about the apocalypse.

I mentally reviewed what had come out of my mouth and was pretty sure I hadn't accidentally said something absurd. I started getting nervous. I shifted from one foot to the other. Seriously, what was the deal?

Then I got it. No one else knew yet.

"Lizzie Lovett?" Mr. Bennett asked.

"Uh, yeah. Lizzie. Disappeared."

From the front of the room, a painfully shrill voice asked, "Lizzie Lovett is *missing?*"

The voice belonged to Mychelle Adler, who I hated not just because of her nails-on-a-chalkboard voice, but also because she spelled her name with a *y*, though I guess that wasn't really her fault. Also, I hated Mychelle because in our four years of high school, asking about Lizzie was possibly the nicest thing she'd ever said to me.

I shrugged. "Yeah, I guess so."

Everyone kept staring, and I was getting more uncomfortable by the second. Sometimes at school—and by sometimes, I mean a lot of times—I feel as if I've turned invisible without realizing it. This makes me a bit panicky, and I get the urge to be outrageous—like jump on a table in the middle of the cafeteria and tap dance—just so people will look at me and prove I still exist. But that morning, being the complete focus of everyone's attention, I started to think maybe being invisible wasn't so bad after all.

"What exactly happened?" Mr. Bennett asked.

"Um, I don't really know. Something about Lizzie going camping, which if you ask me, sounds pretty far-fetched, but whatever. I guess she was with her boyfriend, and he woke up this morning, and Lizzie was gone."

Then everyone started talking and pulling out their phones to send texts, and there was this totally typical and boring moment where Mr. Bennett tried to regain control of the class. I took the opportunity to slip into my seat. Which was, unfortunately, right in front of Mychelle's.

Mychelle leaned forward as soon as I sat down. I could smell her strawberry lip gloss and expensive coconut shampoo she always bragged about. Though I had to admit, she did have absurdly glossy hair, so maybe the stupid shampoo worked. "What do you think happened to her, Hawthorn?"

I shrugged and didn't turn around. "I don't really care."

"*Seriously?*"

"Seriously."

"But she might be lost," Mychelle said.

"She might be."

"Or hurt."

"Or *both*," I said.

"What if she's dead?"

That's when I started to think bad thoughts. Like how I wished someone would replace Mychelle's fancy shampoo with a drug-store brand. I wished she would suddenly forget the name of her five favorite songs. I wished every time she microwaved a frozen burrito, the center would stay cold.

"*Hello?* Hawthorn? Don't you even care that a girl might be dead?"

I spun around in my seat and stared at Mychelle. "She's not dead. And even if she *was*, you don't care any more than I do. You're just looking for an opportunity to be melodramatic. Leave me out of it."

The dumb jock who sits next to Mychelle and whose name I could never remember scowled at me. "What's your problem, Hawthorn?"

"Yeah," Mychelle echoed, "what's your problem?"

This was a good question. What *was* my problem?

✹✹✹

Likely, part of my bad attitude was due to the fact that I really hated Lizzie Lovett. I'd always hated Lizzie, and her vanishing didn't change that.

"But is it just because I hate Lizzie?" I asked.

Emily Flynn, my best friend for the past million years, took a bite of her sandwich and got a serious look on her face—possibly because she was taking my situation super seriously, but probably because Emily looked serious most of the time.

It was lunch period, and we were sitting on the stairs that lead to the back entrance of the gym, which is where we always eat.

Lunch is when social interaction happens. Since the back staircase isn't really the place to be seen, no one goes there much. Exactly why Emily and I like it.

Emily still hadn't commented, but I plowed on anyway. "I mean, at first, I thought I was just in a bad mood because it's Monday and I'm tired and I'm the only person in the school who didn't go to the dance—"

"I didn't go to the dance," Emily interrupted.

"But it's not just that, is it?" I went on. "And it's not *just* that I hate Lizzie. So why am I so bothered by this whole thing?"

"Because you're jealous."

For a second, I was too stunned to speak. "Because I'm *what*?"

"Jealous. You've always been jealous of Lizzie," Emily said, as if it was the simplest, most reasonable explanation in the world.

Obviously, aliens must have abducted Emily and thought she was such a good specimen that they couldn't bear to part with her, so they took her to their planet and put a pod person in her place.

I was wondering how I might contact the mother ship about returning my friend to her earthly body when a new thought occurred to me. "I think what's bothering me is that everyone is making such a big deal over nothing."

Emily tilted her head and looked at me strangely. "I don't think a girl mysteriously disappearing is *nothing*."

"It's *nothing*, because it's Lizzie Lovett."

"What are you talking about?"

I opened a bag of potato chips, only briefly considering how disappointed my mom would be if she caught me consuming empty calories. She'd probably rather find me with drugs. "It's like this, Em. Nothing bad will ever happen to a girl like Lizzie. The world doesn't work that way. The biggest problem she'll ever have is, I don't know, whether to match her shoes to her eyeshadow."

"First of all, who matches their makeup to their outfit anymore?" Emily asked, wrinkling her nose and brushing nonexistent crumbs off her blouse. "And second, you're saying *what* exactly? Some people live charmed lives, and nothing tragic can happen to them?"

"I guess so."

"That's really stupid."

I put another chip in my mouth and crunched loudly, knowing how much it bugged her. "It's true though. Some people are just lucky."

"Let me guess. You think you're one of the unlucky ones?" A smile pulled at the corner of Emily's mouth, which I instantly resented.

"No. That's not what I'm saying. This isn't about me."

Emily raised her eyebrows.

"It's not," I insisted.

Emily shrugged. "If you say so."

We ate in silence for a moment. Rather, I ate while Emily pulled strands of her hair in front of her eyes and examined the ends. As if she'd ever had a split end in her entire life.

Eventually, I had to ask. "What do *you* think happened to her?"

"I thought you didn't care where Lizzie was."

I didn't. Mostly. I smiled sheepishly at Emily. "Well, pretend for a minute I do."

"Maybe she got in a fight with her boyfriend and left. That's what most people think."

"Poor guy," I said.

"Can we stop talking about Lizzie for a minute?"

I put down my bag of chips. I could tell when Emily had something important to say. "Yeah, of course."

"I got a letter about that music composition program. I'm a finalist."

I'm not one of those girls who squeals and hugs her friends all the time, but in certain cases, I make exceptions. Emily laughed and hugged me back.

"This is so exciting! Why didn't you tell me right away?"

"It's not for sure yet. I'm only a finalist."

I rolled my eyes. "You're going to get accepted. I know it."

"We'll see. This is really big. It could help me get a jump start on the rest of my life."

I was glad one of us was thinking about the future.

"This is awesome, Em. I'm really proud of you."

Emily smiled, and I could tell she was proud of herself too, even if she'd never in a million years admit it.

"Do you want to come over after school?" I asked. "We can celebrate."

"There's nothing to celebrate yet."

"Then we can watch the news reports about Lizzie and make up elaborate theories."

If Lizzie was even still missing by then.

"I can't. Piano lesson."

"Oh, right." I was disappointed, even if the news probably wouldn't have new information, and Emily wasn't good at making up theories anyway.

"You should come to the library with me after school tomorrow though. We have that report due on Friday."

The report on the Mills. I'd forgotten. "Yeah, I guess I should."

Then the bell rang, and lunch was over, and Emily and I gathered up our things. I wanted to say more, maybe something about how I was super happy about her music program but a little sad that we might not have one last summer together. And how maybe I *was* a little jealous of Lizzie Lovett and that I appreciated Emily not judging me because of it. And probably something about how she was a really good friend. Instead, I told Emily I'd see her in fifth period and went to my English composition class.

★★★

The first day Lizzie was missing, everyone talked about the disappearance without actually knowing the facts. By the time the final bell rang, I'd heard more about Lizzie Lovett than I had since we were in school together. Which I guess worked out, because no one talked to me about the dance.

I walked home from school, because I hadn't been able to find my car keys that morning. Also because my Volkswagen Rabbit was making huffing noises again. Someday, it'll explode while I'm driving, and my mom will tell people, "I told Hawthorn not to get that old car. I told her we'd buy her something nicer like we did for her brother, but she just never listens," and then the last thing people will ever think about me is that I'm stubborn and made stupid mistakes.

I could have taken the school bus home, but I consider that a last resort. Being in a cramped space with lots of people who all have something to talk about with each other while you're sitting there alone is totally awkward. Also, there are no seat belts on the bus, which has never made sense to me.

Luckily, I don't live far from Griffin Mills High School. In a place as small as the Mills, nothing is very far from anything else. Really, the town is just a bigger version of high school, which is just a bigger version of the bus. Lots of people packed together for their entire lives, all having things to do and people to talk to, and if you're not a part of it, you feel totally broken.

My family should have lived in Pittsburgh. My dad drives forty-five minutes to get there five days a week. Wouldn't it be better to live closer to the place he worked? My parents were pretty opposed to the idea though. My mom had all this stuff to say about a "better quality of life" and whatnot. A better quality of life for her, I guess. Not for me. If I'd grown up in a big city, everything could have been different.

Cities let you blend in. There are so many people that it doesn't matter if you're weird or if no one likes you, because there's probably someone even worse off. And if you're really lucky, you might even meet people who are weird in the exact same way you are and feel like you've finally found a place where you fit in.

There was no chance of that happening in Griffin Mills. I was convinced there was a secret factory somewhere in town, spitting out people from a mold. And I came out defective.

But I only had one more year, and then I could go far away from the Mills. Not that I'd actually made any plans yet.

The walk home mostly takes me through residential areas. The houses close to school are ancient—crumbling Victorians with wraparound porches and turrets that look out on the Ohio River. It used to be where the rich people lived, but that was a long time ago. The farther you go west, the newer the Mills gets. Then all of a sudden, the neighborhoods end, and there's only dense woods and occasional farms.

My house is near the edge of town. It's a typical 1950s house, two stories with white siding and dark-blue trim. The street it's on, the street I've lived on for my entire life, dead-ends in a patch of woods. There are no fences in my neighborhood, just trees separating one house from another. It makes the area seem more isolated than it is but not as isolated as one of those old farmhouses. Which is a good thing. I know what sort of stuff can happen at a lonely farmhouse in the middle of the night. I read *In Cold Blood* for freshman English.

At home, I found my mom and Rush sitting in front of the TV, watching a local news station.

"Anything new?" I asked.

"Not yet," my mom said. "The search party is still out."

I tossed my backpack on the floor and sat in an armchair, my legs dangling over the side. "She couldn't have gotten that far. I mean, it's not like we're dealing with someone exceptionally bright."

"Hawthorn," my mom said with her warning tone.

"Lizzie's mom is about to talk," Rush said. He grabbed the remote and turned the volume up enough to drown me out.

I hadn't planned on watching the news with my family. I didn't really want to spend my afternoon watching Lizzie Lovett's mom cry on TV and ask for help finding her daughter, or wait for updates radioed in from the search party. But it's not like I had much else going on. And besides, I was mildly curious.

CHAPTER 3

FRESHMAN YEAR

❋ ❋

I couldn't sleep that night, which is something that happens
more often than I'd like. How it usually goes is I'm tired and
lay down, but suddenly, my mind is racing, so I go over everything
that happened during the day and all the ways it could have happened better than it actually did.

On the first night Lizzie Lovett was missing, I gave up on sleep
pretty fast. I got out of bed and climbed onto the bench in front
of my window. There aren't any streetlights in my neighborhood,
but the moon was full, so I could see clearly. Not that anything was
happening outside. Was everyone in all the other houses asleep, or
did some of them have insomnia too? I bet Lizzie was sleeping like
a baby, wherever she was.

It was annoying, the way my thoughts kept returning to Lizzie.
She had enough people obsessing over her. I didn't need to add
to the Lizzie worship. But the more I tried to push her out of my
mind, the more impossible it became. Stuff I hadn't thought about
for years kept popping into my head.

Like the first time I saw her.

It was a pretty weird thing to remember, but I did. I was in sixth grade, and my parents forced me to go to one of Rush's freshman football games. I thought it unfair, because he never had to attend any of my activities. But when I brought that up, Rush was like, "What am I supposed to do, sit there and watch you *read*?"

At the game, Lizzie was cheerleading, and she wasn't very good. Her jumps and tumbles were sloppy. Once, she forgot the entire second half of a cheer. But even though she sucked, everyone was watching her. You *had* to watch her. She was so pretty and loud and happy that it didn't matter how much she screwed up. There wasn't one other girl in the stadium who had as much charisma as Lizzie Lovett.

The other cheerleaders were looking at each other instead of at the crowd, trying to stay in sync. Every time there was a break, a bunch of them pulled out compacts and checked their hair and makeup. They were so obviously worrying what people thought of them. What made Lizzie different was that she didn't care. She was grinning and having fun. She was happy.

Instead of paying attention to the game that night, my eyes were on Lizzie Lovett as she smiled and laughed and joked with her friends. And I wanted what she had. I wanted her charisma. I wanted to be that comfortable in my own skin. I wanted to have a high school experience that was as much fun as hers seemed to be.

Clearly, we don't always get what we wish for.

Lizzie and I didn't talk until a few years later, when I was a freshman. It was so early in the year that I still hadn't memorized my locker combination—though I seemed to be the only one in school having that particular struggle.

I also seemed to be the only person who had no friends.

Everyone else was excited about being in high school and embarking on a new journey and all that, but I was pretty depressed. Not only because no one would talk to me, but because I was starting to realize being in high school didn't actually make you any smarter or cooler than you were in eighth grade. You were the same person, just in a new environment where you didn't know the rules.

On the very worst day of my freshman year, I hid in the gym's locker room during lunch period. I hadn't expected anyone to be there. I certainly didn't think Lizzie Lovett would be sitting on one of the benches, talking on her cell phone. But there she was.

I instantly felt awkward, like I was interrupting a private moment. Which meant the polite thing would be to turn around and leave. Except I was already halfway down the bank of lockers when I noticed her, and running away would probably have made me seem even more awkward.

So instead, I stood paralyzed in the middle of the room—which was probably the most awkward option of all.

Lizzie glanced up at me. Our eyes met. I wanted to disappear.

Instead, I forced myself to sit down on a bench and rifled through my backpack like I was looking for something.

Even if I hadn't gone to Rush's football games, I would have known Lizzie. Every single person at Griffin Mills High School knew who she was. And now I was the weird freshman who invaded her space and eavesdropped on her conversations.

"Well, I was planning on it," Lizzie said into the phone. She sounded angry. I wondered who she was talking to. One of her many admirers, I guessed. They were probably fighting over something super incredibly important.

"God, Mom, I know."

Or maybe not. It was weird to think of Lizzie Lovett doing something as ordinary as calling her mom during lunch.

"OK, fine. Yeah. *OK*. Love you too. Bye."

Lizzie sighed deeply and tossed her phone into her purse. Of course she would carry a purse instead of a backpack.

I was still pretending to dig through my own bag. It suddenly seemed oversized and childish. At least it wasn't the *Alice in Wonderland* backpack I'd had the previous year, the one I thought was so cool until my brother made fun of it.

"Aren't you Rush Creely's little sister?" Lizzie asked.

It took me a moment to realize she was talking to me. Which was pretty absurd, because Rush only has one sister.

"Uh, yeah."

Lizzie nodded. I waited for her to say more. She didn't. She didn't get up to leave the locker room either.

I wondered if I should start looking through my backpack

again. Or say something about Rush. Or slink away while hoping she didn't notice.

"Sorry if I interrupted your call," I finally said.

"You didn't. It wasn't, like, private or anything."

"Oh. Cool."

Silence again. *Why wasn't she leaving? Was she waiting for me to leave?*

"What are you doing in here?" Lizzie asked.

I figured I should make up some awesome and elaborate story that explained why I was in the locker room, rifling clumsily through my backpack. The reason would be really great, and the story would make me sound cool, and then Lizzie would respect me.

"I'm sort of hiding," I said instead.

"From what?"

"My friends."

Lizzie shrugged as if it wasn't a big deal at all. She seemed vaguely bored. I wished she would stop looking at me, because her gaze made me feel like I was taking up all the space in the room, sucking up all the air.

I looked down at my backpack. I looked at the locker room door. I looked at Lizzie, who was still looking at me.

"I guess I kind of screwed up," I said, because I had to say something. "My friend Amy had this thing happen…this thing with a teacher."

"Oh my God," Lizzie said, her face lighting up. "You're friends with the girl who was hooking up with Mr. Kaminski?"

"Yeah. I mean, I *was*. Not anymore. I was sort of the one who spilled the beans."

"Really?" Lizzie scooted down the bench closer to me.

"I didn't mean to," I said.

I had no intention of telling Lizzie how I'd been pretty sure I saw Mr. Kaminski on a TV show about fugitives and thought he was the guy who bombed that bridge in Pennsylvania, and how when I saw Amy getting into his car, I assumed it was because he was trying to get her to join his rebel cause and go on a suicide mission or something.

That was the only reason I'd called Amy's mom to tell her about it. I hadn't imagined Amy might be *sleeping* with him. Which, honestly, was maybe as disturbing as her becoming a suicide bomber, because Mr. Kaminski is not an attractive man.

Later, after everything got crazy and the whole school was talking about the secret relationship, Emily asked me why, if I was sure Mr. Kaminski was a terrorist, I called Amy's mom instead of the police. Which was a really good question. One I didn't have an answer to.

"I heard they started fooling around in, like, July or something," Lizzie said.

"Yeah. Amy was taking this summer class. Getting ahead with her credits."

Lizzie laughed. "And she ending up dropping out of school instead."

"She didn't drop out exactly. Her mom is sending her to private school."

"Well, you were right to say something."

Lizzie pulled out her phone and checked her messages, which was good, because it meant she didn't see the look on my face. The look that said I was surprised and totally thrilled that she thought I'd been right.

"I wish other people thought so. All my friends hate me."

"So make new friends," Lizzie said.

I glanced over to see if she was joking, but she wasn't. As if making friends was that simple. Maybe for her, it was.

Lizzie didn't have any idea what it was like to be a regular person. In her world, she was the one calling the shots. She got to decide what was cool and what was worth worrying about and who she'd be friends with. I wondered what it felt like to have all that power. Did she even realize she had it? Probably not. Girls like her were oblivious.

"Everyone hates me," I said. "The whole school is talking about what I did."

"Look, it's not that big of a deal, OK? So your friend fucked a teacher. So you told some people. Who cares?"

"Um. It seems like a lot of people care."

"Listen, Little Creely," Lizzie said matter-of-factly, "none of this matters."

"Are you sure?" I asked, hating how insecure I sounded.

"You did what you thought you had to do. Stand by it."

I wanted life to be as straightforward as she made it sound, as straightforward as it apparently was for her.

"You'll get through this," Lizzie said, standing up to go.

I wanted to ask her to stay, to tell me over and over again that everything was going to be OK. Instead, I said, "Thanks for the advice."

"It's nothing. Anytime."

Then she left. But her words stuck with me.

Anytime.

Though I knew it was probably just something she said to be nice, I got a weird thought in my head. Maybe Lizzie really wanted to help me. Maybe she was someone I could talk to about my problems without her judging me.

I had this image of a Lizzie who wouldn't tell me I was crazy if I suspected Mr. Kaminski had bombed that bridge. She wouldn't even flinch if I said I didn't *actually* think he was a terrorist, that it just popped into my head and almost made sense, so I said it out loud. That even as I was calling Amy's mom, I knew I was doing something stupid, but I couldn't stop myself.

I could tell her how disconnected I felt since starting high school. How suddenly life was all about dances and football games and who was hooking up with who, and I didn't know how to be a part of that world and just wanted things to go back to the way they used to be. I wanted friends who talked about characters from books like they were real people, friends who would make up elaborate games with me because anything we imagined was better than something that already existed. I wanted friends who loved me even if I didn't wear the right clothes or know the lyrics to the right songs or have crushes on the right celebrities.

Maybe I could even tell Lizzie it seemed as if everyone else wanted a completely different life than the one I dreamed about and how lonely that made me feel. I wanted more than high school, then college, then some stupid job I didn't care about. I wanted to be swept away on a magical adventure. But so far, I was still waiting for that to happen, and I was starting to suspect I'd be waiting forever. And maybe Lizzie would look me in the eyes and say, "Little Creely, I know *exactly* what you mean."

Lizzie could teach me how to ignore all the people who thought I was broken and strange. She'd teach me how to fit in, how to be likable. How to be like *her*. She'd take me under her wing so it wouldn't matter what I said or did, because if I had her approval, I'd have everyone's. Even if no one else understood me, *she* would. We could dream together.

Even at the time, I knew it was stupid to imagine Lizzie as some kindred-spirit/mentor person. But I couldn't stop my train of thought. That's why, when I went to the locker room during lunch the next day, I was kind of hoping Lizzie would be waiting there for me.

She wasn't, but Emily was.

"I've been looking for you," she said.

"You're speaking to me again?"

"I never stopped speaking to you."

Technically, this was true. She might have tried calling, but I'd turned off my cell phone and told my mom I was never talking to anyone from school ever again. I said it was because I didn't want everyone telling me how much they hated me and threatening my life. But really, I was most afraid of turning my phone back on and finding out no one had tried to get ahold of me at all.

I sat down on the bench next to Emily.

"Do you want to talk?" she asked.

"There's not much to talk about. I really messed up."

"No, Mr. Kaminski messed up."

"Then why is everyone so mad at me?"

"*Amy* is mad at you," Emily said. "Everyone else just likes to gossip."

That didn't change the fact that I could feel people staring at me when I walked down the hall and hear them whispering behind my back. It didn't change the fact that I'd pretty much ruined my chances of having a normal high school experience. I would always be the girl who couldn't keep a secret.

"What about the terrorist thing?" I asked Emily.

"Well. That part was stupid."

"I just wanted something interesting to happen."

"You got your wish," Emily said, laughing a little.

"No. Not like this. I mean I wanted to uncover a terrorist plot and save the school seconds before we were all blown to pieces or something."

"I know. That's not how the world works though."

"The world sucks."

"Come on," said Emily, standing up.

"I can't go back to the cafeteria."

"We'll find somewhere else to eat."

"Won't you miss everyone?"

"Believe me, Hawthorn, I don't fit in with them any more than you do."

So we left the locker room, and though I was happy to have Emily on my side, I couldn't stop thinking of Lizzie. I pictured her going to the locker room, expecting to find me but being disappointed when I wasn't there. I wondered what would happen when we ran into each other again.

I didn't see Lizzie for nearly a week, which gave me plenty of time to build up our connection in my head. I was running down the hall, late for the bus, when I passed Lizzie at her locker with some of the other cheerleaders.

I didn't want to approach while she was with her friends, but it didn't seem like a better opportunity was going to present itself. Pushing aside my fear of the bus leaving without me, I walked up to Lizzie.

"Hi," I said.

I could immediately tell it was a mistake, because Lizzie gave me a blank look, as if she'd never seen me before.

"Who are you?" asked one of the other cheerleaders.

"I, um..."

Who was I? The girl from the locker room? The girl who snitched on a creepy teacher? The awkward girl with no friends? I couldn't think of a single way to describe myself without sounding like a complete loser.

"Oh, right, Little Creely," Lizzie said after a moment. "This is Rush's sister."

I guess that was my answer. I was a footnote in the book of Rush.

One of the girls nudged Lizzie. "Are you using Creely's sister to get close to him?"

Everyone giggled. Except me.

"Yeah, right," Lizzie said, rolling her eyes. "Like I'd need an excuse."

"He's totally in love with you," said the brunette cheerleader who was always two feet behind Lizzie, like she was being pulled by a leash. The other girls nodded.

"Who isn't?" asked another girl, and they all laughed. Lizzie didn't bother denying it.

In the locker room, alone with Lizzie, I'd felt too big for my skin. In the hallway with her friends, I felt tiny. So small that I was barely visible. A speck of dust. Little Creely.

Their conversation, centered entirely on Lizzie, continued around me. I stood there, shrinking more and more every moment.

None of the girls were paying attention to me, and I didn't know what to do. I had just decided to walk away when Lizzie fixed her eyes on me and asked, "Did you want something?" as if finally remembering I was there.

Yes, I wanted something. I wanted her to like me. I wanted her to be my friend. I wanted her to make me cool.

"Um…"

Everyone stared at me, waiting. I knew my face must be red.

"Well?" Lizzie prompted.

It would have been easier if she had been mean to me. Then I could say she was a terrible person and shrug off the incident. It was her indifference that hurt the most. I didn't mean anything to her. The locker room conversation had been nothing more than a way to pass the time. She hardly remembered it—or me. I was insignificant.

"It's nothing," I said and slunk away.

Behind my back, I heard one of the girls say, "*She's* related to Rush?"

And everyone laughed. Even Lizzie.

By the time I got outside, the bus had left. I walked home, burning with shame the entire way. I knew I would never speak to Lizzie again. I vowed not to think about her. For the rest of the year, the rest of the time we were in high school together, I pretended Lizzie Lovett didn't exist.

But I couldn't completely block her out. Every once in a while, I'd pass her in the halls, laughing with her friends, carefree and enjoying every second of her charmed life. Then the bitterness would creep in, and I'd wonder why she got to have it so easy.

The thing is, Emily was right. I *was* jealous of Lizzie, but not of how pretty and popular and perfect she was. I envied Lizzie's *happiness*. It seemed unfair that she should have so much of it when other people had so little.

I still cringed when I remembered how naive I'd been, thinking Lizzie and I had some special connection.

In between my last conversation with Lizzie and her disappearance, three years had passed. After the situation with Mr. Kaminski blew over, I went through high school mostly unscathed. Sure, I never really made new friends, but I had Emily, and that was enough. Lizzie graduated and moved away. She was part of another life, one that only vaguely resembled the one I was living now.

But still, her disappearance was enough to turn back the clock and make me an embarrassed, awkward freshman again. It didn't matter that it had happened a long time ago. I would always hate Lizzie for the way she made me feel in the hall that day.

Like I was nothing at all.

I looked out the window at my dark neighborhood, willing myself to think of something else, anything else, but I couldn't get

Lizzie off my mind. I wondered where she was. If she was happy. How long it would be before she turned up.

Mostly, I just wanted Lizzie to be found so I could go back to not thinking of her.

There was another part of me though, a very small part, that wanted her to stay missing a while longer. Not that I hated her so much that I wanted her to be lost or in pain, but it was kinda nice to have a mystery in the Mills. Once it was solved, the explanation was sure to be totally boring, like when you read a whodunit and end up wishing you'd stopped before you got to the end. The truth was always a letdown.

Besides, when Lizzie eventually showed up, it was going to be a huge deal. The town would celebrate, and everyone would act like Lizzie's homecoming was the biggest miracle that had ever happened. When it came down to it, I'd rather listen to speculation about Lizzie's whereabouts than watch everyone worship her when she returned. I'd already experienced enough Lizzie worship to last a lifetime.

CHAPTER 4

THE NEW LIZZIE

* *

On the morning *after* the morning Lizzie disappeared, there was a big article about her on the front page of the *Griffin Mills Daily Journal*. The paper was sitting on the kitchen table when I went downstairs, and I figured I'd hear people talking about it at school all day, which is why I almost ignored it. But my curiosity got the best of me.

My family wasn't around, so I sat down and grabbed the paper without them making annoying comments about how they thought I wasn't interested in Lizzie.

I didn't read the article at first, because it was impossible to pay attention to anything other than Lizzie's photo, which was obnoxiously big. In it, Lizzie was staring straight at the camera with a half smile on her face. The sun was behind her, making her hair into a halo. It was Lizzie all right, pretty Lizzie Lovett. But she wasn't how I remembered her.

Where was the cheerleader who always looked like she was on her way to a photo shoot? This Lizzie wasn't wearing any makeup.

Her long hair was messy, as if she hadn't bothered to comb it. She was wearing a loose-fitting men's dress shirt, which was nothing like the clothes she wore in high school, meaning you couldn't see her perfect body at all.

This new Lizzie was almost more annoying than the old one. You could imagine old Lizzie waking up three hours early every day to make sure her eyeliner was expertly smudged and the ends of her hair had just the right amount of curl. You could tell yourself that old Lizzie spent her free time exercising and tanning and moisturizing, and that was why she looked as perfect as she did. That if you were willing to dedicate the same attention to your appearance, you could look "effortlessly" gorgeous too.

The Lizzie who stared out from the front page of the paper actually *hadn't* put in any effort, and she was about a thousand times prettier than she'd ever been before.

I directed my attention to the article and skimmed it, even though I was pretty sure it wouldn't say anything new, which turned out to be correct. Elizabeth Lovett, twenty-one years old and formerly of Griffin Mills, Ohio, had gone camping in the woods off Wolf Creek Road. She'd been with her boyfriend, Lorenzo Calvetti, twenty-five, of Layton, which was two towns over. They hiked, set up camp, made s'mores, and all that jazz. According to Calvetti, everything seemed normal; his girlfriend seemed happy. They went to bed around ten. The next morning, Lizzie was gone.

I flipped to page three where the article continued. There was another photo, smaller and in black and white. It was also way more fascinating than the one on the front page, because it showed the new, disheveled Lizzie with her arm around Lorenzo Calvetti.

I brought the paper closer to my face. It was a pretty terrible picture, taken from far away and too grainy to show many details. But you could see the huge grins on Lizzie's and Lorenzo's faces. They looked like the sort of couple who never had a single bad thing happen to them, certainly not the sort of couple in which one member disappears in the woods.

"Is that article about Lizzie?"

I jumped.

Rush hovered in the kitchen doorway, still looking a little undead.

"Don't sneak up on me."

My brother shrugged and sat in the chair across from me. He nodded at the paper. "What do you think?"

"He's not as handsome as I expected him to be." I glanced down at the picture again. "Actually, he's not really handsome at all."

"Not about him. I don't care about him," Rush said, which was certainly a lie.

"I bet they'll find her today," I said.

"Or find her body," Rush said darkly.

I rolled my eyes. "She's not dead. And even if she was, what's it to you?"

He didn't answer, so I went back to the article. There wasn't much more to read. A search party had gone through the woods near the camp. Today, they'd be expanding their area of focus. There was a list of Lizzie's stats at the end, twenty-one years old, five feet six inches tall, one hundred and twenty pounds. Blond hair, blue eyes. Last seen wearing jeans, a red sweatshirt, hiking boots, and a pendant in the shape of a wolf's tooth. Then the obligatory plea to call the police with any information that might assist them, blah, blah, blah.

I tossed the paper on the table and wondered about the wolf pendant.

"You already read it?" I asked Rush.

"Online."

"Then you saw the picture."

"She looks different, huh?"

"What happened to her after high school?" I asked.

"Don't know. I haven't seen her since the graduation parties. I don't think anyone's seen her."

"She moved to Layton, not Africa. Certainly, someone has hung out with her."

"If they have, they didn't tell me."

Maybe that's how it was after high school. Maybe you just left and became someone new. That gave me hope for the future.

I stood up. "Wanna get a breakfast burrito with me before mom tries to feed us soy sausage?"

Rush hesitated, and I had time to imagine that he'd say yes, and we'd leave the house to get drive-through and sit eating greasy burritos in the parking lot, talking and laughing like we used to when he was just Rushford Creely, my big brother, before all the distance in the social hierarchy came between us.

But that didn't happen, because it was real life, not some feel-good movie. What actually happened was Rush said he wasn't really hungry, maybe some other time. It wasn't a big deal. A burrito tastes good even if you're eating it alone.

✹ ✹ ✹

The second day of the disappearance, I was prepared for the drama at school, so I wasn't surprised when I heard Lizzie Lovett's name roughly ten times before the first bell rang. Everyone seemed to have their own opinion of what had happened to her.

I think she ran away to start a new life somewhere. Like, one day we'll be watching a movie, and she'll be the lead actress, only her name won't be Lizzie Lovett anymore, and she'll never talk about her past.

I think her boyfriend killed her. Did you see the picture of him? Total creeper.

I heard she was working as a waitress at some dive in Layton. How pathetic. I'd run away too.

My cousin knows a detective working the case, and he said she might have gone into the woods to go the bathroom or something and got ripped to shreds by a wild animal.

I half listened but mostly didn't care, because the people I go to school with pretty much have no imagination.

I was especially not surprised that Mychelle Adler and the nameless jock were talking about Lizzie in first period. While Mr. Bennett collected our homework, they droned on and on behind me.

"She looks totally different," Mychelle whispered.

"Still hot," the jock said.

"If you're into that kind of thing, I guess. My sister's boyfriend has a friend who ran into Lizzie at a concert, like, a year ago, and he said Lizzie was saying all this weird stuff about how people need to connect with nature and open their eyes to what's really important, like she's some kind of flower child now."

I knew what was coming next, like it was scripted and we were performing in a play. Exactly on cue, the jock leaned over his desk and said, "Maybe Hawthorn can tell us more about that. Huh, Hawthorn? How's Sparrow doing?"

Mychelle laughed as if it was the most hilarious thing anyone had ever said, which it clearly was not. I ignored them and hoped Mr. Bennett would hurry up and start class.

It's not fair that kids get made fun of for the stupid choices their parents make. For example, changing their name from Meredith to Sparrow, which is even more embarrassing than being named Hawthorn. My mom said it's the name her spirit mentor gave her when she was in college at Kent State, a school she chose because it was "important to the movement" after some hippie kids were shot there while protesting the Vietnam War. My mom is too young to have been a *real* hippie. She missed out on all the sit-ins and peace marches, which I'm pretty sure is something she's always resented, even though she claims that resentment is a negative emotion, and she purges negativity from her life.

Sometimes, I wonder what it would be like to have a normal mom. A mom who'd tell my friends to call her Mrs. Creely, not *Sparrow*. A mom who always wore a bra, had pictures of Jesus in the house instead of Buddha statues, and took real classes in college, not Intro to Basket Weaving and How to Ruin Your Child's Life 101.

It also isn't fair that Rush never got made fun of for having a hippie mom. That leads me to believe I'm not actually being taunted because my mom made a stupid choice, but because people are looking for any reason to mess with me. Which is much worse.

Mychelle didn't know when to let a joke die. "Maybe Lizzie and Sparrow are, like, running around the woods naked and communicating with tree spirits at this very moment."

"I wouldn't mind seeing that," the jock said.

I wished Mychelle and her stupid jock buddy would win the lottery and lose the ticket. I wished they would only ever be able to take cold showers. I wished every glass of lemonade they drank for the rest of their lives would be just a little too sour.

Before my list of curses could get any longer, Mr. Bennett cleared his throat and started class. Mychelle and the jock leaned back in their seats and forgot about me. For once, I was happy to hear about equations.

✸✸✸

Emily was waiting by my car after school, which was weird until I remembered we were supposed to go to the library together. I wasn't in the mood. I wished I'd walked to school instead of driving. That's what I got for wanting a burrito.

"You forgot, didn't you?" Emily said.

I sighed melodramatically. "This paper is so stupid, Em. The whole thing is stupid. I don't see why we're spending an entire quarter on Ohio's history anyway. Nothing interesting has ever happened here."

"Well, maybe you should make that the focus of your paper," Emily said, laughing. She opened the passenger door of my Rabbit, which she could do before I unlocked it, because my locks haven't worked for well over a year.

My car has a lot of idiosyncrasies like that, things my parents would refer to as broken but I call quirks. My mom was always pointing them out to me because she really wanted me to regret buying the car. She couldn't get that I *wanted* a car that was a little broken. When something starts out perfect, it usually lets me down.

That's why I never mind the broken locks or it taking four tries before my car sputters to life.

"I can't believe this thing is still running," Emily said.

I sighed. "I can't believe I'm about to spend my afternoon at the library researching Griffin Mills."

✸✸✸

It turned out that by "researching Griffin Mills" I really meant sitting at a table with a stack of books in front of me and whispering to Emily, who was *actually* trying to research Griffin Mills.

Emily had a notebook open and was using one hand to jot down bits of information while the other hand twisted the strand of pearls around her neck. The pearls were something Emily got teased about, along with her sweater sets and penny loafers. At some fancy boarding school, she probably would have fit in just fine, but the Mills doesn't have much tolerance for sophistication.

Sometimes, I wondered how Emily became so cultured. Her parents own a drugstore. They aren't the kind of people who know what's playing on Broadway or what wine goes with what entrée. But I guess I'm not all that much like my parents either, so maybe it's not that weird.

"I just keep wondering about him," I said to Emily.

"Who?" she asked, her eyes not moving from the book in front of her.

"*Him.* Lorenzo Calvetti."

Emily looked up at me, clearly drawing a blank.

"Lizzie's boyfriend."

"Oh, jeez, Hawthorn. Let it go." She went back to making notes in her neat, cramped cursive.

"He didn't look special. Just a regular boy. Man, I guess, not boy. The paper said he's twenty-five. But there was something boyish about him, you know? Anyway, I keep thinking he *must* be special for Lizzie to be with him."

Emily looked up again. "I know plenty of guys Lizzie has been with, and there's not a special one in the bunch."

"Really? Like who? She dated that Kyle guy through most of high school, didn't she?"

"I can't believe we're having this conversation. This is stupid gossip."

"People I know? From when we were in high school together?" Then a thought struck. "My brother?"

Emily sighed. "I don't know, Hawthorn. I shouldn't have said anything. I don't think I ever heard about her and Rush."

"They were in the same clique. I think he was in love with her. Or *in lust* with her at least."

"Look. I'm really trying to get my work done, OK? I don't care who some girl who used to go to our school *might* have slept with."

"I don't care either. I was just making conversation," I said.

Emily raised her eyebrows. I decided to busy myself with the stack of books in front of me. I grabbed one about the Ohio canals, which a lot of people have never heard of. I found the section that mentioned the Mills and almost started reading.

"Those guys *were* special though. The guys like Kyle or even Rush. Not that they're super interesting or bright, but they're talented in their own athletic way. They look like models, and everyone loves them."

"Not me. Or you."

"But you understand what I mean. Lorenzo Calvetti isn't like them."

Emily slammed her book shut, and the people around us turned to stare. That's how I knew I'd crossed a line. Emily wasn't one for public displays of emotion.

"Hawthorn, you're my best friend, and I'm glad you found something to care about so deeply. But I don't have a parent who teaches at a university. I don't have guaranteed acceptance into a good school. I work hard to keep my grades above average, and right now, I just want to do my research paper, not talk about Lizzie Lovett."

I felt my face flush. "You're right. I should go."

"You probably should."

"Will you be able to get a ride home later?"

"It's fine. Just go."

"Why can't we do the research online anyway?"

"I'll see you tomorrow, Hawthorn."

I walked out of the library with my shoulders slumped and decided the incident was one more reason to hate Lizzie.

✖✖✖

Both Rush and I were pushing food around on our plates instead of eating. I was doing it because I wasn't a fan of Indian food. I suspected Rush still had no appetite because he was pouting over Lizzie.

"Then he goes on to argue that putting Clarence on the throne would have actually kept the Plantagenets in power," my dad was saying.

My mom chuckled like my dad's student was totally absurd, but I was pretty sure she didn't actually know or care one way or another. She was probably thinking about her garden.

"So I reminded him Clarence had been off his rocker for years and drowning in Malmsey was a better end than he deserved."

"Malmsey?" my mom asked, though I was sure my dad had told this story before.

"A type of wine. See, George of Clarence was quite the drinker. So when his brother, King Edward, ordered him executed for treason—"

"My car is making really weird noises."

"Hawthorn! Your father was talking," my mom said.

"Sorry. I guess I don't feel like talking about Edward IV all night."

Sometimes, I felt like I knew Edward IV better than I knew my dad. I'd heard the story about his brother, George, drowning in a barrel of wine. Just like I'd heard all about their other brother, Richard, the hunchbacked murderer. These were the bedtime stories I grew up with. I didn't get how my dad could give lectures on medieval history all day and still have energy to talk about it at home.

But maybe he *did* get bored with it, because instead of being annoyed with me like my mom, he said, "It's fine, Sparrow. I'm sure there are more interesting things in Hawthorn's life than dead kings."

"I doubt it," Rush muttered.

"Rushford," my mom said in her warning tone.

My dad tried to keep dinner from going completely downhill, which was a role he took on a lot. "What sound is your car making?"

"It's sort of roaring, like it's on the verge of taking flight."

"It's an old car," my mom reminded me. "You knew this was a risk."

"I'll look at it this weekend," my dad said.

"No, James. She can take it into the shop or learn to work on it herself. That was the deal."

Rush sighed loudly to let us all know how tired he was with the conversation.

"I don't have the money to take it to the shop," I said.

"Whose fault is that?" I could tell my mom was in an unreasonable mood and I should stop pushing her, but winter wasn't that far away and I couldn't walk to school in the snow. Which would mean the bus. Every day.

"Really, Sparrow. It won't take me long to open the hood and take a look."

"No. She wanted the car. She has to deal with the consequences."

The tension in the room was rising, and I started to feel really awkward, but apparently not as awkward as my brother, because he suddenly pushed his chair back from the table.

"I can't believe the three of you are just sitting here talking as if everything is normal. Lizzie's missing, and all you care about is car problems and some guy who lived five thousand years ago."

"Edward IV lived five *hundred* years ago, you idiot," I snapped. "And excuse us for not spending every second crying for some girl we don't know."

"Hawthorn," my mom scolded.

"*I* knew her. I guess that doesn't mean anything to you," Rush said.

"*Knew* her, past tense," I said. "You haven't thought about her for years. If she hadn't disappeared, you probably wouldn't have ever thought about her again."

Now my mom was angry. "Hawthorn, stop."

"Why? He's not sad about Lizzie. He's sad because it's just one more reminder high school is over and he's nothing but an ex-football player who's stuck taking classes at the community college."

"Fuck you," Rush said. He stomped out of the room, and a moment later, the front door slammed.

The dining room was quiet. Then my dad cleared his throat. "I don't want to ever hear you talking to your brother like that again."

I guessed I'd crossed some sort of line. Not that what I said wasn't true. But just because something's true doesn't mean it's OK to say, as my dad frequently told me.

"As for your car," my dad said, "your mother is right. If you want it fixed, take it to a mechanic. If you don't have the money, get a part-time job."

A job was the last thing I wanted. I was still feeling scarred from working at the mini golf course over the summer.

The problem wasn't the screaming kids or the monotony or that I had to give up most of my weekends. What frustrated me was thinking about how little money I was making compared to how much I was *doing*. And that made me think about how some people end up working at a mini golf course for their entire lives. And then I realized if I didn't hurry up and figure out what I wanted to do after high school, I might turn into one of those people.

After that, the job changed. Instead of just being a way to make spending money during the summer, working at the mini golf course became a purgatory of cleaning up spilled ice cream cones and fishing stray golf balls out of the algae-filled pond. That was about the time I started to dread going to work every day. Then I started to dread the idea of having a job at all.

On the other hand, if I had a job like Dad suggested, I wouldn't spend so much time sitting around the house thinking about how boring my life was.

"I didn't mean to say that to Rush," I said, partly because it was true and partly because I knew my parents would be angry until I apologized. "I'm sorry. Really."

My mom put her hand over mine. "I know you didn't mean it, honey. This situation with Lizzie is making everyone tense."

"I've noticed."

Noticed but didn't understand it. How was it possible for

Lizzie to have such a strong hold on everyone? She could be a hundred miles away for all we knew. But still, our lives were centered on her. She was causing fights, creating tension, making people worry. Even when Lizzie was absent, she was the star.

CHAPTER 5

THE HUNDRED DEATHS OF LIZZIE LOVETT

B y Friday morning, people were starting to think the worst. The search parties had been at it for four straight days. There was nothing—not a footprint, not a piece of fabric torn from Lizzie's clothes, not a strand of her long, blond hair. It was like she just snapped her fingers and *poof*, disappeared.

From the start, people said all sorts of stuff about how maybe Lizzie was dead. But as the first week of her disappearance neared its end, I realized none of them had really believed it. They'd been talking just to talk, trying to shock each other with gruesome scenarios. It was more of a game than anything else. But on Friday, it was different.

Maybe it was because five days was a long time for someone to be missing. Maybe it had to do with the vigil planned for that evening. Maybe it was because when the reporters interviewed Lizzie's mom, she didn't seem urgent anymore. She seemed defeated. Whatever sparked the change, the whole school was grim that day, and it made every second seem as long as an hour.

Personally, I was getting for-real bored with Lizzie Lovett. I got why everyone was so upset, but I just couldn't buy into it. If anything, it seemed like no sign of Lizzie should be good news. If Lizzie had died in the woods, there'd be some evidence. But there wasn't. Which is exactly what I would expect from a girl who slipped away from camp, trying to make sure no one would follow her.

Unfortunately, no one in school cared what I had to say, no matter how logical it was. That's why, on Friday, I didn't hear anyone debating where Lizzie ran away to or what had made her run in the first place. Instead, I heard the Hundred Deaths of Lizzie Lovett.

She was mauled by a wild animal.

She was killed by her boyfriend.

She fell into a ravine and wasn't able to climb out.

She was butchered by a serial killer.

She was butchered by her boyfriend.

She ate some wild berries and was poisoned (or possibly bitten by a poisonous insect).

She got lost and died of starvation, thirst, or exposure.

She was stabbed, shot, strangled, bludgeoned, drowned, hanged, burned. By her boyfriend.

At school that day, everyone had a theory of their own. And most of the theories involved Lorenzo Calvetti.

Some people thought he accidentally killed her and panicked. Others thought he must have been planning it from the moment they met. I even heard a story about how he proposed to Lizzie that night, and when she turned him down, he murdered her in a fit of rage.

I kept thinking of the picture in the newspaper and how boyish Lorenzo Calvetti looked. Young and in love. Not like a killer. The police chief had even made a statement about how he wasn't a suspect. The cops thought Lorenzo Calvetti was inno-cent, and my gut told me they were right. But most of Griffin Mills High School disagreed.

First period came and went, then other equally boring hours passed, and everyone talked about the girl they were sure was dead and the boy they were sure had killed her. I wanted to tell every-one Lorenzo didn't do it. He was the real victim, ditched in the woods by the girl he loved. But I knew what people would say and how they would look at me, so I kept my suspicions to myself. I figured Lizzie would turn up soon, and everyone would forget the whole thing anyway.

✻ ✻ ✻

I ended up eating lunch in the library instead of on the back steps. How that happened was, before I'd taken a single bite of my sand-wich, Emily said, "How'd your paper turn out?"

I almost asked Emily what she was talking about. Then I remembered.

"You didn't do it? Seriously?" Emily asked when she saw the look on my face.

"I meant to," I said. The paper was probably a great example of what my teachers meant when they said I was bright but didn't apply myself.

"You had plenty of time," Emily said. "What have you been doing?" I didn't like how she sounded like my mom.

I gathered my stuff without answering. I hadn't been doing anything important. I never did much of anything, which is probably why I was always bored.

"I'm going to the library. I can skip fourth period and get something written."

"Good luck, I guess."

"Thanks, I guess."

I could feel Emily's disapproval the whole time I walked away.

✸✸✸

They were calling it a vigil, but it felt more like a funeral. Everyone was crying, and the whole event was totally awkward, and I wished I'd stayed home. It was even worse than it should have been, because I went with my mom. I'd been planning on asking Emily to go with me, but after the blowup about my paper, I decided it was maybe, probably, a bad idea. So there I was, at a vigil for a girl I hated with my hippie mom and surrounded by pretty much every single person I went to school with except for the one person who was actually my friend.

Lizzie had been living in Layton, a town about fifteen minutes away. But her mom still lived in Griffin Mills, which I guess is why they chose to do the vigil here. It was at the biggest park in town, the one with a man-made lake and old-fashioned bandstand. Lizzie's mom was on the bandstand with Mayor Thompson and some other people I didn't know, though one was clearly a priest and another a police officer.

A crowd of people surrounded the bandstand. My mom and I were in the middle of the mess. People crushed against us like we were at a concert, making the September evening seem warmer than it actually was. I saw kids from school, neighbors, and people who graduated the same year as Rush. There were a bunch of people I didn't recognize though. Lizzie had lots of friends. Or, at least, a lot of people who wanted to be her friend.

Volunteers from the middle school were weaving through the crowd, handing out white daisies and telling people they were Lizzie's favorite flower.

"Daisies? Aren't we supposed to have candles?" I asked my mom.

"I think the flowers are nice."

You could tell who the reporters were, even the ones who didn't have camera crews with them or little notepads in their hands. They were dressed too professionally, watching everything too closely. I wished I were one of them, that I didn't have any-thing to do with Griffin Mills and had only shown up because it was my job.

"There's your brother," my mom said. She waved her hand above the crowd, trying to get his attention.

Either Rush didn't see her or he pretended not to. That's what I would have done. He was with his best friend, Connor, and the two of them had the attention of some giggling middle school girls. That's how it is for people who used to play football in the Mills, especially the guys who are still young and attractive. They're minor celebrities young girls dare each other to talk to.

"He doesn't see us. Let's go say hi."

"Mom, no. Just no."

"I'm not going to embarrass him, Hawthorn."

"You're going to embarrass *me*."

Before my mom could respond, the mayor stepped up to the microphone, tapped it once to see if it was working, then launched into a speech about how in tragic times, it's so important for a community to come together and blah, blah, blah. I shifted from foot to foot and looked around at the crowd, at all the people who loved Lizzie gathered in one place.

Part of me wished something terrible would happen. Like maybe there was a fault line running through the park, and there'd be an earthquake, and the ground would split open, and we'd all be swallowed. Or a flash flood would wash away everyone at the vigil. Then the world would pretty much be free of anyone who cared about Lizzie. It would be like she never existed.

Only she did exist. And she was probably out there some-where watching the news coverage, laughing about how easily she'd tricked everyone. Then she'd go to a new town and start over. Make a whole new group of people love her. And maybe, if they were lucky, she'd deem a few of those people worthy enough to get her love in return.

Lizzie's mom took the microphone next. She was a tired-looking woman in wrinkled clothes. A woman whose appearance had clearly stopped mattering to her since her daughter disappeared.

"I want to thank everyone for coming," Ms. Lovett said. "I wish Elizabeth could see us gathered together like this."

She paused and blinked back tears, trying to stay composed while she pleaded with the crowd to find her only child.

"I also want to thank everyone who's been part of the search party and answering phones on the tip line we've set up. I know my daughter is out there, and I know we'll bring her home."

Another pause. Ms. Lovett pulled a tissue from her pocket and dabbed at her eyes.

"Father Patrick is going to lead us in a prayer, but first, I wanted to say a few words about Elizabeth."

She reached into her pocket again and pulled out a piece of paper. She unfolded it and held it in a hand that shook as much as her voice.

"Those who know Elizabeth know how full of life she is. Even as a baby, she was always smiling."

Ms. Lovett droned on and on about how great Lizzie is, as if everyone hadn't heard it a million times already. Lizzie was the reason her squad had won the state cheerleading competition years ago. She was so friendly that she got Christmas cards from people she'd only met once. She was so selfless that she donated a third of every paycheck to some wildlife conservation society. Smart, pretty, talented, humble. Lizzie Lovett was perfect.

I stopped listening and started looking around.

That's when I saw movement on the other side of the bandstand. People parted as someone pushed through the crowd. He climbed up the steps toward Lizzie's mom. Shoulders slouched, hands shoved into the pockets of a wrinkled gray cardigan. His longish, dark hair hung in his eyes. Lorenzo Calvetti, late for his own girlfriend's vigil.

Even from where I was, I could see the head of police frowning at him. Ms. Lovett paused and motioned Lorenzo to her, wrapping an arm around his skinny shoulders.

"Elizabeth's absence has left a hole in many lives. She... I know my daughter. She didn't run away. She's out there in those woods, and she's alone and scared. I just want her to come home safely. I need her to come home."

Ms. Lovett broke down. Lorenzo shifted his weight, like he knew he was supposed to comfort her but didn't know how.

Mayor Thompson ended up being the one to do it. He stepped forward and whispered some things in Ms. Lovett's ear and pulled her back from the microphone.

The police officer took over and talked about where the search parties would be meeting the next day and what people could do to help. Then the priest led the gathering in prayer. I watched the people on the bandstand. Ms. Lovett wiping her eyes. Lorenzo Calvetti running his hands through his hair. Lorenzo Calvetti looking down at his feet. Lorenzo Calvetti looking like he wanted to be anywhere else. Lizzie was missing, but Lorenzo was the one who seemed in need of rescue.

It wasn't until people started waving their daisies in the air that I pulled my attention away from the bandstand. It seemed spontaneous but probably was planned, because somehow, everyone else knew that's what the flowers were for. People held them above their heads and swayed back and forth. Father Patrick prayed, and hundreds of tiny white petals blew around in the breeze, making something beautiful out of something ugly.

I didn't wave my daisy. I felt small, the way an ant must feel looking up at a field of wildflowers. I was nothing. I was trapped below the flowers, buried under them, while girls like Lizzie Lovett danced overhead. That was life. We all have a place.

I wondered where Lorenzo Calvetti belonged.

CHAPTER 6

UNDER THE LIGHT OF THE MOON

I pretty much expected my parents to drop the whole part-time job idea, but they didn't. That's why, on the Saturday after the vigil, I spent the day driving around, pretending to look for work.

Except at first, I wasn't pretending. I went to the video rental place that had been on the verge of closing for, like, five years. They weren't hiring. So I went to the trendy shoe store next door. It's a place I'd always hated, not just because they call themselves a boutique, but also because all their shoes are ugly. I wanted to tell my parents I'd put in a lot of applications though, so I was about to fill out the paperwork when Mychelle Adler appeared from nowhere. She was all, "Oh my God, don't tell me you're actually applying to work here." I put down the application and walked out.

After that, I drove to the sporting goods store where the jock manager didn't look interested in hiring me and looked *super* uninterested once I told him I didn't have a cell phone where he could reach me. I do have a cell phone, but it usually sits on my desk or in the bottom of my backpack, uncharged. What did it matter? It's not like people ever called me. There was a sign outside the fast-food taco shop saying they were hiring, but the greasy teenager behind the counter gave me a creepy look, so I walked right back out.

That's when I decided to spend the rest of my day driving around aimlessly and making up places I could tell my mom I'd applied.

I ended up in Layton, and that made me think of Lizzie, and that made me think of how she'd worked at some diner. Since I was already in town, I decided to look for it.

It was actually pretty easy. Layton only has a few major streets running through it, so there wasn't a lot of area to cover, and I only saw one diner that fit the newspaper's description of where Lizzie worked. The Sunshine Café. I pulled into a parking spot.

The café was a sad brick building at the edge of an even sadder shopping center. It looked like it had been painted yellow a billion years before and never touched again. The name of the diner was written on the side of the building next to a big, orange, smiley-faced sun, and the specials sign in the window still said it was June.

A bell jingled when I stepped in, and I was relieved to see the inside was a little more inviting. It was a small place, with a single row of booths along one wall and a counter along the other. The kitchen was behind the counter, and I could see into it through the window where food was set out to be delivered by the waitresses. Waitresses like Lizzie. I tried to picture the Lizzie Lovett I knew working there. It was sort of impossible to imagine.

The only patron was an old man hunched over the far end of the counter, doing a crossword puzzle. I was deciding where to sit, or if I should even stay, when a girl came out of the kitchen. She was in her midtwenties and had bouncy curls and a big smile. She looked like the kind of person who'd been friends with everyone when she was in school, even the nerdy, weird kids no one else wanted to talk to. I smiled back at her, even though I'm not usually the type to smile at strangers.

"Hi!" she said. "Let me grab you a menu."

"Uh, actually, I was wondering if you were hiring."

The girl seemed thrown off. I was too. The words had come out of my mouth without getting permission from my brain.

"Well, I guess we are," she laughed. "You have good timing. Let me tell the manager you're here."

She disappeared into the back, and I sat down on a stool at the opposite end of the counter from the old man. I didn't have a plan. I didn't know why I'd said anything about a job. I'd only wanted to see where Lizzie worked. I wanted to prove to myself that she did work, since Lizzie seemed like someone who could go her entire life without having responsibilities.

I was thinking about jetting out the door, but I hesitated too long. The waitress bounced over, saying Mr. Walczak would be out in a second, and he'd act really stern, but he was totally laid-back, and I should just be myself, and then the job would likely be mine.

"I'm Christa, by the way."

"Hawthorn Creely."

"Hawthorn. That's an interesting name."

I made a face, and she laughed.

"Do you live in Layton?"

"No, Griffin Mills. No one's hiring there though."

Christa rolled her eyes. "There's no one hiring *anywhere*. I got lucky. Half my friends have to drive all the way to Pittsburgh for work."

"There's an opening here though, huh?" I said, as if I didn't know *why* there was an opening. I patted myself on the back for casually working that into conversation. I told myself I was awesomely sneaky and maybe, probably, had what it took to be a secret agent.

Christa got a look on her face, which I was super familiar with from my time at Griffin Mills High School. Her eyes went wide, and she cast furtive glances around the dining room. It was the look of someone who wanted to gossip. She lowered her voice and leaned over the counter. "You know about Lizzie Lovett, right? The girl who's missing?"

I tried to keep my face neutral, as if Lizzie was just a name from a newspaper article.

"Sure," I said. "Everyone knows about her."

"Well, she worked here."

"Really?"

Christa nodded. "At first, Mr. Walczak was holding Lizzie's job for her, 'cause we all thought she'd come back. Then yesterday, he started talking about putting a listing in the newspaper just in case."

"Wow. That's crazy. So you think she's gone for good?"

Christa lowered her voice even more. "I don't know for sure, but I think her disappearance has something to do with her boyfriend. I always thought he was a weirdo."

I wanted to tell her weirdo and killer aren't always the same thing, but that would likely blow my slick super-spy cover, so I didn't.

"You think he killed her?" I asked.

"I'm not saying he *killed* her. Not for sure, anyway. I just think it's all a little suspicious."

"Like her being in the woods in the first place," I said. "She doesn't seem like the outdoorsy type."

"Oh, no." Christa shook her head. "That part isn't suspicious. Lizzie is totally into camping and hiking. She went out in the woods all the time. Looking for wolves or something."

Well, that wasn't what I expected to hear.

"Wolves?" I asked.

"Weird, right?"

It *was* weird.

"Personally, the last thing I'd do is go looking for a wild animal," Christa said. "I don't even like domesticated ones. My sister has a dog, and her entire house is covered with fur."

Before I could pump Christa for more information about Lizzie, a nervous-looking man with a ruddy complexion came out of the kitchen and told me to follow him to his office. I hadn't planned on taking the charade that far. I wasn't ready for another mini golf experience, especially when I'd probably get fired as soon as Lizzie decided to come back.

But I sat down in the manager's office. I answered his questions and told him I thought I'd be a really, really great waitress. At the end of the interview, when he shook my hand and said I'd be a welcome addition to their staff, I knew I'd reached the point of no return.

★★★

I couldn't sleep that night. It was close to midnight, and I was lying on the swing on the front porch. Maybe my insomnia wouldn't have been a big deal if I had Saturday night plans like everyone else in the entire school. Everyone else was probably at parties. Everyone else was enjoying what some people would call the "best years of life." Not me. I was hanging out alone on my front porch.

Sometimes, when it's late at night and I'm feeling especially lonely, I think about middle school me. Eighth-grade Hawthorn knew what high school was supposed to be like. I'd watched movies, read books, attended high school football games, and heard stories from Rush. I knew exactly what to expect.

And then I got there, and it was all wrong.

Actually, my expectations weren't wrong. I was. High school *was* full of crazy adventures and friendships and dating and stuff. It's just, it was wrong for *me*. I didn't know how to be a part of all that or even if I really wanted to be.

Which made it impossible to get excited about applying to college. Because I had certain expectations of that too. And if they were as spectacularly misguided as my expectations for high school, I had another string of disappointments waiting right around the corner.

I closed my eyes and tried to clear my head. Tried not to think of next year and how dissatisfying it would probably be. I tried not to think of anything at all. I just wanted the night to end. The whole week, really.

But I couldn't turn off my brain. Even though I was tired, I couldn't stop thinking of high school and college and everything that came after. Sometimes, it felt like I'd already missed my chance to become something awesome. I was too old to find out I was a musical prodigy or a child genius or a superhero. I wasn't even awesome in an ordinary way. Like Lizzie.

I bet she was never alone on a Saturday night. Not in high school for sure. A party wasn't a party unless Lizzie Lovett showed up. My brother was at those parties. Him and all the other jocks. He was probably at a party that very minute, drinking beer with his friends while they discussed their old friend who was lost in the woods.

Where *was* Lizzie Lovett? Six days in the woods without any supplies. She couldn't have gotten far. How did she just disappear?

How was there no trace of her around Wolf Creek when so many people were looking so hard? I wondered how many people would search for me if I went missing. My guess was not a lot.

I yawned. My mind kept skipping around like it usually does right before I drift off. But I didn't want to go inside yet. Was Lizzie outside too? Was she looking up at the moon at the same time I was?

I wondered why it was called Wolf Creek anyway. For that matter, I wondered what Lizzie was doing looking for wolves in the first place. There aren't wolves in Ohio. Except...

When I was eight or nine, there were these reports of a wolf in Griffin Mills. People saw it in the woods, in neighborhoods, at the edge of downtown. Maybe it was just a big dog that escaped from someone's backyard. It probably was. I never found out one way or another.

Back then, it wasn't Emily and me against the world. We had a whole group of friends. I felt like I belonged, and life was an adventure where anything could happen.

We spent the whole summer searching for that wolf, scouring the woods, setting traps, collecting evidence. There was never a moment when we lost hope, when we considered that we might not find it, that there might not be a wolf at all.

Then, in the fall, the wolf disappeared. There were no more sightings. Everyone got distracted by school and forgot all about the search. Everyone but me. I kept thinking about those magical few months when we really believed it was out there. We were certain we could find the wolf and make it bite us so we could change too. Because, of course, we didn't think it was an *ordinary* wolf.

I missed being a kid. I missed having friends who would spend the entire summer hunting for a werewolf.

If there were werewolves, they'd probably hang around a place called Wolf Creek. I smiled at the thought. Maybe that's what got Lizzie. Maybe it was late at night, and she had to go to the bathroom, so she'd slipped away from camp. Only in the woods, something wasn't right. Something was watching her. She knew she had to get back to the tent. She wanted to shout for Lorenzo but was too afraid to make a sound. So she silently crept toward the clearing. The thing in the dark growled at her. She froze. It stepped out into the moonlight. It wasn't an animal or a man. It was both. She opened her mouth to scream, but before she could, the beast lunged, and its teeth were at her throat, sinking into the soft skin and—

No. That wasn't right.

I pulled myself into a half-sitting position. A chill went down my back. A wolf didn't kill Lizzie.

It was her idea to camp at Wolf Creek. Wolf Creek, where she looked for wolves while wearing a wolf pendant around her neck. I remembered the night after she disappeared, how I'd looked out my window, and the whole neighborhood was lit up because of the moon. The full moon. Lizzie the wolf lover wanted to camp at a very specific spot during the full moon.

I thought about how Lizzie had changed since high school.

No more glossy-magazine-cover Lizzie. She became unkempt. A little wild looking. She became a girl who loved nature and had a thing for wolves.

All signs pointed to her walking into the woods that night of her own free will. She wasn't dragged out of the camp. There was no evidence of a struggle. She *left*. Lorenzo Calvetti told reporters Lizzie seemed happy before she went to bed.

Some people thought Lizzie was lost, and some people thought she was dead. I'd been certain Lizzie took off because she was bored or wanted attention. But maybe we were all wrong.

Maybe Lizzie Lovett turned into a werewolf.

It was probably because I was so sleepy, but the image of pretty, perfect Lizzie Lovett turning into a wolf suddenly seemed like the most hilarious thing in the world. I started laughing. There, alone on my porch, in the middle of the night, I started to giggle like an idiot. If any of my neighbors would have looked out their windows, they would've thought I was insane.

Even after my laugher dried up, as my eyes were getting heavy, I couldn't get the image of werewolf Lizzie out of my mind. Honestly, it wasn't the craziest theory I'd heard in the past week. It almost made sense.

I was still thinking of it when I drifted off to sleep.

Lizzie the werewolf.

That explanation made her disappearance *much* more interesting.

CHAPTER 7

THE WOLF GIRL

✳ ✳

A car door slammed and woke me up. I rubbed my eyes and shifted my weight. *What was wrong with my bed?* Then I realized I wasn't in bed. I'd slept through the whole night on the porch swing. I groggily sat up as Connor climbed the front steps.

"Your parents kick you out?" he joked.

"You're way too cheerful for this early in the morning."

"Probably because I didn't sleep outside on a swing."

Connor smiled at me, looking like the perfect, all-American jock that he was. He tried to hide it with his stubbly beard and slightly too-long hair, but it didn't work. It looked too intentional. He could have been on one of those TV shows where everyone was perfect and no one had real problems. I felt very aware of my messy hair and morning breath.

"Rush is inside. You can go in."

"Thanks. Didn't mean to wake you, Thorny."

"Yeah, well, I guess that's what I get for sleeping on the porch."

Connor laughed and let himself in the house. As soon as the door shut behind him, I lay back down. My back hurt from the hard swing. My head was achy like I was hungover. Not that I know exactly how a hangover feels, since my experience with alcohol is pretty limited.

Though it seemed like I *should* have been drinking. Because, you know, falling asleep contemplating werewolf cheerleaders is a lot more acceptable if you're drunk. Having those thoughts when you're sober makes people wonder if you're crazy.

Not that I really thought Lizzie was a werewolf. Obviously. That would have been absurd for a million different reasons. Starting with the fact that werewolves don't exist.

But still.

There *were* some oddities about Lizzie's disappearance, oddities that centered on wolves. It made sense that if someone isolated those details and kept an open mind, they could conclude that Lizzie turned into a werewolf. When you added up all the clues, the whole thing seemed very reasonable.

Well, maybe *reasonable* wasn't the right word.

It wasn't that much of a stretch though.

And really, as far as paranormal creatures went, werewolves were probably the least unlikely phenomenon.

An image popped into my mind of the police chief somberly leading Lizzie's mother into his office and motioning for her to sit. Ms. Lovett would look at him with wet eyes, tissues clutched in her hand. And the police chief would say, "I'm sorry, ma'am, but your daughter has turned into a wolf." And Ms. Lovett would be like, "We always knew this day would come." Then the police chief would open a drawer and take out a box of silver bullets.

I started giggling all over again.

It was messed up to laugh. Totally disrespectful. But I couldn't help it.

I was still laughing when Rush and Connor came out of the house. They stopped and looked at me like maybe I'd gone off the deep end.

"What's wrong with you?" my brother asked.

"Nothing," I said, trying to calm myself with a deep breath. "Or maybe everything. It could go either way."

❧ ❧ ❧

"Please tell me you're joking," Emily said when I called her on Sunday afternoon. "Please tell me you didn't steal Lizzie Lovett's job."

"I would hardly call it *stealing*," I said defensively.

"Hawthorn, what are you doing?"

"I need money to fix my car."

"Did you even look for a job in the Mills? Or did you immediately go to Layton?"

"I looked here first. Everything sucked. And I knew the diner had an opening." I was getting pretty annoyed about Emily's reaction, especially since what I really wanted to talk about was my werewolf idea. If Emily couldn't deal with my new job, then I couldn't imagine her reaction to the rest of my news.

"I just think it's really weird, OK?"

"It's only a part-time job."

"You hate people. How are you going to be a waitress?"

"Look. I admit that I went because I was curious," I said.

"About what?"

"I wanted to see where she worked. Then everyone was really nice, and they offered me a job, and I took it."

"How convenient," Emily said.

"It is, actually. I need money, and this way, maybe I can get some information too. About the disappearance."

"So you think you're going to solve the mystery, is that it? Don't you think the police talked to everyone who works at the café?"

"What does it matter if they don't know the right questions to ask?"

"What's that supposed to mean?"

There was a long pause. Then I said, "Listen, Em. What if Lizzie turned into a werewolf?"

"Oh, here we go," Emily said with a sigh.

She didn't laugh or act shocked. She didn't tell me to stop messing around. Like I wasn't even worthy of a *reaction*. It made me feel a million miles away from her.

"Look, Hawthorn, I need to get to my piano lesson."

"No, wait," I said. "Hear me out."

Another sigh. "Three minutes."

And that's how I shared my theory about Lizzie Lovett being a werewolf out loud for the first time.

✖ ✖ ✖

My mom's vegan chili was surprisingly good, though it would have tasted even better over a hotdog. There was something called textured vegetable protein in the chili, which made me a little squeamish, but if I didn't pay too much attention to it, I could pretend it was ground beef.

While my mom told my dad and Rush her plans for a winter garden, I thought about my conversation with Emily. She wasn't a fan of my werewolf theory. In fact, the more I talked, the more annoyed she got. I hadn't expected her to buy into my reasoning, but I thought maybe we could have one conversation that wasn't about school assignments, college, and real life. Would it have killed her to play along?

"Earth to Hawthorn," my dad said, nudging me.

I looked up. "Huh?"

"Your mom asked you to pass the cornbread. What are you thinking about over there?"

"Werewolves."

Rush rolled his eyes.

"You know," my dad said, "werewolf legends were very popular in medieval Europe."

"They were?"

"It was a coping mechanism. People preferred to believe murders were committed by beasts rather than by men. Most accounts of werewolf attacks from that time would be considered serial killings today."

"So you don't believe in werewolves?" I asked.

"Well, no. Do you?"

"Maybe. I mean…they *could* exist."

"Yeah," Rush said. "They probably hang out with vampires and mummies."

"You know, mummies are real, Rush. That's not a debate," I shot back.

"Hawthorn," my mom said in her warning voice.

"Why the sudden interest in werewolves?" my dad asked.

"I was just thinking what if Lizzie Lovett turned into one?"

Rush pushed his chair back from the table. "That's it. I'm out of here."

I thought my mom would use her warning voice and tell him to sit back down, but she let him go.

Instead, she turned to me. "That was very insensitive."

"What?"

"I know you don't understand why Rush is upset about Lizzie. But that doesn't mean it's OK to make jokes."

"How do you know I was joking?"

"Hawthorn."

"She *could* be a werewolf. You don't know."

"You have more imagination than is good for you," my dad said.

"And we love your imagination," my mom added. "But you need to learn boundaries."

Boundaries. She meant I had to say and do what was expected of me. Keep any weird thoughts to myself. Not rock the boat. I bet her mom told her the same thing when she was my age. I bet she got some pretty weird looks when she changed her name to Sparrow and painted peace signs on her face.

For someone who called herself a hippie, my mom had become quite the conformist.

❋ ❋ ❋

I couldn't sleep again. Every time I closed my eyes, I saw the disgust on Rush's face when I brought up werewolves. It was the same tone I'd heard in Emily's voice. Which made me angry. I had to let it make me angry, because otherwise, I would just feel sad.

Couldn't they have humored me? I wasn't asking them to launch a werewolf investigation. Why was everyone so desperate to be logical all the time anyway? As if growing up meant you couldn't even talk about something unless you thought it was real.

Who were Emily and Rush to say what was real or not anyway? It's not like either of them knew all the secrets of the world.

Legends exist for a reason after all. Those stories are based on *some* truth.

I thought about what my dad had said, how hundreds of years ago, people believed serial killers were half-beast because it was easier than admitting what horrors men were capable of. But couldn't it be the other way around? Maybe it was present-day people who couldn't accept the truth. Maybe a man turning into an animal was too magical for a society that values logic and reason. Maybe those medieval villagers with their werewolf lore were the ones who had it right.

The more I thought about it, the angrier I got.

Werewolves *could* be real.

They probably weren't.

But they *could* be.

All I'd wanted was to talk about the possibility.

I felt very alone. I lived in a world with practical people, like Emily and Rush and my parents, people who had stopped believing in the impossible a long time ago. Where were the other people like me? Locked up probably. Getting called crazy and delusional.

Sometimes, the crazy people turn out to be right though.

I shut my eyes and pushed my brother's disapproving face out of my mind. Instead, I pictured a world where there was magic, a world where Lizzie Lovett really *was* a werewolf, and I was the one who found her and proved it.

The night before, I'd laughed myself to sleep thinking about werewolves, but my theory wasn't funny anymore.

It felt possible. Inevitable.

Why *shouldn't* werewolves exist?

And if werewolves were real, what other creatures might be out there?

Anything.

Everything.

I just needed to find Lizzie. I could start my own investigation—talk to the people who knew her, search the woods myself. And yeah, maybe Lizzie had simply run away, but at least I'd have some fun until the case was solved.

That night, I came up with my own version of counting sheep. Over and over again, I thought, *Lizzie is a werewolf, and I am going to find her. Lizzie is a werewolf, and I am going to find her. Lizzie is a werewolf, and…*

I fell asleep in no time.

CHAPTER 8

A BRIEF HISTORY OF GRIFFIN MILLS

I was pretty sure I'd get my history paper back with a big F written on it, maybe a D if I was lucky. Instead, something totally weird happened. Mr. Romano wanted me to read my paper to the class.

I froze.

Mr. Romano handed my essay to me. It was only a page long, which was three pages shorter than it was supposed to be. "Hawthorn had a very interesting take on the assignment, and I'd like you all to hear it."

"Are you being sarcastic?" I asked. Some kids laughed, and they weren't laughing *with* me.

Even Mr. Romano seemed amused when he told me that no, he was not being sarcastic. I felt like I was the only one not in on the joke.

Reluctantly, I walked to the front of the classroom and took my report from him. Everyone was staring at me, including Emily, who had her jaw clenched really tight. It was probably the first time my schoolwork had been singled out before hers.

I cleared my throat and looked down at the paper.

"Go on, Hawthorn," Mr. Romano said.

The skater kid who sat in the back of the room shouted, "Yeah, we don't have all day." The class laughed, even though it wasn't funny.

When it was silent again, I figured I'd better start, or I'd just be prolonging my agony. I cleared my throat again.

"Every town has a story. And every story has a beginning and an end. For Griffin Mills, the beginning was around the turn of the century when Samuel Griffin came to the Ohio River Valley."

I figured everyone's essay started with Samuel Griffin. But I was probably the only one who skipped over the glory days of Griffin Mills and the advances that were made in the mining and milling industries. Instead, I focused on the Griffin Mansion, the big abandoned house on the hill, where kids tried to catch a glimpse of Samuel Griffin's ghost.

"Griffin Mills *is* a haunted town," I read. "Not by the ghost of Samuel Griffin but by generations of people who told his story simply because there was nothing better to do."

Kids who'd been shifting in their seats and rustling papers stopped. The room was totally quiet.

"This will always be a steel mill town, even though the last mill closed more than twenty years ago. It's a place where boys enlist in the army and are disappointed if there's not a war to fight. It's a town of mechanics and plumbers, of drunken brawls and Friday night football games. Kids who grow up in the Mills dream of what life would be like elsewhere and count the days until they can get out and experience it, even though, deep down, they know they never will."

Someone coughed, that awkward sort of cough when you want to say something, but you have no idea what that something is.

"Griffin Mills is a town that's perpetually bored with itself but too stubborn to dry up. So instead of dying gracefully, it's a slow, painful process, one that's embarrassing to watch. Because Griffin Mills *is* dying, and the people who live here are dying with it."

I heard a few whispers. I was pretty sure they weren't about my fantastic writing ability.

I said the last lines in a rush. "Every story has a beginning, and every story has an end. The Mills has reached its epilogue."

If my life were a movie, I would've been all nervous about reading my paper, but I'd do it anyway. There would be a really dramatic pause at the end, an awkward silence, but then someone would start a slow clap, and the rest of the room would join in, and just like that, I'd go from being me to being someone who is brilliant and likable.

My life isn't a movie.

A glance around the classroom was enough to determine my essay wasn't going to do much for my popularity.

Mike Jacobs, who's the captain of the football team, said, "Nice, Hawthorn."

Some kids laughed.

Jessica Massi raised her hand and, without waiting to be called on, said, "I thought we were supposed to write a history of Griffin Mills, not insult the whole town."

The kids around her nodded in agreement.

I looked at Mr. Romano. Sympathy was written all over his face, as if he was just realizing he'd made a terrible mistake.

"I think Hawthorn's paper raises a lot of interesting points for us to discuss."

"Yeah, like how she's pathetic."

I couldn't tell where that last comment came from, but it didn't matter. I retreated to my desk while Mr. Romano tried to regain control of the class.

Emily leaned across the aisle. "It really was a good paper."

"It was stupid."

"No, they're stupid."

She was right. They *were* stupid. But not so stupid that they'd write an essay like mine. So really, who was the biggest idiot?

✭✭✭

I had my first shift at the Sunshine Café after school that day. Christa trained me. There wasn't much to learn.

"As long as you're friendly, you'll be fine," she said.

If that was the case, I was a long way from fine, but I didn't tell her that.

The same old man was at the same spot at the end of the lunch counter. Christa told me his name was Vernon and he was always there. Other than that, there were only two tables of people the entire night. It seemed like working at the Sunshine Café mostly meant sitting around.

"So there's no word on Lizzie Lovett, huh?" I asked, trying to sound causal.

Christa was showing me how to work the coffee machine, as if it were complicated.

"Nope. But her boyfriend was in here the other night."

"In the diner?"

Christa nodded. "He used to come here while she was working. I didn't expect he'd show up *now*."

"I saw his picture in the paper," I said. "They looked sort of mismatched to me."

"I couldn't say. I didn't really know either of them."

"But you and Lizzie worked together for a while, right?"

"That doesn't mean you *know* someone," Christa said. "Lizzie kept to herself."

"Did you like her?" I asked, wondering if I was pushing the conversation too far. Christa was going to think I had ulterior motives. Which I did.

"We got along."

If I'd known her a little better, I would have told Christa that didn't answer the question. Instead, I let her lead me from the coffeemaker to the closet where extra napkins and sugar packets were stored.

A little later, Christa asked me to watch the diner while she called her boyfriend. There wasn't much to watch, so I sat down next to Vernon. He was halfway through a word search.

"Hi."

Vernon didn't respond.

"My name's Hawthorn. I'm the new waitress. Lizzie's replacement. Did you know her?"

Still nothing.

"This is my first shift. Which is sort of bad timing, because my day sucked."

Vernon still didn't speak, but he made a harrumph sound, which I figured meant it was OK to continue.

"I had to write this paper about Griffin Mills, and I wrote the truth, which is that the town is totally lame. I didn't think anyone besides my teacher would ever read it."

Vernon found the word *stellar* and circled it.

"They can't all think the Mills is a great place to live. Can they?"

Lizzie Lovett must not have thought so. She left after graduating. Though, admittedly, she didn't get far. Only down the road to Layton and a job at the Sunshine Café. Where, apparently, her boyfriend Lorenzo would visit her sometimes.

I wondered how much Lorenzo Calvetti loved Lizzie and if her turning into a werewolf would ruin his life forever.

"Why didn't you leave Layton, Vernon?"

Vernon finally looked at me and said in a high, crackly, old man voice, "Did leave. Fer nearly thirty years. Din't git far though. Come back in the end."

"Why?" I asked.

"Cuz it's no difference wheresabouts yinz live, girlie. Zak same trouble everywhere."

I sighed. "Well, that doesn't give me much hope for the future."

"Hope? Wah good ya think hope gonna do?" Vernon said, then threw back his head and cackled.

I laughed too. Because maybe, probably, it was a better response than I'd get from anyone else.

I spent the rest of my first waitressing shift reading *The Book of Werewolves* by this guy named Sabine Baring-Gould. It was written a long time ago but is still considered one of the most important werewolf texts. Every once in a while, I jotted down notes in a composition book.

"Is that something for school?" Christa asked.

"Uh. Sort of."

"Looks like a lot of work."

It was. I didn't mind though. I wished I could show my teachers and Emily and everyone else that I *could* apply myself. I just needed the right subject to come along. Werewolves seemed to be just my thing.

CHAPTER 9

LORENZO CALVETTI

✳ ✳

Sometimes, I thought I was really observant, like I saw all this stuff that other kids at school missed, like how ninety-five percent of what they cared about was actually totally pointless. Then there were other times when I missed something so super obvious that I wondered how observant I was after all.

What happened was, on my fourth night working at the Sunshine Café, I walked right by Lorenzo Calvetti without noticing him.

I spent so much time wondering about him, what he was going through, how he was dealing with having a missing girlfriend who was possibly dead but more probably a werewolf, that I had a whole picture of how I would meet him and what we would talk about. I thought of Lorenzo Calvetti only slightly less than I thought about Lizzie. But I still walked right by him.

Christa was the one who pointed him out while I was putting on my apron in the kitchen. I'd gotten to work late, since my car keys had gone missing again.

"Did you see who's here?" she whispered, nodding toward the dining room.

I glanced out the little window. Vernon was at his usual place, and a guy was sitting alone at a booth near the door. I shrugged at Christa, who was acting weird and flustered, like Adolf Hitler was out there chowing down on biscuits and honey butter.

"That's *him*," Christa said. "Lizzie's boyfriend."

I froze.

"He probably killed her, and I've been bringing him coffee for the last hour. That's all he wants. Black coffee."

I looked out at the dining room again. Lorenzo Calvetti. Lizzie's boyfriend. It *was* him in the booth. I'd only seen him twice, once in a newspaper picture and once from far away at the vigil. He looked even skinnier up close. His hair was greasy. His clothes looked slept in. But since he was maybe, probably, going through a really awful time, I figured I should cut him some slack. I shouldn't expect him to look the way he did in the newspaper photo when Lizzie was snuggled up next to him. That picture had been taken when he was happy. When he had a girlfriend. When he didn't have half the county pitying him, which was better than the other half, who thought he was a murderer.

Christa moved closer to me, as if Lorenzo could hear us from across the diner. "He totally creeps me out."

"I'll take over," I said.

I could tell Christa was relieved, which sort of made me feel good but sort of made me feel guilty, because Christa's discomfort hadn't inspired me to make the offer.

"Really? You don't mind? My shift is almost over anyway."

I told her that it really wasn't a problem until she looked like she believed me. I just had to make a quick phone call first.

✖ ✖ ✖

"Emily? You won't believe who's here," I whispered.

"Who's where?"

"At the café. I'm working." I'd gone into Mr. Walczak's office to make the call, because I'd forgotten to charge my cell phone again. I was pretty sure he wouldn't mind, due to the obvious importance of the situation.

"Is it Lizzie wondering why you stole her job?"

Since when was Emily such a comedian?

"This is serious, Em." I was so anxious that I was practically bouncing. The conversation was taking too long, and if Lorenzo was gone by the time I got back, I was pretty sure my plan would be ruined.

"OK, Hawthorn. Who's there?"

"Lorenzo Calvetti."

There was a pause on the other end of the line. "Lizzie's boyfriend?"

"Yep."

There was another pause. This one was longer. I was thinking

Emily and I'd gotten disconnected, but she finally said, "Please think about what you're doing."

"Well, I'm not going to walk up and tell him Lizzie's a werewolf."

"I have no idea *what* you're going to do, Hawthorn. That's what worries me."

Her response was too sad to bear. Emily and I used to have adventures. We used to talk about our lives and all the possibilities, and the future seemed so amazing. Emily didn't lecture me back then.

"I have to go," I said.

"Wait. I didn't mean to upset you. Just… This guy is grieving. You know that. This is serious for him."

"It's serious for me too." I hung up without waiting for her response.

✶✶✶

"More coffee?"

Lorenzo barely glanced up. "Sure."

I filled his mug, and my heart was pounding so hard that I was sure it would burst right out of my chest and cover half the restaurant in blood and gore. Which would remind Lorenzo of his potentially dismembered girlfriend, and he'd probably go home and commit suicide or something. Then all three of us would be dead, me and Lizzie and Lorenzo, and Emily would walk around telling people, "I *told* Hawthorn not to talk to him."

But that didn't happen. I finished pouring the coffee. He

didn't say thank you. I was about to walk away. But that didn't happen either.

"Hey, you're Lorenzo Calvetti, right?"

He looked up. "Yeah."

"Your girlfriend is missing."

"Yeah."

"That really sucks."

He didn't say anything, just stared at me. His eyes were dark blue and bloodshot. He must not have been getting much sleep lately.

I was getting uncomfortable and wondered if I'd said something totally inappropriate, which I guess wouldn't have been unusual.

"Look," I said, "I didn't mean to be weird or anything. I just thought I should say something, because it would be weirder to act all quiet around you so you'd wonder if I was, like, thinking you killed her, which I wasn't. Well. Maybe a tiny bit. You didn't kill her, did you?"

He stared at me like I was an escaped mental patient, like I was the only one who'd straight-out asked him if he was a murderer.

"No," he said. "I didn't kill my girlfriend."

"Well. That's good."

We stared at each other for another second, and there were so many important things I wanted to say, but I didn't know how. So instead, I said, "Let me know if you need more coffee."

I started toward the kitchen.

"Hey, wait," Lorenzo called.

I turned back to him.

"It's Enzo. My parents are the only ones who use my full name."

"Enzo. Got it." I smiled and then scurried into the kitchen.

❧ ❧ ❧

I paced back and forth in front of the stove, still carrying the coffee carafe. I didn't know what I was doing. Emily was right. Everything about the situation was getting out of hand. Vinny, the cook, watched me with a bemused expression, which I didn't really appreciate.

Enzo. People called him Enzo. His friends called him Enzo. Was I a friend? Of course not. I didn't even know him. *Could* I be his friend? Maybe. Did he kill his girlfriend? Certainly not.

I peeked into the dining room. Enzo was hunched over his coffee mug again. He looked like the kind of guy who shopped at thrift stores and wrote poetry, which was considerably different from the kind of guy who dismembered beautiful young girls in the woods.

But how did I know that? I didn't. I hadn't even known he went by a nickname until five minutes before. I'd spent so much time thinking about Lizzie and Enzo but hardly knew anything real about them. It had started to feel as if they only existed in my head. As if I'd made them up or could make them into anything I wanted them to be.

Meeting Enzo changed everything.

It was Mark Twain getting on a bus and sitting down next to Huck Finn. Or F. Scott Fitzgerald running into Jay Gatsby at the grocery store. It was meeting someone I invented and realizing I hadn't actually invented him at all.

For once, I wasn't just pretending.

Something interesting was really happening.

Vinny pulled me out of my thoughts. "You got a crush or something?"

"No," I said with as much scorn as I could muster. "I don't have a crush."

"What then? You're blocking the grill."

"Oh, because we have so many customers putting in orders?" I moved to the other side of the kitchen anyway, because there was no point in arguing.

Enzo. I'd met Enzo Calvetti, the guy with a missing girlfriend. But not a dead girlfriend. And for sure not a girlfriend he'd killed.

I thought about the full moon and Wolf Creek and the two of them in the tent that night. Something had happened to Lizzie; that was for sure. And maybe Enzo had been there, but her disappearance wasn't his fault. No matter what people called him, he wasn't a murderer.

Maybe he just had the bad luck of dating a werewolf.

I could see Lizzie so clearly, rushing into a clearing, not knowing what was happening to her and being afraid but at the same time feeling more alive than ever before. She would have understood that she was finally becoming what she was always meant to be.

I saw Lizzie tilt her head back to look at the swollen moon, saw her golden hair falling over her shoulders. Her lips pulled back to reveal her perfectly straight, white teeth starting to lengthen, and then the beautiful young girl snarled and fell to her knees as the snarl became a howl and her bones reshaped themselves.

I wished I'd been there to see it.

When I looked at the dining room again, Lorenzo Calvetti was gone. *Enzo*, I corrected myself. I wished I'd had a chance to talk to him more, but it wasn't too much of a concern. I was sure he'd be back.

✷✷✷

I was sitting outside on the porch reading *The Werewolf of Paris*, which a lot of people consider to be *the* werewolf novel, when a car door slammed shut. There were muffled voices and shuffling sounds and then another door slam.

It was around midnight, and the neighborhood was dark. I got off the swing and walked to the edge of the porch to see a shape emerging from the darkness. It was looming, too big to be a person, and moving in an inhuman way. It figured that just when something fascinating was finally happening in my life, a monster would come along and kill me, ruining everything. The monster drew closer and split in two, and I saw that it wasn't a monster after all. Rather, two people, one leaning on the other for support.

My brother was clearly very drunk, and Connor struggled to keep him upright. When they neared the house, Connor noticed me.

"Thorny. What are you doing out here?"

"I live here. Is he going to throw up?"

"I don't think so. He already lost most of his dinner in my car."

"Gross."

Connor half dragged Rush up the porch steps.

"Where'd you park?" I asked.

"Down the street. I didn't want to wake up your parents."

I helped Connor dump Rush on the swing, where he instantly passed out. He reeked of beer and vomit, which was not a combination I enjoyed. Since my seat had been stolen, I sat at the top of the porch steps. Connor sat down next to me.

"*The Werewolf of Paris*," he said, pointing to the cover of my book. "Any good?"

"Yeah. It's pretty dark. There's a lot of rape and incest and stuff."

"Sounds charming." He paused. "I hear you've taken an interest in werewolves lately."

I winced. How many people had my brother been babbling to?

"Rush told you about the Lizzie thing, huh?"

"He did."

"And you think I'm crazy."

"Nope," Connor said.

I looked over at him, surprised.

Connor grinned. "I'd only think you were crazy if you really believed it."

"I do believe it," I protested.

"Sure you do, Thorny."

I rolled my eyes and opened my book. A minute later, when Connor hadn't left, I closed it again.

"What do you think of Lizzie?" I asked.

"I think she probably got lost."

"No, not about her vanishing. About Lizzie as a person."

"I don't think anything about her," Connor said.

"You must think *something*. You were part of that group when you were in high school."

"Not like Lizzie and Rush were. I played football because I grew up thinking I had to. I didn't like it much. And I wasn't very good."

"You don't miss it?"

Connor laughed. "Not even a little bit."

"Rush does."

"Rush thought football was going to be his life."

That was true. My brother had thought he'd get into Ohio State on a full football scholarship. They didn't even want him on the team. Maybe, probably, he could have gone somewhere else and played, but his stupid jock pride wouldn't let him. Now, he wasn't playing football anywhere and taking classes at the community college.

"What's going to be *your* life?" I asked Connor.

"I'm majoring in electrical engineering. So I guess at the moment, it's that."

"Sounds sort of boring."

"I'm having way more fun than I ever did on the field."

The whole conversation was weird. Connor had been hanging around my house since I was twelve, but I'd never talked to him so much at once. Rush had always kept his friends separate from me.

"I don't believe you weren't in love with Lizzie," I said after a while. "Everyone was."

Connor looked at me and seemed genuinely curious. "Why are you so sure of that?"

"She was perfect."

"She was just a girl. And not really my type. Honestly, she was kind of dull."

"Then you're, like, the only person on the planet who thinks so."

"Don't confuse being popular with being interesting," Connor said.

That made me pause for a second, even though I was positive Connor was lying. A girl like Lizzie was everyone's type, and anyone who said otherwise was making an excuse for why she never chose him.

"I met her boyfriend tonight," I said. "Enzo. He seemed sad."

"I'd hope so. His girlfriend disappeared."

I suddenly desperately wanted to be alone. I wanted to keep reading my book. I wanted to think about everything Enzo had said to me. I stood up.

"I'll check on Rush in the morning, OK? Thanks for bringing him home."

"No problem," Connor said.

I watched him walk down the street to his car and wondered if it was possible he actually meant the part about Lizzie not being his type. Were there people who were immune to her charms? It seemed more unlikely than the existence of werewolves.

CHAPTER 10

DAY SEVENTEEN

The search parties started to lose their enthusiasm. At school, people talked about Lizzie's disappearance as if it had happened in the distant past. Every once in a while, Lizzie's mom went on TV, begging anyone who had any information about her daughter to come forward. That was the saddest part. Other people could forget about Lizzie, but not Ms. Lovett. She'd always feel the pain of her daughter's disappearance and the pain of watching everyone around her slowly stop caring.

I thought about calling Ms. Lovett. I knew how stupid it was, which is why I only *thought* about it. But I wanted her to know someone still had Lizzie on their mind. And I wanted her to know Lizzie was in a better place, which didn't mean dead but out in the woods where she belonged. But I couldn't say that, because people didn't agree with the notion of werewolves, which had become increasingly awkward for me.

Like when Mychelle Adler came up to my locker and said, "So I hear you think Lizzie Lovett turned into a werewolf."

"Where'd you hear that?"

"Is it true?" Her expression said that she really, really wanted it to be true, because then she could make fun of me forever.

School had been bad enough since I'd read my Griffin Mills essay. For years, I'd been mostly ignored for being weird and nerdy. The essay made it different. People started actively making fun of me. It was hard to walk into school every day knowing I was going to be mocked. I didn't get why everyone was treating what I wrote like it was a huge insult. I didn't think I was the only one who wished she'd grown up somewhere else.

"Didn't your parents ever tell you there's no such thing as werewolves?" Mychelle asked.

"Didn't your parents ever tell you opinions should be left to people with brains?"

For a second, I thought Mychelle might hit me. It would have been an extremely unexpected addition to my day and slightly fascinating, because I'd never been in a fistfight. But she backed off.

"Watch yourself, Hawthorn Creely."

I burst out laughing. "Seriously? Watch myself? Are we in the remake of *Mean Girls*?"

Mychelle gave me one last unamused look and went on her way. The good thing was I didn't have any classes with her for the rest of the day. The bad thing was Griffin Mills High School was pretty small, and there were plenty of other people I had to avoid.

✱✱✱

"If you didn't want people making fun of you for thinking Lizzie's a werewolf, then you shouldn't have *told* anyone you think Lizzie's a werewolf," Emily said at lunch.

She had a point.

Though I'd only told four people, and I couldn't imagine Emily or my parents running around town spreading gossip. Rush had really outdone himself.

"I wish you'd just entertain the possibility that I'm right," I told Emily.

"Hawthorn, you can't will werewolves into existence because you're bored."

I took a bite of my sandwich, which was some sort of avocado concoction I wouldn't have chosen to eat.

"I wonder if Enzo will come back to the diner."

"Why?" Emily asked. "Because he's so desperate to see you? You're lucky he hasn't."

"He's not a killer."

"Maybe not. But he's damaged."

I was pretty sick of everyone acting like they knew what I needed when no one really knew me at all. I was about to tell that to Emily when the gym door opened and a guy walked out.

"Sorry. I didn't think anyone came out here," he said when he saw us. I'd noticed him around school because he wore skinny jeans and had all sorts of piercings, which was not the usual style in the Mills.

"Well, we do," I said.

"Mind if I smoke? There's nowhere else to go on campus."

I shrugged, and he lit a cigarette. Then he nodded at Emily.

"Hey, you're in my guitar class, right?"

"Yeah," Emily said. "Sixth period."

"You're really good."

Emily blushed, and I felt embarrassed for her.

"I'm OK. Piano is my instrument. I just took guitar for fun."

"Maybe you should think about switching instruments. I'm Logan, by the way."

He held out his hand. They shook. Emily told him her name. I wasn't addressed at all. I focused on my sandwich as if I was *choosing* not to be a part of their conversation.

"You've been playing guitar for a long time, haven't you?" Emily asked.

"I got my first guitar before I could walk."

I rolled my eyes. Emily smiled at him.

"It shows."

"I'm actually in a band," Logan said. "Strength in Numbers? You might have heard of us."

I couldn't believe he actually uttered that clichéd line. I looked at Emily to see if she was equally amused, but she was gazing at Logan like he was the first boy she'd ever seen.

"Yeah, I've heard some kids mention you guys," Emily said. "I've never heard you play though."

"You should come to one of our shows. It's pretty intense. We do this sort of metal-bluegrass fusion. I think you'll like it."

I snorted.

"Let me know when you have your next gig," Emily said.

"Sure thing." He threw down the cigarette and crushed it with the heel of his Doc Marten. "See you in sixth."

I gaped at Emily as soon as the door shut. "Metal-bluegrass fusion? What does that even mean? Does he scream obscenities while strumming a banjo?"

"Don't be so judgmental."

"Seriously? That guy is clearly inviting judgment on himself."

"Sort of like someone who believes in werewolves?"

I scowled.

"Besides," Emily went on, "I've heard that his band is actually really good."

"Heard that from who?"

"People."

"What people?" I pressed.

"Friends, Hawthorn. My *friends*. You're not the only person I talk to."

I wasn't?

"Are you going to see his band play?" I asked.

"Maybe. Do you want to come?"

"Maybe."

I didn't know why we were arguing over something so stupid.

The last thing I wanted to do was fight with Emily. But I was still uncomfortable with her having friends I didn't know, talking about music things I didn't get.

How long before Emily's new friends, the people who shared her interests, stole her away from me? Pretty soon, maybe Emily wouldn't have any use for me at all. Why would she? She belonged to a world I had no place in.

CHAPTER 11

IN THE WOODS

✳ ✳

I was sitting on a stool at the back of the Sunshine Café, updating the specials on the whiteboard, when Vinny the cook came in from his smoke break and said, "Your boyfriend is here, Creely."

I knew he meant Enzo and didn't bother telling Vinny that calling him my boyfriend was not as hilarious as he thought it was. I also didn't tell him we weren't in a locker room, so there was no reason to call me by my last name.

I got up and peeked through the window to the dining room. Sure enough, Enzo Calvetti was sitting at the booth by the door, wearing the same ratty sweater as last time I saw him. I grabbed the coffee carafe and made my way out of the kitchen.

"Coffee?"

"Yeah, thanks," Enzo said.

"Any news on your girlfriend?"

"Nope."

"Sorry."

I finished pouring and stood there, hating myself because I

knew I was being awkward, but not wanting to walk away, even though I didn't really have anything more to say.

"Are you coming here because it makes you feel close to her?" I blurted out.

"I come here because no one bothers me."

"Sorry," I mumbled, thinking maybe I should take a vow of silence to prevent stupid things from coming out of my mouth.

"Hey, that didn't come out right," Enzo said. "I didn't mean you."

"No, I'm probably being invasive. Let me know if you need anything else."

The next thing he said startled me. "What's your name, kid?"

"Hawthorn Creely."

"Hawthorne like the writer?"

I usually said yes when people asked that question, though it was a lie. It would have been nice to be named after a writer.

"Hawthorn like the tree," I said, making a face.

"Your parents named you after a tree?"

"They sure did."

Enzo smiled. "There's got to be a story behind that."

"There is, and it's one of my least favorite stories ever."

"Now you have to tell me."

I sighed. "Apparently, I was conceived under a hawthorn tree."

Enzo laughed, and I smiled, though I didn't think there was anything remotely funny about it. I was still angry at my mom for sharing that information with me in the first place.

When Enzo stopped laughing, he looked me in the eye, which made me sort of uncomfortable. I didn't know if I should stay or go.

"Why are you being so nice to me?" he asked.

My surprise must have shown on my face.

"Most people are treating me like a criminal."

"I'm not like most people," I said.

"I can tell."

He didn't sound put off by it. It was possible he even thought it was a *good* thing.

"And I know you're not a criminal," I said.

"How?" Enzo asked. "You don't know me. And if I'd killed Lizzie, I'd hardly go around broadcasting it."

"Are you trying to convince me you *are* a murderer then?"

Enzo smiled. That was the third time. When he smiled or laughed, it felt like a victory.

"I guess I'm being nice to you because I know how it feels," I said.

"How what feels?"

"Being an outsider."

As soon as I spoke, I wished I could take it back. I waited for him to say, "Now that you mention it, you *are* kind of a loser." Or maybe, "Please don't compare me to you."

Enzo looked at me for a long time. I held his gaze, even though it made me feel completely exposed, even though I wanted the floor to open up and swallow me whole.

And then he said, "You want to get out of here?"

It took me a second to process what he was saying, because it was so close to something I would have imagined that I almost thought I was experiencing an auditory hallucination.

"I have an hour before the diner closes."

"The cook will cover for you. He did it for Lizzie all the time." I hesitated.

"I'm not going to kill you, if that's what you're thinking."

"No. I wasn't thinking that." I paused a moment longer, which was just long enough for me to make up my mind. "I'll get my things."

❉ ❉ ❉

Enzo didn't have a car.

"I can barely afford a bus pass," he said.

I shrugged, and we climbed into my Rabbit.

"Where do you want to go?" I asked.

"Anywhere. Just away from people."

Mostly, we didn't talk. I drove around aimlessly, sneaking glances at him from the corner of my eye. Only maybe it wasn't *that* aimless, because we ended up near Wolf Creek Road.

"Are you driving to where Lizzie disappeared?" Enzo asked, right about the same time I realized where we were.

"Not on purpose. I swear. I'll turn around."

"No, it's OK. Go there."

That's how, not even a month after Lizzie Lovett disappeared, I ended up at her campsite with her boyfriend.

"I haven't been here since that night," Enzo told me as we walked around a small clearing. "I haven't gone out with the search parties."

"Why not?"

"I guess I kept thinking, what if I was the one who found her? Her body, I mean. I couldn't deal with seeing her that way."

I wanted to tell him there wasn't a body to find. Instead, I made myself busy looking around the campsite.

The tent was long gone, but the ring of stones where they'd built their fire was still there. What had it been like that night? Did they laugh and talk while roasting marshmallows? What were they talking about right before they went to sleep and Lizzie disappeared?

I wanted to ask Enzo a million questions. But he seemed skittish. If I said too much, he might dart off into the woods and become as lost to me as Lizzie was. So instead, I just watched him and hoped he would share some clues.

He pulled something out of his pocket, and for a moment, I thought it would be a gun or knife. Then, right before he murdered me, I'd have time to reflect on how dumb it was to go off with him, and Emily would tell people, "I told her not to trust Lorenzo Calvetti."

But a second later, Enzo was rolling a cigarette, which I guess was still dangerous but not a weapon. He walked around the clearing, his shoulders hunched and the tip of the cigarette glowing. I thought maybe, probably, I'd never seen someone look so broken.

"This place seems haunted now," Enzo said.

"The woods always seem haunted to me."

He took a long drag on his cigarette and blew smoke at the sky. "Have you heard about that suicide forest in Japan?"

"Um, I don't think so," I said, trying not to sound too intrigued, since it was kind of morbid.

"People from all over the world go there to die. It happens so often, they have signs up, you know, encouraging people to think twice. It's, like, the most fucked-up tourist destination ever."

"How do you know about it?" I asked.

"Read it somewhere. I wrote a song about it a few years ago."

"You're a musician?"

"Not really," he said. He circled the clearing silently, and I wondered if that would be the end of it, but then he spoke. "I always wondered if a place could be bad. Not what a person did there, but the place itself. Like, if you went to the suicide forest, would you feel that something was wrong as soon as you stepped in?"

It was the most fascinating thing anyone had said to me in a long time.

"Do you feel that way here?" I asked.

He laughed and ran a hand through his shaggy hair. "Yeah, I

guess. I know it's in my head though, because I didn't have that feeling when I was here with Lizzie."

"What happened that night?"

"What happened? Nothing. We had fun. Then I went to sleep and woke up in a parallel universe."

"You didn't hear anything weird during the night?"

Enzo sighed. "No, officer. I didn't hear anything. I didn't see anything. Lizzie's mood was fine. We hadn't fought. Everything was normal. Wherever Lizzie went, I slept through it."

"Sorry," I said. "I guess you've been getting a lot of questions."

"It's a wonder I'm not in jail."

"In the paper, the police chief said you aren't a suspect."

"Sure, that's what he *said*." He tossed his cigarette on the ground and crushed it out.

The silence was uncomfortable. I searched for something to fill it.

"I went to high school with Lizzie," I said. "Well, sort of. I was a freshman when she was a senior. She was friends with my brother."

"Really?" Enzo looked surprised. I didn't know if that was good or bad.

"She was the homecoming queen that year. There's still a picture in the trophy case of her riding around on the float."

"Homecoming queen? Huh. She never told me that."

I decided it was probably in my best interest to keep quiet

about the rest of it. How I'd hated Lizzie and spent half my fresh-man year having horrible thoughts about her.

I sat down on a flat rock near the middle of the clearing. A minute later, Enzo sat down next to me.

"We never talked about high school. It wasn't a time I like to think about much," Enzo said.

"I don't like to think about it, and I'm still there."

Enzo started rolling another cigarette. "What's your deal, kid?"

"What do you mean?"

"Why are you out in the woods with me?"

I shrugged. "You asked me to hang out."

"You aren't afraid? I could be a killer."

"But you aren't."

"You don't know that."

There hadn't been many moments in my life where there were two clear paths to take. This was one of them. I could tell Enzo he seemed like a nice guy who missed his girlfriend and go home and forget about the night altogether. Or I could tell him the truth.

My mom always says when we're honest with others, we're honest with ourselves, and that leads to a purer state of being. My dad puts it simpler. He just says honesty is the best policy.

"What if Lizzie turned into a werewolf?"

Enzo laughed. Then he saw my face. "You're not joking, are you?"

So I went ahead and told him everything.

✻✻✻

Enzo didn't talk for most of the ride to his apartment. When he did, he said, "You're a weird kid, Hawthorn."

"I'm not a kid."

"It wasn't an insult."

Then we were silent again, except for when Enzo gave me directions.

I tried not to be disappointed but couldn't help it. I had sort of thought Enzo was going to be an ally. Instead, after I'd spilled my whole werewolf theory, he sat quietly for a long time, then said it was an interesting explanation, then said he should probably get home.

I considered apologizing. Or trying to convince him I was right. Or telling him that we could hang out again, and I would keep my mouth shut about the supernatural. But I didn't say any of that.

I pulled up in front of Enzo's apartment complex. There were bars on the windows, and the other cars in the parking lot were worse off than mine. It made me feel even more depressed.

Enzo looked at me for a moment before he got out of the car. I didn't look away, even though I wanted to.

"I wish I lived in your world, Hawthorn."

I wish you did too, I thought.

I watched him walk into the building, watched until a light came on in one of the second floor apartments. It felt like something very important had slipped out of my grasp.

I got the urge to call Emily, to pour out details of my and Enzo's conversation. But she'd just lecture me for hanging out with him in the first place. So instead, I sat in the parking lot with my car running until I realized how awkward it would be if Enzo looked outside and saw me still parked there.

Not that it mattered what he thought of me now. I doubted I'd ever see him again.

CHAPTER 12

SUNDOG AND THE CARAVAN

✳ ✳

The thing about high school is that you have to pretend you don't care what people think even though that's *all* you care about. I was pretty sure that whether you're a cheerleader or on the chess team, you spend a crazy amount of time wondering what people are saying about you or if they're saying anything at all. It used to be that I thought it was worse to be forgotten, that even being made fun of was better than being invisible. Then there was my essay, and the rumors about me thinking Lizzie was a werewolf, and then the caravan arrived.

My dad and I peered through the living room window as it drove up the street. Some of our neighbors were on their porches, alerted by all the honking. They were acting like it was a parade. Being blatantly curious is OK when it's not your life that's about to be ruined.

"I'll never be able to show my face at school again."

Instead of comforting me, my dad grimly stared out the window. Which confirmed that our house was the caravan's destination. Not that I'd had much doubt.

"Sparrow!" my dad shouted. "Come in here, please."

"What is it?" my mom asked, coming down the stairs.

I gestured to the window.

My mom peered outside and instantly looked flustered. My dad's mouth had turned into a very straight line. That's when I figured it would be in my best interest to pack my bags and flee the county.

Rush came in the room and asked what was going on.

"Our lives are being ruined," I said.

Then he joined us, and the whole Creely family watched the hippie caravan make its way up our quiet, suburban street.

The lead car wasn't a car at all. It was an old school bus that was painted purple and had curtains hanging in the windows. It was also the vehicle playing the music, some jangly sounding rhythm, with lots of bells and maybe a fiddle. Emily would have known. Three cars followed the bus, two no-name sedans and a beat-up VW Bug that made me ashamed to be a Volkswagen owner. One of the sedans was painted like a psychedelic hippie car from the sixties, complete with peace signs and flowers and swirly lines. The other sedan would have passed for normal if it hadn't been in the middle of such craziness.

I could have crawled faster than the procession was moving. They were taking their time, making sure every single person in the neighborhood had a chance to get outside to witness the Creely family's shame.

"Sparrow," my dad said. "What is this?"

I could tell from my dad's voice that he was not even a little bit entertained, and I could tell from my mom's face that she knew it too.

"I...well, it's the group I used to go with."

"What the hell are they doing *here*? Did you know about this?"

My mom shook her head, and I believed her, but I didn't blame her any less. I wished she'd discover she was allergic to soy. I wished all her crystals would spontaneously shatter. I wished her yoga DVDs would get replaced with war movies.

By that time, the caravan had reached our house. The bus pulled in front of the driveway, completely blocking it. While the other cars found parking spaces along the street, the door to the bus opened, and the driver stepped out. He was old. In his sixties at least, but maybe, probably, even older. He had long, gray hair and wore a paisley shirt and Birkenstocks. He was pretty much a walking stereotype.

I glanced at my mom, who looked even more surprised than before, except in a good way. Two seconds later, she was out the door and in the old hippie's arms.

"Dad, this is really weird," I said.

"Yes, Hawthorn, it is."

"Who's the old dude?" Rush asked.

My dad sighed deeply and ignored my brother. "Come on. Let's see what he's doing here."

✿ ✿ ✿

There were twelve of them in all. The old guy was clearly their leader, and he'd apparently once been my mom's.

"You remember James," my mom said to the old guy, "and these are our children, Rushford and Hawthorn. Kids, this is Sundog."

Rush snorted, which I thought was a little unfair, considering his own name.

Sundog bowed to us. I wondered if I was supposed to bow back, but I couldn't without feeling like an idiot, so I smiled at him instead.

"Well met, Rushford and Hawthorn. May the blessings of light be upon you."

Then my mom and Sundog started talking, and half their words were nonsense. Apparently, a message he'd received during cosmic meditation told him to seek out our house. I zoned out and looked at the rest of the group. Some of them were standing behind Sundog, waiting to be introduced, and the rest were doing something that filled me with dread: unpacking.

None of the other hippies were as old as Sundog, but there were a couple around my mom's age. One girl with long dreadlocks looked like she was only a few years older than me. Another woman, whose age I couldn't tell, had her head shaved bald. Half the caravan had bare feet, and all of them wore clothes that looked like they hadn't been washed in way too long. I felt queasy from the competing smells of pot and patchouli.

Sundog named the other hippies, and they were all Dakota and Journey and Marigold. I made a point of not putting names to faces. I refused to accept that they'd be around long enough for me to know who they were.

As Sundog told my mom about his recent travels through space and beingness, a small dog ran off the bus. It looked like a miniature coyote, one that had been in the wild for a long time without knowing how to care for itself. Its black-and-brown coat was mangy and standing on end. The dog ran up to us, yipping, and Sundog scooped it off the ground.

"This here is Timothy Leary," he said. "We found her on the side of the road near Phoenix."

"You named a girl dog Timothy Leary?" Rush asked, as if that was the most troubling thing about the whole situation.

"We try not to place gender limitations on ourselves," Sundog said.

The dreadlocked girl spoke up. "Yeah, man. That kind of thinking holds you back from true cognitive enlightenment."

Rush just stared.

I wasn't on board with the girl's philosophy, but I knew how it felt to get those kind of looks. I tried to keep my own face neutral.

After that, I stood by numbly and listened to details. Yes, they needed a place to stay. No, they didn't expect to be put up in the house. They had tents. They preferred to be outside anyway. Yes, they knew it was fall and would be cold soon, but they'd be gone before the first snow.

I looked up at my dad and saw the resignation on his face. He was going to let this happen. He had the power to turn the hippies away, to keep our house free of incense and bongo drums and spiritual enlightenment, and he was choosing not to.

I was angry at all of them: my mom, my dad, Sundog. I was even angry at Timothy Leary—the dog, not the man—who was probably the most blameless in the entire situation.

"Kids," my mom said, "why don't you help unload the bus?"

"Are you serious?" I asked.

Her frown told me that she was indeed.

"It's like being forced to dig our own graves," I said to Rush as we trudged over to the bus.

My brother laughed. We'd finally found something we could agree on.

CHAPTER 13

ANIMA AND ANIMUS

✻ ✻

At school on Monday, most people were talking about homecoming, which annoyed me, because I was already worried about the caravan and how many people in school already knew about it. Probably everyone, because news travels fast in small towns.

"Why are we even having a homecoming dance?" I asked Emily at lunch. "We just had the Welcome Back dance, like, a month ago. It's the exact same thing."

"Homecoming is formal. The Welcome Back dance is more of a social."

"It's the same thing, Emily. It literally means the same thing."

"One has a football game and a queen and king. That's different."

"People just make up excuses to have dances and parties. Like the President's Day dance last year. Totally weird and pointless."

"That *was* sort of bizarre," Emily admitted.

"These dances exist just to torture me."

Emily looked down at her salad as if it was the most interesting thing she'd ever seen. "People go to dances to have fun, Hawthorn. Not to torture people."

"Obviously you haven't read *Carrie*."

"You think someone's going to invite you to the dance to play a prank on you?"

"No," I said. "I don't think I'm going to get invited at all. I'll be the only loser in the school sitting at home alone that night."

I waited for Emily to chime in and say *she* wouldn't be at the dance. Instead, she speared a piece of lettuce with her fork but didn't eat it. "I went out with Logan on Saturday."

"What?" I didn't bother hiding my surprise. "Metal-bluegrass fusion?"

Emily nodded, looking guilty.

"Like, on a date?"

"I guess so," Emily said, still looking at her salad instead of at me.

Since when did we go on dates without telling each other first?

"What did you do?" I asked, trying to sound casual, since that was apparently how Emily wanted to play it. I refrained from asking her if she was going to start wearing fishnet tights and get her face pierced and ditch me for people who knew what metal-bluegrass fusion was.

"We saw this concert in Pittsburgh. Jazz. It was really good."

"Oh. Do you like him?" I braced myself for the answer, even though I already knew what it would be.

Emily thought for a second. "Yeah, I think so."

"I'm pretty sure he wears eyeliner."

"Hawthorn."

"I'm just saying."

I tried to imagine them together at a jazz concert. Emily wearing pastels and Logan with his dyed-black fauxhawk. I knew the saying about opposites attracting, but *really*?

I was deeply bothered, and I wasn't sure why, but I suspected it had something to do with jealousy. Not jealousy because I wanted Logan for myself. That would be absurd. And not jealousy because Emily having a boyfriend would mean she spent less time with me like when she was dating Marc, otherwise known as the most boring person on the planet. But because I had been alive for seventeen years and no one had ever liked me enough to go on more than a few awkward dates and share more-awkward first kisses. I was pretty sure there was a sign on me that said I was one hundred percent undateable.

"Did you kiss him?" I asked.

Emily's face turned bright red, and it was charming enough to make me feel less jealous. Slightly.

"Did that stupid lip ring feel weird?" I asked.

"It was…interesting. His tongue is pierced too."

"Your mom is going to have a fit."

"I know. I wish she was more like your mom."

I laughed. "Emily, right now, *Sparrow* has a band of hippies set up in a shantytown in our backyard. Believe me, your conservative mother isn't so bad."

Emily laughed too, and for a second, we were having fun together, and everything felt like it used to.

✻✻✻

It was dark when my shift at the Sunshine Café ended, which is why I was uncomfortable that someone was hovering around my car. Maybe I was wrong, and Lizzie Lovett really had been taken into the woods and killed, and I was going to be next.

Then the potential serial killer spoke. "Hey."

It was Enzo. My fear turned to surprise, then excitement, then nervousness.

"Hi. What's going on?"

He leaned against the passenger-side door, smoking a cigarette. He hesitated before answering me. "I keep thinking about what you said. The werewolf thing."

"What about it?" I asked cautiously.

"I don't know. Maybe we're both crazy."

Sometimes, people say I have a tendency to jump to conclusions, so I paused, even though I was pretty sure I knew what Enzo was getting at. "Do you believe it then?"

"How can I say I believe something like that?"

"You're here."

Enzo took a long drag on his cigarette. "Yeah. I'm here."

"And you've been thinking about it."

"Yeah."

I waited.

"And I guess your theory is better than any of the alternatives," Enzo finally said.

It wasn't the perfect response, but it was enough to make me want to jump up and down and do cartwheels and shout to the entire world that someone was finally on my side. But I was afraid of scaring Enzo, so I bit my lip and tried to restrain myself.

"The thing is," Enzo continues, "even if Lizzie *did* turn into a werewolf, what are we supposed to do about it?"

That was the easy part. "We find her."

✶✶✶

Enzo took me to a pizza place in the basement of an old office building. There was no sign out front, just steps leading down from the street. The redbrick walls were covered in graffiti, and it was dark and cramped and my feet stuck to the floor when I walked.

We sat at a table in the corner, away from the college kids who were drinking pitchers of beer and arguing about religion and philosophy and everything else they could think to argue about. I asked Enzo about the raised platform on the far side of the room.

"Bands play sometimes," he told me. "They have poetry readings too. Everyone here is trying to be a beatnik."

I didn't know much about beatniks, except it was a movement

that came before the hippie movement, and my mom sometimes mentioned it.

"Are you?" I asked Enzo.

"I'm not trying to be anything."

Our pizza showed up, and I attempted to eat some, even though I was too excited to be hungry. How could I think of eating when I'd finally found an ally? Enzo finished a slice, took a long drink of beer, and then got down to business.

"So, you're the werewolf expert. How does all of this work?"

"Well, I'm not exactly sure. Werewolf lore isn't consistent. It's not like becoming a vampire. There are werewolf legends from all over the world, and none of them match up exactly."

Once I started talking, words poured out of my mouth. I hadn't realized how much I'd wanted someone to ask about werewolves and actually listen to my response. "In some legends, a werewolf is created when a person is bitten and the wolf virus, or whatever you want to call it, gets into their blood. In other legends, someone *chooses* to become a werewolf, and there's a whole ceremony and ritual. Magic, I guess. The last way is that someone is just born a werewolf. That's what makes the most sense for Lizzie."

"So she's always been a werewolf?" Enzo asked, frowning.

I talked fast, before his skepticism could take over. "Yeah, but she probably hadn't turned yet. Think of puberty. You reach a certain age or a certain point in your life, and it's just your time. Imagine that Lizzie goes her entire life not knowing much about werewolves, but sometimes, she has intense cravings for red meat, or she always has tons of energy on the full moon. And as she gets older, things get stranger and stranger. She has weird dreams. She hates being inside. Her sense of smell becomes much more developed. Then there's some significant day, like her twenty-first birthday, and all of the stuff she's been feeling gets overwhelming. She has this sense that something isn't right. It's as if her body isn't the body she's supposed to be in. And one night, she suddenly understands what it all means, what she's supposed to do. So she goes into the woods."

Enzo's elbows were on the table, and he leaned forward, hanging on every word I said. It made me feel more alive than I had in a long time.

"You really think that's what happened?"

I nodded.

I went back to eating my pizza and gave Enzo time to think. He pulled out his zippo lighter and absently flicked it open and shut. I watched his hands, mesmerized. His fingers were long. Emily would have said he'd make a good piano player. The sleeve of his sweater pulled up slightly, and I could see a tattoo on the inside of his wrist.

"What's your tattoo say?"

Enzo pushed up the other sleeve and held out both arms for me to see, the pale insides of his wrists exposed. "Anima and animus. It represents the dual nature in all of us."

"Lizzie must love that."

"She does, actually."

I wanted to ask if he had any more tattoos but figured I shouldn't change the topic. "Now it's your turn. Tell *me* something."

"I don't know anything about werewolves."

"But you know Lizzie. Start with Wolf Creek. She was the one who wanted to camp there, right?"

Enzo nodded. "She loves that place. Said she used to look for wolves there when she was a kid."

"She loves wolves."

"She likes them a lot. But she's not fanatical about them or anything."

"Fanatical enough to wear a wolf talisman."

Enzo laughed. "Talisman? That's a little melodramatic. It's a necklace."

"With a wolf tooth."

"It has to do with some Indian tribe around here, I think."

I started to feel a little defeated. "There must be something else."

Like hadn't he noticed that Lizzie's legs were unnaturally hairy? Maybe he'd heard a howl or two?

Enzo's gaze was back on his lighter. He brought the flame to life and extinguished it. Finally, he set the zippo down decisively. "There's this shitty petting zoo, like, half an hour from here. You know where I mean?"

I nodded.

"Well, they have all these animals you can touch, you know, pigs and goats and whatever. And in the back, there are some big animals in cages."

"Wolves," I said. I leaned forward too, anxiously waiting.

"Yeah. They have a couple wolves. Lizzie wanted to see them, so we drive out there and pay fifteen bucks a person to get in. Lizzie goes straight to the wolf cage and kneels down in the dirt. Wolves are nocturnal though. They're asleep in this den structure, and we can't even see them."

My heart was pounding, and a chill ran down my spine, but not the kind of chill like when you're cold or scared. The kind you get when you realize you're about to hear something incredibly important.

"So Lizzie's kneeling there, and she whistles. And just like that, one of the wolves comes out of the den. She called it, and it came. It walks right up to her, and they stare at each other. The wolf is this massive gray animal. It towers over Lizzie, just watching her. A minute later, it turns and goes back to the den, and Lizzie finds some guy who works there and tells him the brown wolf is sick. The zookeeper guy goes and checks it out, and sure enough, the brown wolf is sick."

"The gray wolf told her!"

"That's what it seemed like, yeah. Like they were communicating. I asked her what the hell had happened there, but she never said. We didn't talk about it again."

I picked a piece of pineapple off the pizza and chewed slowly, taking in Enzo's story.

"If she's a werewolf, why didn't she just change into a wolf and come back after the full moon?" Enzo asked quietly.

I wondered the same thing.

"I don't know. In most werewolf legends, the person can change at will. They're at their strongest during the full moon, but they don't need its power. In other legends, werewolves are forced to change on the full moon whether they want to or not. But the rest of the time, they can shift when they choose. So maybe Lizzie hasn't been back in human form since the night she disappeared."

"You really believe all this, kid?" Enzo asked.

That was maybe, probably, a really good question.

"Yes," I said. And if Enzo noticed my hesitation, he was nice enough to not call me on it.

I met his gaze, and we stared at each other for a long moment before he said, "So, what do we do?"

"I told you—we find her. And help her figure out how to, you know, balance her two forms. You can have your girlfriend back."

"And what do you get out of it?"

I shrugged. "Knowing for sure."

"Knowing what happened to Lizzie?"

"Knowing there's more to the world than what we see every day."

Enzo nodded. Maybe he wanted the same thing.

CHAPTER 14

THE HUNT BEGINS

✳ ✳

Things in my house had been tense since the caravan arrived. My dad constantly made passive-aggressive comments about the hippies, and I didn't bother with the *passive* part. My mom was annoyed at both of us for not embracing—or at the very least *accepting*—Sundog and his followers.

Rush was the only one who was indifferent to the caravan drama. He'd gotten a job as assistant coach of the peewee football league, and he seemed happier in general since then. He was also keeping weird hours and wasn't saying where he was spending time, which pretty much meant he had a new girlfriend.

I couldn't ignore the caravan as easily. I couldn't even eat breakfast without seeing their camp out the back window. I wished all their tents would blow away. I wished the government would place a ban on tie-dye and unwashed hair. I wished their pot would turn into oregano.

"When I first met your mother, I thought all of this was

charming," my dad said on Saturday morning when we were alone in the kitchen together. "She seemed so free."

Through the curtains, we could see the dreadlocked girl named Calliope playing guitar with Timothy Leary curled up at her feet. Someone had put a tie-dyed bandana around the dog's neck.

"Free of what? Besides responsibility, I mean."

My dad gave me a look. "You're one to talk, kiddo."

I ignored the comment. How could I take on *more* responsibility when all my efforts were concentrated on just surviving high school?

"Is that why you fell in love with Mom?" I asked. "Because she seemed free?"

"In a way. I loved that she saw the world in a way no one else did. Does that make sense?"

It did.

"Before I met your mom, I spent every second doing the right thing. What people told me was the right thing anyway. I studied, played sports, applied to the right schools. I was exactly what I was expected to be."

"And Mom changed you?"

"I like to think we changed each other."

Outside, one of the older men walked up to Calliope and offered her a joint. She stopped playing guitar long enough to accept it.

"Someone's going to call the police." My dad sighed. "You can smell marijuana from the street."

The guitar started again. Timothy Leary raised her head lazily. I wondered if she was high too.

"Do you know what a sundog is?" my dad asked.

"Besides the guy in our backyard?"

"When your mom told me about him, I thought I'd impress her by telling her the definition of sundog."

"What is it?"

My dad leaned forward eagerly, with a professorly look. "It's a weather phenomenon that creates the illusion of multiple suns in the sky. The Greeks and Romans first wrote about it, but the most notable sundog in history occurred on the day Edward IV won the Battle of Mortimer's Cross. Later, he made it his badge."

I should have known it had something to do with medieval history.

"Edward believed the three suns in the sky represented the three sons of York."

"Wow. Mom must have been captivated."

My dad laughed. "She said thanks for the history lesson, but she was more interested in what she could learn from the living."

"Do you blame her?"

"I suppose I don't."

It wasn't a very cute "how we met" story. But that's how things go in real life. And it worked out OK for them, because twentysomething years later, they still acted like they were in love.

"Speaking of college," my dad said, though we hadn't really been, "have you looked through the catalog at all?"

I looked out the window to avoid his gaze. "What catalog?"

"The one I put on your desk."

"I didn't see it," I said, though what I meant was that I had seen it, then stuffed it into a drawer where I could pretend it didn't exist.

"I'm not trying to pressure you," my dad said.

But that was exactly what he was doing.

The problem was, I had no clue what I wanted to study in college. It was unfair that you had to decide how to spend your life before you'd been out in the world and seen what the options were. Not to mention my dreams weren't exactly viable. I doubted college offered courses on how to be an adventurer.

Even if I choose a path that seemed interesting and exciting, what if college turned out to be the same as high school, only with slightly more interesting classes? Then I'd graduate, start my career, and it would turn out to be a disappointment, just like everything else. Nothing is ever as exciting as you imagine it's going to be.

If I reached that point, and I was disappointed with just about everything, then what could I look forward to anymore? And if I had nothing to look forward to, what was the point of living at all?

"There's no need to get upset," my dad said.

"I'm not upset."

"Then why won't you talk about this?"

I figured I owed him some honesty. It wasn't his fault I dreaded the upcoming years. "I guess I'm afraid of making the wrong choice."

"I understand how scary that can be. But you can't let it stop you from making *any* choice."

Sure I could.

I watched out the window as members of the caravan assembled for their morning prayer circle or whatever it was. I wondered if they really believed all the stuff they talked about. I wondered if they were happy.

Then I told myself to stop wondering and stop stressing about the future. Wasn't my mom the one always saying to live in the now?

Now I had more important things to think about than college courses and how much I'd hate my eventual job. I had a werewolf to find.

The future could wait.

"We can talk more later, OK?" I said, standing up. "I have to be somewhere."

"Where?" my dad asked, like he couldn't fathom anything more pressing than our conversation.

"I'm going hiking."

He raised his eyebrows. "Alone?"

"With a friend," I said.

"Emily hikes?"

And mess up her penny loafers? Yeah, right.

Instead of answering, I hugged my dad and told him goodbye. I was out the door before he could ask any more questions.

***

I got to Wolf Creek earlier than Enzo. I guess it wasn't surprising since I drove and he took the bus, which was probably late and maybe even broken down somewhere since that's what all the buses in our area seemed to do.

I walked around the campsite, looking for signs that Lizzie had visited in the last few days. There were no paw prints or tufts of fur or whatever else a wolf might leave behind.

For a second, I freaked out that the police would show up and want to know what I was doing at the site of Lizzie Lovett's disappearance. I, of course, would get all weird and mumble something incoherent, because I was too embarrassed to tell them I was looking for evidence that she was a werewolf, and that would make them think I was suspicious and had maybe, probably, murdered her, so then I'd get locked up in jail.

To shake off my worries, I sat down on the flat rock and pulled *The Howling* out of my bag. I tried to concentrate on the words on the page, but the woods were too quiet. Being there alone made me uncomfortable. What if wolf-Lizzie was in the trees watching me, waiting for the right opportunity to pounce?

"What are you reading?"

I startled.

Enzo wore a beat-up leather jacket to protect him from the chill in the air. It was finally starting to feel like fall.

"Research," I said, holding out the book so he could see the cover.

"I saw that movie when I was a kid. Didn't even know it was a book."

"They're kind of drastically different."

Enzo sat down on the rock next to me and started rolling a cigarette. "So, what's the plan?"

"I guess just walk through the woods and see if we spot anything."

"Do you know how many people have been through these woods recently?"

"They were looking for a girl, not a wolf. They could have missed the signs. I picked out the areas where we'll probably have the best luck."

I pulled out a map, and Enzo examined the sections I'd high-lighted. A breeze rustled the leaves on the trees. Birds and bugs gave us their own soundtrack. It felt like I was in the place I was meant to be, doing exactly what I was meant to do. Enzo and I were on the edge of an important discovery.

Lizzie Lovett went into the woods and never came out. But I would. I would come back with all her secrets.

✼✼✼

The trees were dense past the clearing. It would be easy for some-one to get lost. To disappear. The ground cover was so thick that it was hard to look for wolf tracks. Occasionally, I stopped to push some aside and hoped I hadn't stuck my hands in poison ivy. Mostly, I just watched for tamped-down areas where a wild animal might have stopped to rest.

"Can I ask you a question?" I asked Enzo.

"Go for it."

"What made you change your mind?"

"About what?"

"The first night we came here, you acted like I was crazy. So what changed your mind?"

Enzo took so long to answer that I started to think he wasn't going to.

"When I was a teenager, I had this fascination with weird sto-ries," he said. "Mysteries, I guess. I'd cut out articles from maga-zines and newspapers and paste them into this notebook."

"What kind of articles?"

"Oh, you know. Alien abductions. Parallel dimensions. People who remembered past lives. Anything bizarre."

"Anything that couldn't be explained," I said eagerly.

"Yeah. Every few months, I'd flip through the old stories and try to find out if any of them had been solved. They never were. Remember what you said the other night? About wanting to know there's something more to the world? I think that's why I did it."

"Do you still have it?"

"The notebook? No. I got rid of it a long time ago. But your werewolf theory got me thinking about it again. Made me wonder when I'd become so *logical.*"

A weird, fluttery feeling filled my chest. I couldn't remember the last time I'd heard someone mirror my own thoughts and feelings so closely. Not since I was little. I wanted to stop and tell Enzo he was totally awesome, that I wished we'd known each other when we were younger. I would have helped him fill his notebook with mysteries. Instead, I said, "So, what was your favorite weird story?"

"The creepiest one was about these hikers in Russia in the 1950s. You know it?"

"No, tell me."

We were in the perfect place for scary stories. The trees blocked out the sunlight, casting sinister shadows on the ground. I had to keep my eyes on my feet so I wouldn't stumble. I could have walked right up to a monster or serial killer and not realized until it was too late.

"Well, these hikers didn't get back from a camping trip when they were supposed to, and people went looking for them. Their tent was found, ripped open from the inside, like there had been a struggle to get out. They'd even left their shoes behind. But there was no other sign of them. It took weeks to find their bodies. None of them survived."

"Pretty creepy," I said. And by creepy, I meant fascinating.

"It gets better," Enzo said, talking faster and gesturing. For the first time since I'd met him, he didn't seem weighed down by grief. "The hikers were found scattered all over the area, and most of them were naked. One of them was missing a tongue. A couple had fractured bones, like you'd get after a major car accident, but there was no evidence of external damage. Well, other than their hair had turned white and their skin was some weird shade of orange. And all of the hikers tested positive for radiation."

I stopped walking and looked at Enzo. "Then what?"

"Nothing. No one has ever figured out what happened."

I scowled at him. "That's the *end*?"

"Sometimes, you never get answers, kid," Enzo said with a grin.

"Doesn't not knowing make you crazy?"

"Not at all. The truth would only be disappointing."

He was right, of course. I couldn't even count how many times I'd been disappointed by the truth. Enzo *got it*.

My fluttery feeling grew stronger. I turned away from Enzo and started walking again so he wouldn't see me smile.

We hiked for nearly an hour and never saw a sign of Lizzie, in either werewolf or human form. The terrain got steeper the farther we went, and after a while, we were both too winded to talk. When we reached a section of flat ground, Enzo stopped walking and leaned against a tree, breathing heavily.

"I'm not in good enough shape for this."

"I'm sure that doesn't help," I said when he started to roll a cigarette.

I expected a laugh or maybe a sarcastic retort, but Enzo only shrugged. His good mood had vanished.

"We should call it a day," he said.

He was right. I was worn out. Neither of us were really dressed for hiking. And we hadn't seen anything to indicate we were on Lizzie's trail. I tried to swallow my disappointment. I knew it was unlikely we'd find her on the first day anyway. It never happened that way in books or movies. It would have been anticlimactic.

"You know she's been gone almost a month now?" Enzo stared into the woods, like he wasn't really talking to me.

"Yeah," I said softly.

"It seems impossible. Like time should have stopped when she disappeared. I guess in a way, for me, it did."

His shoulders were hunched, and his hair fell into his eyes. He looked so broken, and I wished I knew how to make him whole.

"Do you want to talk about it?" I asked.

"About what?" He finally looked at me.

"Anything. Everything. What the past month has been like. Have you had anyone to talk to?"

"Oh, I've talked to the police and reporters and Lizzie's mom."

"That's not what I mean. Someone to talk to, you know, the way you would talk to Lizzie."

The way he'd talked to me earlier, telling me the story about the hikers. Like I was a real person who he wanted to share some-thing with. A friend.

Enzo shrugged. "Lizzie and I wouldn't talk about this kind of stuff. She's not really big on analyzing her feelings. Or listening to other people's for that matter."

It took me back to my conversation with Lizzie in the locker room, how good it made me feel that she acted like she cared. And how devastated I was when I realized she didn't. Maybe *she* wasn't concerned about feelings, but other people were. What happened when one of her cronies got dumped or didn't get nominated for prom court and needed someone to pour out her heart to? Did Lizzie just shrug and tell her friend to deal with it?

"That's really sad," I said.

"Actually, it's awesome. She doesn't overthink anything or let anything bother her. She just lives."

"It doesn't sound awesome," I blurted out. "It sounds like being in a relationship with a robot. How can you date someone you can't *talk* to?"

"There's more to relationships than talking," Enzo said.

I assumed he meant sex, which made my face heat up, because clearly, he thought I was too much of a *kid* to know anything about that. Enzo must have read my mind, because he winced, which only made the whole thing a million times more awkward.

"No, I mean…we go out and do things, OK? Go to concerts,

poetry readings, whatever. We have experiences. We just don't have to analyze every single one or talk about what it means to us."

But weren't those experiences *meant* to be analyzed? Weren't you *supposed* to share how they made you feel?

"And you like that?" I asked.

Enzo didn't answer right away. I wasn't sure if he was figuring out what to say or deciding if I was worth saying it to. Or maybe he was following the Lizzie Lovett school of thought and wasn't thinking anything at all.

"Sometimes, I feel like I'll go crazy if I don't find a way to turn off my thoughts," Enzo said. "When I'm with Lizzie, I can do that."

In my head, I said, "What thoughts? Tell me, no matter how weird or depressing they are or how much you want to forget them. Maybe they're my thoughts too."

Out loud, I casually said, "I guess I can understand that."

Considering everything Enzo said about Lizzie, I was hesitant to ask more questions. Hesitant to make him *think* too much. But there was one more thing I had to know.

"Is she happy?" I asked. "Or was she, before she disappeared?"

"Yeah," he said, sounding surprised, as if Lizzie's happiness was a given. "She's always smiling. Always makes the best of a situation. Like, her car could break down, and she'd just say she finally had a reason to buy a bike."

"What about you? Are you happy?"

Enzo took a long drag of his cigarette. He watched the smoke drift up to the sky. "I'm a different kind of person."

I figured I was too.

Maybe that was OK.

As we hiked back to my car, I tried to reconcile the Lizzie I knew with Saint Lizzie, who Enzo had apparently been dating. I couldn't do it. Was it really possible for someone to change so much in just a few years? Or maybe she hadn't changed. Maybe I'd read Lizzie wrong from the start.

There was so much to puzzle over, I didn't even mind that our first werewolf investigation had been unsuccessful.

CHAPTER 15

SPECIAL

❋ ❋

I knew what would happen if I ventured into my backyard. But I went out anyway, which made me think maybe, probably, part of me *wanted* it to happen, which was totally weird.

I hadn't even been on the back patio for a full minute when Sundog saw me and broke into a grin. There was something child-like about his smile, which was startling to see on such an old face. Getting a genuine smile from an adult was about as rare as seeing multiple suns in the sky.

"Hawthorn," he said, crossing the yard to meet me. "Join us."

He put his arm around my shoulders and guided me into his little backyard tent city. He smelled like sweat and campfire and incense. It wasn't exactly a good smell but not as bad as his unwashed hair and clothes suggested.

"I've been hoping you'd spend some time out here."

"Why?"

"I'd like to know you. Your mom was about your age when we first met. Seeing you is like going back in time."

I wasn't sure if that was a compliment or not, so I didn't say anything.

Sundog led me to the middle of the yard, which the hippies had turned into their gathering place. They'd set up a fire pit and ringed it with blankets and beat-up lawn chairs. It was where they had their prayer circles every day at dawn and dusk.

One of the men, Journey, I think, was meditating near the smoldering remains of the fire. He was in the lotus position, eyes shut, face turned up to the sky. I briefly wondered if my and Sundog's intrusion would disturb him but decided probably not. He was only a few feet from us in body, but his mind was on another planet.

Otherwise, the camp was empty. Sundog and I sat down on a tattered Indian blanket.

"Where is everyone?"

"In town looking for work."

"What work?" I asked warily. I imagined one of the caravan members getting a job at the stupid shoe boutique and deciding to stay forever.

"Odd jobs mostly, yard work and that sort of thing. Or they sell our goods."

He meant hemp necklaces and organic shampoo and who knew what else. They'd conned Rush into making purchases on at least three separate occasions.

"Do *you* work?"

"Not anymore," Sundog said. "I'm too old for that now."

"Do you ever feel like Charles Manson?" I asked.

Sundog laughed. I hadn't meant to make a joke.

"Why would you say that?" he asked, his eyes twinkling.

"I mean, you're the leader of this…I don't know, commune."

Sundog took both of my hands in his and looked me straight in the eye, which was sort of uncomfortable. Most people don't really look at you for more than a second. It also made me want to listen to what he had to say. Maybe that's the trick to getting whatever you want from life—making people feel like you *see* them.

"Hawthorn, Charles Manson took something beautiful—the idea of community, of oneness—and turned it into evil. We embrace the light."

"But this *is* a commune, right? A traveling one?"

"Commune is just a label. What does it even mean?"

"Um, the dictionary would have me believe it's a group of people living together and sharing everything."

"We love and respect each other, Hawthorn. That's what matters."

I pulled my hands away, because it was getting a little weird. Journey was still meditating, deep in some other cognitive state. Which was good, because I had another question for Sundog, and I didn't want anyone eavesdropping.

"Can I ask you something?"

Sundog laughed again. "You should never ask to ask a question."

It wasn't that I thought Sundog had all the answers. He was

my mom's mentor, not mine. But I suspected he'd at least take me seriously, and that was better than what I usually got.

"OK, well, do you believe in werewolves?"

I was right—Sundog didn't flinch. He didn't look surprised. He quietly considered the question, and that made me love him a little bit.

"I believe there are two sides to every individual. I believe we all have a beast."

"But what about a human turning into a wolf?"

"The most beautiful thing about the world is how much is unknown to us. There are so many secrets, Hawthorn. So much awaiting discovery. We are merely dust motes in the vastness of the universe."

Something wet touched my arm, and I jumped. Timothy Leary was rubbing her cold nose against me. I reached out to pet her and wondered if she understood what we were talking about. Maybe some canine connection had prompted the dog to come over and vouch for the existence of werewolves.

"Did you hear about the girl who disappeared a while ago?" I asked.

Sundog nodded. "It's a bad time to be an outsider in Griffin Mills."

I didn't break it to him that the caravan members would be treated with suspicion in Griffin Mills whether there was a missing person or not.

"I thought maybe she turned into a wolf," I said, keeping my eyes on Timothy Leary. She craned her neck so I could scratch under her tie-dyed bandana. "Yesterday, I went looking for her. Her boyfriend went with me."

"And did you find a wolf?"

"No. But we only searched a small area."

Sundog reached out and touched my hands again. Timothy Leary tried to wriggle between us.

"Absence of proof is not proof of absence."

"So you think it could be true?"

"We all have cosmic awareness inside of us. We're born knowing everything about the world, and then society makes us forget it. But there's still a part of us that remembers. What do you see when you look inside yourself?"

"I don't know."

"Then you need to look deeper."

"And what if I see Lizzie as a werewolf?"

"Stranger things have happened."

I stood up and brushed the dog fur off my clothes.

"I have to get ready for work," I told Sundog. "But thanks."

I expected him to say, "For what?" and I would tell him, "For believing that anything is possible."

Instead, he smiled and said, "*Namaste*, Hawthorn."

Whatever that meant.

✖✖✖

My car keys had gone MIA, and I was losing hope that I'd make it to the Sunshine Café on time. This was apparently very amusing to Connor. He'd come over to hang out with Rush but had settled for watching me tear the living room apart.

"How would your keys have ended up there?" Connor laughed as I peered behind the entertainment center.

I took a moment to scowl at him before moving to the couch and lifting the cushions. There were no keys, but I did find part of a candy bar wrapper. I wondered whether it had been my dad or brother who snuck the contraband food into the house.

"I heard you had an adventure yesterday," Connor said casually.

I replaced the couch cushions. "Do you and Rush sit around and talk about me all the time or what?"

Connor shrugged. "It just came up."

It was stupid of me to tell Rush about looking for Lizzie in the first place. But I'd been too excited to keep it to myself, and my brother was the first person I saw. Not a mistake I'd make again.

I got on my hands and knees and looked under the coffee table. Nothing.

"Find anything?" Connor asked.

"No. My keys aren't here."

"I mean in the woods."

"Oh." I sat back on my heels, scanned the room for anywhere I hadn't checked. "No, nothing there either."

"So what's Lorenzo Calvetti like?"

"It's Enzo. He's pretty cool," I said.

"He seems weird."

I looked at Connor and frowned. "What? No, he doesn't."

"You don't think it's weird for some dude in his midtwenties to go hunting for his were-girlfriend with some random teenager?" Connor asked.

"No. What I think is weird is that sometime in the last twenty-four hours, my car keys ceased to exist. And the term wouldn't be were-girlfriend. That doesn't make sense."

Connor laughed. "But werewolves are totally sensible, right?"

"Why are you even here right now? Where's my brother?"

As if I summoned him, Rush bounded down the stairs. "Ready to go?"

"Yep." Connor stood up.

"Isn't anyone concerned that my keys are missing?"

Rush rolled his eyes. "They're on the kitchen counter."

"Really?"

"That's where you put them down."

Connor laughed. "Good job, Thorny."

I went into the kitchen, and sure enough, there they were. I grabbed them, then went back into the living room to tell Connor that no, I didn't think Enzo was weird for thinking his girlfriend could be a werewolf, but he and Rush were already gone.

✖✖✖

The truth about working at the Sunshine Café was that they didn't need a waitress to fill Lizzie's spot, because mostly no one ate there. I never said that to Mr. Walczak, since I didn't want to look for a new job, and it meant I could do whatever I wanted during my shifts. Besides, it was way better than the mini golf place.

That night, I was reading *The Werewolf Book*, which was basically an encyclopedia of everything that had to do with werewolves, and taking notes. I sat at the lunch counter a few stools down from Vernon, who also never seemed to mind how boring the café was.

"You know what's interesting about werewolves?" I asked.

Vernon made a sound that could have been "*Huh?*" but didn't look up from his crossword puzzle.

"It wasn't until pretty recently that people started questioning their existence. Before that, werewolves were just accepted as part of life."

Vernon didn't respond.

"Almost every culture has some kind of shape-shifter myth," I went on. "Take Native Americans, for example. They didn't have werewolves exactly, but they believed in skinwalkers, which is pretty close."

I assumed Vernon's continued silence meant he was fascinated by my wealth of werewolf information and that I should keep talking.

"There's actually a psychological disorder called clinical lycan-thropy. Have you heard of it? It's when people believe they're werewolves and do crazy stuff on the full moon."

For a second, I considered that maybe Lizzie wasn't a were-wolf but had gone into the woods because she *believed* she was one. Believed it so much that being a werewolf became real to her in her heart and in her head. Rather than a werewolf roaming the Ohio River Valley, it was just crazy Lizzie.

I dismissed the idea as interesting, but it didn't really fit.

"There are all these methods for killing a werewolf," I told Vernon. "But no one seems to care much about *saving* them. Occasionally, people in medieval Europe attempted to keep were-wolves alive but only to perform these weird surgeries and exor-cisms, so the end result was usually death anyway."

Vernon finally raised his head. "Ya wanna see a werewoof, ya should looky at my Pap Pap. Drunk blood on the first of every month."

I was sure Vernon's grandpa, or Pap Pap, did *not* drink blood. I also didn't necessarily think that would have made him a werewolf. But I figured when I reached Vernon's age, I'd probably appreciate someone humoring me.

I smiled. "What happened to him?"

"Nazis." Vernon went back to his crossword puzzle and wrote an answer with his shaky, old-man hand. I waited until I was sure he didn't have more to say, then went back to my book.

There was a German legend that said you could cure a were-wolf by saying its name three times.

I could picture myself out in the forest. A branch would snap behind me. I'd know something was there. I'd turn around slowly, and there she'd be. Crouched down, ready to strike, coiled as tightly as a rattlesnake. Her fur would be white and gray. She'd start to stalk toward me, and I'd look her right in the eye and say, "Lizzie Lovett, Lizzie Lovett, Lizzie Lovett." Or maybe I wouldn't. Maybe, probably, I would shut my eyes and wait to be bitten.

There was so much to think about. There was so much to learn. I read about King Lycaon, who Zeus punished by turn-ing into a wolf. I read about wolfsbane and the lunar effect and the werewolf's connection to demons and vampires and witches and a million other things. Humanity had spent hundreds of years gathering information about werewolves and making up their own stories. I didn't know how to separate the truth from the fiction.

Then I had a thought that made my hands tingle and my vision get super focused, like a jolt of electricity was running through my body. How many people had actually encountered a werewolf? Out of everyone who'd researched and studied and written about werewolves, how many people had firsthand experience? A hand-ful? Possibly none?

If werewolves were real and Lizzie was a werewolf, I could be one of the only living people to ever spend time with one. Well, me and Enzo.

What would it be like to experience something that no one else had? It would be special—*I* would be special. And not in the way that kids at school, like Mychelle, called me special. Special like important. I'd never felt that way before.

Maybe, if I showed the world that werewolves existed, people would stop asking me about my plans for the future. No one would care about the future, because I would have already proven myself, accomplished something great.

"Vernon, do you think that pioneers know they're about to make a great discovery right before they make it?"

Vernon didn't look up from his puzzle. He'd already said his piece for the night.

CHAPTER 16

THE PAINTING

✳ ✳

Emily didn't want to talk about anything besides Logan and how awesome he was. I pretty much stopped listening to her, because it was getting really boring. Instead, I concentrated on my lunch and on my strategy for finding Lizzie.

After a few minutes, I realized Emily had stopped talking and was staring at me.

"What?"

"I asked if you wanted to go with me."

"Where?"

"You're not listening at all."

"I am. I just got distracted for a second."

"Strength in Numbers is playing at the Barn this weekend. Do you want to go?"

There wasn't even a tiny part of me that wanted to find out what metal-bluegrass fusion meant. I was sort of intrigued by the location though. The Barn was an abandoned farm on the edge of town. Kids had been going there to have parties for forever, and even though it was right off the highway, cops turned a blind eye. The farmhouse was gone except for the chimney, but the barn itself was in good shape, and local bands played there. The plot of land was backed by woods, which meant it was easy for kids to sneak off and hook up. Or so I'd heard. I'd never been to a party there. I'd never really been to a party at all.

"Since when do you go to parties?"

"It's important to Logan."

"Well, I'll see if I'm free."

"Hawthorn, you're always free."

"I might have to work," I said. "Or I might be doing something with Enzo."

Emily made a face to let me know she thought as much of Enzo as I did of Logan.

"I don't think you should be hanging out with Enzo," she said.

"You haven't even met him."

"He's old."

"He's twenty-five. That's not old."

"It's too old for you."

"I'm not dating him."

"What *are* you doing then?"

I wasn't in the mood to get into the werewolf debate again. I took too big a bite of my sandwich and responded with my mouth full, which Emily hated. "What about you and Logan? Is this supposed to be your rebellious phase?"

Emily narrowed her eyes at me. "Maybe you shouldn't come to the party after all."

"Fine."

I wished Emily and Logan would knock their teeth together every time they tried to kiss. I wished Strength in Numbers would spontaneously only be able to write lyrics in Greek. I wished the Barn would get torn apart in a freak storm.

I wished Emily and Logan had never met.

✖✖✖

In English composition, Mrs. Doyle was explaining how to write a persuasive essay, which was the next paper we had due. Sophie Walker, who was probably going to be homecoming queen in a few weeks, raised her hand.

"And we can write on any topic?"

"This isn't creative writing, but I still want you to be creative," Mrs. Doyle reassured her.

"So if I wanted to write about, say, how I think werewolves are real, that would be OK?"

Pretty much everyone in the class snickered. Mrs. Doyle looked a little confused but told Sophie that would be fine. I could feel my face go red.

From the back of the classroom, Mike Jacobs asked, "What if I wrote about the benefits of living in a tent and not showering and stuff? Would that be cool?"

"I suppose so."

Everyone stared at me, waiting for me to respond so they could make even more jokes at my expense. It was like all the things I most dreaded about high school were actually happening. There was an entire roomful of people mocking me. I glanced around to see if I had a single ally but only saw smirks. I wanted to disappear.

"What if someone tried to persuade the reader they're normal and not a total pathetic loser, even if everyone knows otherwise?" Sophie asked.

I got up and walked out of the classroom. I still had two classes left, but I couldn't deal. I knew ditching class and running away was the exact opposite of what you're supposed to do if someone is being a bully. But you're also not supposed to let the bully know she's getting to you, and I was about two seconds from screaming at Sophie that I hated her and hoped her homecoming gown made her look fat.

I hurried through the parking lot and climbed into my car, praying that it would start. The jet plane sound came from the engine, as if the car might take flight at any moment only to crash and burn. But at least the car was running. I needed to take it to the shop. Really take it, not just swear to myself over and over I was going to. That's why I'd gotten a job in the first place. Sort of.

I was relieved when I pulled out of the parking lot without the security guard stopping me. I didn't usually ditch school and didn't have an excuse to give them. Probably, I would have been honest and hoped for sympathy. Hoped that I was *persuasive* enough.

I didn't really think about where I was going. But, of course, that was a lie.

★★

Enzo took so long to answer the door that I had time to panic. What if he had a roommate? What if I'd gotten the apartment number wrong? What if Lizzie had come back and they were inside together, reconciling?

Maybe I should run away. But then Enzo might look out the window and catch a glimpse of my car tearing out of the parking lot, and it would be so awkward that I'd have to spend the rest of my life avoiding him.

My worries were unfounded. Enzo lived alone, and no one was inside with him. He didn't exactly jump for joy at the sight of me, but he let me inside.

I immediately looked around for signs of Lizzie, but the studio apartment didn't have any traces of a feminine touch. The cramped room was lit primarily by a lava lamp and a fish tank that didn't have any fish. Amateurish artwork covered the walls, and there were stacks of notebooks and papers on every surface. The apartment was cluttered but not really messy. Enzo apologized anyway.

"Don't be sorry. I like your place."

I tried to take in everything at once. Like I thought he was going to kick me out or something.

"Shouldn't you be in school?" Enzo asked.

I looked at him. He was wearing torn jeans and a ratty sweater. He looked like a dark-haired Kurt Cobain. I could imagine Enzo sweating under hot stage lights, scrawny but strong, made into a god by the crowd below him. He'd told me he was a drummer in a band once. He said they hadn't been very good.

"I left."

"Why?"

I tried to sound flippant. "Because I hate everyone there."

"Something happen?"

"Just the usual," I said. "They're all awful. I try to ignore them, but it's pretty much impossible. I end up spending most of the day wishing horrible things would happen to them. Like every time they try to stream a video, it's laggy, or that all their important emails get sent to the junk mail folder."

"Whoa there, kid. You don't want to inflict too much damage."

I laughed. "When I was little, I got mad at my mom and told her I wished she was dead. She gave me this whole lecture about being careful not to wish for something you don't really want to come true. So, you know, I try to moderate."

Enzo's brow furrowed, like I'd grown a second head, so I changed the subject. "Did you paint all these?"

"Not all of them. But most."

I didn't know enough about art to name the different styles, but there were a lot. I wondered if I could pick out the ones Enzo had done. I felt like they would be the darkest of the bunch, the paintings that were anxious and angsty.

I was wrong.

The strongest painting was of a beautiful young girl sitting in a field, knees pulled up to her chest. Her head was tilted up to catch the sun, eyes closed, a half smile on her face. It was a smile I knew. Even in Enzo's painting, Lizzie Lovett was hard to look away from.

"This is really good."

"It's probably the best thing I've done. The last thing too. I haven't painted since she disappeared."

The painting was hung so it was visible from the bed. It was the last thing Enzo would see before he went to sleep and the first thing he'd see in the morning. I wondered if every time he looked at the painting, he thought of the day Lizzie had posed for it. Had they talked while he was working? Had Enzo made jokes? Had Lizzie laughed? Did she already know what she was and that it was almost her time to turn?

I sat down on the bed, because there was nowhere else to sit. "So you're a painter. I didn't know that."

"I try. I've been getting more into photography lately. I work part-time at a photo studio."

"I didn't know that either."

"There's a lot you don't know about me."

He was right.

"Do you like your job?"

"The pay is shitty, and I mostly shoot weddings and baby portraits. But it's something."

I didn't know what to say. I didn't even know what I was doing there. Enzo was practically a stranger, and I'd burst into his life. I felt sure he wanted me to leave.

"Maybe I should go," I said.

"You just got here."

"I feel awkward."

Enzo laughed. "Telling someone you feel awkward just makes the situation more awkward."

"Talk about something that's not awkward then. Tell me about Lizzie."

"What about her?"

"Anything. How did you meet her?"

Enzo sat on the opposite side of the bed from me. "There isn't much of a story. We knew some of the same people and ended up at a concert in Pittsburgh. Neither of us was into the music. I went outside to smoke, and she followed me, and that was that. She was wearing this beaded headband with a feather stuck in it. That's what I remember most."

It was so normal. I'd expected something cinematic, like Enzo pushing Lizzie out of the way two seconds before she got flattened by a runaway train. Not that Enzo gave off movie-hero vibes.

"And you've been dating for a year?" I asked.

"A little less."

"Do you ever wonder why she chose you?"

"*Chose* me? Thanks, kid."

"But do you?"

"We chose each other. That's how it works."

I suspected that Enzo was wrong. Lizzie always got to choose. But I decided to let it drop.

My eyes wandered back to the painting of Lizzie. It was so lifelike, she could have been in the room with us. How would she feel about me sitting on her boyfriend's bed, quizzing him on their relationship?

"What's your favorite thing about her?"

"Her laugh," Enzo said without hesitation. "She laughs all the time. She makes life seem so easy."

"What else?" I pried.

"She always sees the best in everyone, even when they don't deserve it. And she's just…nice. Not that many people are nice, I guess."

"I don't think she was like that in high school," I said.

"People change. Thank God. I can't imagine a world where everyone's the same as they were in high school."

I wanted to know more about Lizzie. I wanted to know *everything* about her. But the truth was, Enzo could only tell me so much. I wanted to crawl into Lizzie's head and know her thoughts and feelings and what made her tick. I wanted to slip into her life. I wanted to be the kind of person who made life seem easy.

"What were *you* like in high school?" I asked Enzo.

If I couldn't learn everything there was to know about Lizzie, at least I could find out more about him. Besides, Lizzie loved Enzo. Don't the things we love say a lot about us?

"High school was miserable," he said.

Now *that* was something I could relate to. I turned my back on the painting of Lizzie and tried to push her out of my mind, focus on Enzo instead.

In the woods, he'd told me he liked Lizzie's outlook on life, that he was happy she didn't overanalyze everything. But from the way he started spilling out information, I wondered if that was entirely true. He seemed like someone who had plenty to say.

Maybe he'd just been waiting for someone to ask.

CHAPTER 17

IN LIZZIE'S WORLD

✳ ✳

A few days later, a body was pulled out of the Ohio River just north of Wheeling, and everyone was like, *Oh my God, they found Lizzie.* It was less than a day before the police announced the body wasn't hers. It wasn't even a female.

"That should teach people not to jump to conclusions," I told my family at dinner.

Rush gave me an incredulous look. "Seriously?"

After dinner, I went outside to talk to Sundog, partly because I wanted to talk to Sundog but mostly because my mom would make me do the dishes if I stuck around the kitchen.

"Join us," Sundog said.

I took a spot next to him near the fire. A few of the other hippies were sitting around, talking or meditating or doing whatever it was they did. One of the older women was making jewelry out of twine and beads.

"You know, marshmallows would really make this campfire better," I said.

Sundog laughed, even though I was pretty sure he was morally opposed to marshmallows since they were made with gelatin, which was made from animal bones and skin, which my mom told me all about when I was little. I couldn't remember the last time I'd eaten a s'more.

"Do you think everyone changes after high school?" I asked Sundog.

"Young Hawthorn, everyone changes *always*. The universe is in a constant state of flux."

"But let's talk about high school specifically."

Sundog thought for a moment. "You could say high school is a time to figure out who you want to be, so you can go out into the world and work toward becoming that person."

"I hope you're right."

Timothy Leary wandered over to us and plopped down in front of me. I used my fingers to comb through her tangled fur.

"Where'd you live before you became the commune pet?" I asked her.

She tilted her head at me.

"Timothy Leary is a companion, not a pet," Sundog explained.

"Right. Of course."

"On the subject of animals, how fares your werewolf hunt?"

I thought for a moment. "It's progressing, I guess. You know the guy I told you about? Lizzie's boyfriend? I went to his apartment the other day. He had this painting of Lizzie. It was so…I don't know, so *real*. Like I could see her whole self captured in it."

"True artists know how to cut their subjects open and bleed them onto the canvas."

"That's probably not the best phrasing, considering, but I get what you mean," I said.

I let the fire warm me and imagined I was in Enzo's apartment again. Art covering the walls. Blue light coming from the lava lamp in the corner. Books stacked on the floor instead of on shelves. A tiny kitchen where it didn't look like any cooking had ever been done.

"It was interesting," I told Sundog. "Being in Enzo's apartment was like being in his mind."

I stopped.

I thought about what I'd just said.

I had an idea.

★ ★ ★

"I was thinking," I said to Enzo.

"Oh?"

I had an hour before I got off work. Enzo sat in his usual booth, drinking coffee and waiting for my shift to end. I pretended to wipe down the table next to his, even though it was already clean and no one was watching me.

"You can tell a lot about someone by where they live."

"I guess so."

"All their stuff is there. Like, if something mysterious is going on with the person, you'd probably find evidence in their bedroom or whatever."

Enzo raised his eyebrows. "Get to the point, kid."

"Well, don't you think we should check out Lizzie's apartment?"

Enzo didn't reply, and I feared I'd crossed some sort of line. Maybe going to her apartment was too much of a personal invasion. Maybe he didn't want to take me that deeply into Lizzie's world.

"It was just a thought," I said, backtracking. "We don't need to."

"No, you're right. I haven't been there since...before."

"Is it too weird?" I asked.

"No, it's a good idea. The police might have missed something. We can go tonight."

"We can get in?"

"I have a key," Enzo said.

That gave me pause. He had a key to her apartment. I wanted to ask if she had a key to his place too, if she could go there anytime she wanted. If she could drive over on a whim, simply because she wanted to be in his home, surrounded by his art, surrounded by the *Enzoness* of it all.

"Hawthorn?" Enzo asked.

"Sorry. Just thinking. Yeah, let's go tonight."

An hour later, we were on our way to the place where Lizzie

Lovett lived. I hoped we'd find something telling. Maybe an essay titled "Where I'd Go if I Ever Turned into a Werewolf."

✖✖✖

Lizzie's apartment was only a couple blocks from the Sunshine Café. The building was old and run-down, not much better looking than Enzo's.

"Lizzie Lovett lives *here*?" I asked.

"The diner doesn't exactly pay well."

We got out of the car, and Enzo led me to a ground-floor apartment.

"Why didn't you two move in together?" I asked.

Enzo hesitated. "I don't think either of us was really at that place yet."

I wanted to ask a million questions, like what was preventing him from *being at that place*, but we'd arrived at a door, and Enzo was putting his key in the lock.

"I feel like we're breaking in," I said.

"Yeah, well, I'm sure the cops wouldn't be thrilled to find us here."

But he opened the door anyway and gestured for me to go ahead. I stepped into Lizzie's apartment. It was dark and silent. Behind me, Enzo fumbled with the light switch.

When the lights came on, I imagined it would be like the curtain rising on the show of Lizzie's life. I'd cross the threshold and step into Lizzieville. Instead, I found myself looking at an apartment that was bare except for a few pieces of furniture.

"Someone cleared it out," I said.

"No. This is how she keeps it."

"What?" It seemed impossible. There was no clutter, no art on the walls, no dishes in the sink. Everything was impossibly clean. "It's like this all the time?"

"She started going through this Spartan phase a little while ago."

It could have been a hotel room. Completely impersonal, a place you don't intend to stay very long.

The apartment was only a little bigger than Enzo's, but the emptiness made the difference seem vast. I walked through the living area and into the bedroom. Enzo followed behind.

The white comforter and pillowcases made Lizzie's bed look like it belonged in a hospital. The only other furniture was a nightstand. But on the nightstand, there was finally a sign of life. A picture frame—an indication that Lizzie had loved ones. I picked the frame up. There was no photo in it.

"What used to be in here?"

"A picture of the two of us," Enzo said. "Lizzie's mom gave it to the police."

I wondered if it was the picture I'd seen in the newspaper right after Lizzie had gone missing.

"How does she live like this? There's not even a TV."

"She doesn't spend much time at home, I guess."

"You guess? She's your girlfriend."

"I don't make her report every detail of what she does when we're not together."

"But you must have some idea," I pressed.

"She goes hiking. She reads a lot. There's not that much to say."

I knew all about reading a lot. About how it could take you to a world that was better than the real one. A world where there were adventures and mysteries and magic. Except, of course, books ended eventually, and then you had to go back to being yourself.

"It's kind of like she was living in a prison cell," I said. "I'd be too freaked out to sleep here."

Enzo shrugged. He opened a drawer in the dresser, closed it, and opened another. "Nothing scares Lizzie."

A memory suddenly came flooding back to me.

"Did you know she made it to the second floor of the Griffin Mansion?"

"The what?"

"The mansion on the hill. The founder of Griffin Mills haunts it or whatever. Kids dare each other to go in, but no one usually makes it past the entryway. Except I heard Lizzie did."

"That doesn't surprise me," Enzo said. "How far did you get?"

"No one's ever dared me to go in. You have to have friends for that."

That wasn't exactly true though. In the third grade, Robbie Larson, who lived down the street, dared me. I was too afraid to take the challenge. High school kids snuck into the Griffin Mansion. Or middle school at the very least. I wasn't ready for it. And I figured it wasn't a big deal, because I'd have plenty of chances to make up for it when I was older. But, of course, I never did.

It taught me a good lesson about taking opportunities when they're presented.

"Why do you need someone to dare you?" Enzo asked.

"What?" I hesitated, poised to open the closet.

"If you want to do something, just do it. You don't need someone to dare you or give you permission."

"Is that what you do?" I asked.

"No. But I wish I did."

Enzo reached around me and opened the closet door, which distracted me from our conversation. There were clothes and shoes and even some books on a shelf. It was a normal closet. I pulled out a long, flowy dress. It was pale yellow. Lizzie would have looked like sunshine wearing it. I put the dress back and pulled out a crocheted top. A worn pair of jeans. A soft blue T-shirt.

"Hey, look at this," Enzo said.

He pulled a book from the top shelf. I looked over his shoulder. It was a yearbook.

"That's not from Griffin Mills," I said.

"No. Somewhere in Pennsylvania. Middle school, it looks like."

"I don't really know anything about Lizzie before she moved here."

"Let's see what we can find out."

We sat next to each other on Lizzie's bed. It felt like maybe, probably, a terrible thing to do. Being alone in Lizzie's apartment, alone on her *bed*, with her boyfriend. Going through her things. But I figured since we were doing it to help her, Lizzie would understand. At least, I hoped she would.

Enzo flipped through the yearbook until he found Lizzie's class. He traced his finger over the names.

"Wow." He pointed to Lizzie's picture.

It was Lizzie. Same flawless skin. Same wide eyes. She was in seventh grade but didn't seem to be going through the awkward puberty phase that the rest of the girls in her class were experiencing. Which figured.

Except it wasn't *our* Lizzie. It wasn't the cheerleader Lizzie I'd known or the laid-back Lizzie Enzo was dating. Thirteen-year-old Lizzie had dyed-black hair chopped off at her chin. Her eyes were ringed with heavy liner. Her nose was pierced.

"Did Lizzie have an *emo* phase?" I asked. In slightly different circumstances, like if Lizzie wasn't missing, it would have been hilarious.

"This is just...weird," Enzo said.

"It's like every few years, she becomes a different person."

I stared at the picture, trying to make sense of it. Make sense of *her*. Then something clicked.

"Think about it," I told Enzo. "Lizzie was born a werewolf.

So she's always had this duality, probably always felt like part of her was pretending to be something she wasn't. So she tried on different personalities, never guessing that she'd *never* find one that fit. Not until she had her first transformation anyway."

"Yeah," Enzo said, still flipping through the yearbook. "I guess so."

"I want to see if there's anything like this in any of my werewolf books." I jumped to my feet. I was suddenly buzzing with energy. We'd found another piece of the puzzle. We were one step closer to solving Lizzie's mysteries.

"I actually think I'm going to stay here," Enzo said quietly.

"Oh."

"I kind of want to be around her stuff for a while longer."

I deflated. He'd rather be around the *idea* of Lizzie than chase a lead with me. Who would have thought you could be rejected for someone who wasn't even present?

"Yeah, sure," I said. "Don't you need a ride home though?"

"I can take the bus."

I hesitated in the doorway.

I was stupid. I'd been so happy to have an ally that I'd let myself forget why Enzo was hanging around in the first place. It wasn't about discovering magic. It wasn't because he felt some kinship with me. He missed his girlfriend. He missed his girlfriend, whom he loved very much, and he wanted to find her. I was just a means of making that happen. I was a pit stop on the road back to Lizzie.

"Really, it's OK," Enzo said. "I've taken the bus from here a million times, kid."

"Yeah. Of course you have. I'll give you a call later, OK?"

Enzo nodded and looked back at the yearbook. I left him sitting in Lizzie's sterile, white apartment.

There was a weird feeling in my stomach that I tried to ignore.

CHAPTER 18

FULL MOON

✳ ✳

At work, Christa was babbling about how she had so much to do to get ready for her cousin's bridal shower and how her cousin was being a bridezilla and checking her registry, like, once an hour to see what gifts had been purchased. Which made Christa not want to throw the shower at all, but she had to. I nodded like I cared, even though weddings are not at all interesting to me.

"Want me to take your shift tonight?" I asked. I got off at eight, and Christa was scheduled to close. "It sounds like you could use a few extra hours."

"That's sweet, but you don't need to do that."

"It's not a big deal."

"Hawthorn, you're seventeen, and it's Saturday night. You have better things to do than hang out with Vernon."

The thing was, I didn't. I'd rather be at work than sitting at home feeling sorry for myself, because what could be more boring than that? I thought about telling Christa that, but she'd maybe, probably, think I was a loser, because she likely always had weekend plans when she was my age.

"Yeah, I guess I do have plans," I mumbled.

"A date?" Christa asked, her eyes all sparkly at the prospect of gossip.

"Not really."

"You aren't still hanging out with Lizzie's guy, are you?"

No one had sat at the counter since I'd last wiped it down, but I grabbed a cloth and hit the Formica with some elbow grease.

"Enzo, you mean? We hang out, but it's not like that."

"Good. You should be dating someone more…wholesome."

I frowned. "What if the wholesome boys don't like me?"

"Then make them like you."

"What if I don't like them?"

Christa laughed and patted me on the back. "We've all had that problem."

She wandered to see if Vernon needed anything, and I continued to clean.

Did Christa really think I could just *make someone* like me? It sounded like something Lizzie would say. It wasn't that simple. Either someone liked me or they didn't, and it was out of my control.

Or was it? Christa was the kind of person who'd probably show up to a party whether she was invited or not. And she'd be so friendly and easygoing that no one would think anything of it. Christa accepted everyone, so everyone accepted her too.

Maybe it was my own fault that I didn't have a real boyfriend. Or friends. Or a social life. Maybe I should have been putting myself out there instead of waiting for people to come to me. If I had nothing to do on a Saturday night, maybe it's because I wasn't really looking.

Before I could talk myself out of it, I went into Mr. Walczak's office and called Enzo.

"Hello?" he said, sounding like I woke him up, even though it was evening.

"Do you want to go to a party tonight?"

✖✖✖

The scene at the Barn was pretty much what I expected: drunk teenagers making stupid decisions while listening to bad music.

Enzo and I parked and walked across the empty highway toward the lights and noise. The full moon was high in the sky, and I wondered where Lizzie was and if the moon was on her mind too.

The barn doors were thrown open, creating a sort of half-inside, half-outside party. There were people everywhere. Small groups leaned in to hear each other over the sound of the band. Other kids were dancing and playing drinking games that had rules I'd never been taught. Enzo and I passed a girl who was on all fours, puking beside a trash can instead of into it. I was finally experiencing the sort of party I'd seen in a thousand movies. And I didn't particularly like it.

"I can't believe I'm here," Enzo said, leaning close so I could hear him over the music. "When I was a teenager, I had night-mares about places like this."

"We'll just stay long enough to hear the band play, OK?"

"I'm the oldest person here," he said, looking around like he expected the police to jump out of the bushes and arrest him for being too adult.

"Well, everyone here hates me, so we're equally out of place."

I strode into the barn like I had purpose, because I didn't know what else to do. We squeezed by a group of football players and their girlfriends who were clustered around a keg. One of the guys shouted, "Holy shit, Hawthorn Creely at a *party*?"

"Don't you have werewolves to hunt?" one of the girls taunted.

I ignored them and kept walking.

It was warm inside despite how cool the night was. The whole place reeked of beer. A stage was set up opposite the doors, and a band was playing. I didn't see Logan though, so it must not have been Strength in Numbers. I looked around for something to do or someone for Enzo and me to talk to, and even though I recog-nized almost every face, there wasn't a group we could join.

Enzo and I stood awkwardly at the edge of the crowd, and I was thinking what a mistake it was to have come when I heard someone shout my name in a much friendlier way than the jock outside had.

Emily ran up to me and gave me a hug. "I can't believe you came!"

I was pretty sure she'd been drinking. Otherwise, she looked like regular Emily, wearing a peach cardigan. That made me feel better. Normal.

Logan was right behind her, and she introduced me to him, even though technically we'd met before. Then I introduced both of them to Enzo.

Emily was polite. She smiled at Enzo and told him it was nice to meet him. I was probably the only one who noticed that the smile didn't quite reach her eyes. Or that Emily, with her impeccable manners, hadn't offered to shake Enzo's hand.

"Hey," Logan said, "aren't you the guy whose girlfriend is missing?"

I could tell how uncomfortable Enzo was without even looking at him. It's like the feeling was radiating off his skin. "Yeah. I am."

"That sucks, man. I'm really sorry."

"Thanks."

"So, are there, like, any updates?"

"No," Enzo said, glancing around the room as if not looking at Logan would make him disappear.

Emily and I looked back and forth between them. I wished for something clever to say that would take the whole conversation in a new direction, but instead, I just stood there.

"You think an animal got her?"

"Maybe."

"That's harsh. I can't imagine what you're going through."

Enzo ended the conversation by saying he was going to find us some drinks. Emily, ever helpful, pointed him in the right direction. For the second time in just a few minutes, I felt relieved.

"Why did you bring him here?" Emily asked as soon as he was out of earshot.

"I didn't want to come alone."

If it were any other time, she would have pressed the matter, and it would have turned into an argument. But we were at a party, and no one wanted to think about unpleasant things.

"You're *not* alone," Emily said, putting her arm around my shoulder. "You have me."

I laughed and squeezed her back. The alcohol was probably responsible for her uncharacteristic display of affection, but I'd take what I could get.

✸✸✸

An hour later, Logan's band was onstage, and I was probably the closest to drunk I'd ever been, which was OK, because I felt great. Strength in Numbers was better than I thought they would be, Emily and Enzo were getting along, and I'd stopped caring about everyone else and what they thought of me.

"They have so much energy!" I said to Emily, and I wasn't sure if she could hear me, because we were so close to the stage, but she nodded and grinned like she knew exactly what I was talking about.

Some people next to us were dancing, and I thought that was a great idea, so I started swaying back and forth too. Emily burst out laughing, then grabbed my hand and joined me.

While watching the revelry in the Barn, I'd had an epiphany. Parties weren't just about who was who and being seen. It was about letting go. About celebrating that we all made it through one more boring week. Everyone came together in one place, and for a while, it was as if nothing mattered except the music and the energy and being away from all of the adults in our lives. These parties were about freedom.

And friendship. They were about friendship too. All the tension I'd felt between me and Emily during the past weeks faded away. I remembered why I loved her so much and why she was my best friend. Emily was smart and talented, and she never apologized for being her own person. She was so much better than everyone in the Mills, and she didn't even know it. And she got me. We clicked in a way that I just couldn't with other people. What did it matter if she had a weird boyfriend? What did it matter if she was about to leave me?

"I'm going to miss you," I shouted.

"What?"

I leaned and tried again. "I'm going to miss you."

"Where am I going?"

"The music thing."

"Don't jinx it," Emily said, but she was laughing. She knew she'd get in.

"And college."

"You're going to college too!"

I wasn't even sure what I'd be doing the next day, let alone the next year.

"You're my best friend in the entire world," I said.

Emily hugged me in response, and I knew what she was trying to say. That she wasn't leaving me, even if we wouldn't be in the same place anymore. That we would always be best friends, no matter what. That somehow, everything would be OK.

"Come on," I said and pulled Emily closer to the stage. "Let's go watch your boyfriend."

We danced, and the room swirled around, and I could hear Logan playing the guitar through it all. I was sweaty and tired, but I was alive. What was more important than that?

✖✖✖

When Logan's band finished playing, Emily went to find him and tell him how good they'd been. I had no idea where Enzo was. It was very suddenly too warm, and even though I stopped spinning, everything around me kept going.

I pushed my way through the crowd. If I could get outside in the fresh air, I figured I'd feel better. But I didn't really. I stumbled around the side of the barn and promptly threw up, hating myself the whole time. I was just as bad as the rest of them.

That's when I heard a voice that I one hundred percent had not expected. "Thorny? What the hell?"

I heaved a couple more times and looked up. Connor was standing a few feet away. Before I even had time to think that the situation couldn't get any worse, Rush came up behind him.

"I don't feel good," I told them weakly.

"You don't look good either," Rush said. "Are you done throwing up?"

"I think so," I said, hating how pitiful I sounded.

"Hawthorn Creely, I never thought this day would come," Connor said, as if my being drunk at a party was some big joke.

"Don't," Rush warned him, then moved to my side.

I leaned against my brother and tried to clear my head, make the world stop tilting back and forth.

"I want to go home," I said.

"Who'd you come here with?" Connor asked.

I didn't know why he thought that was any of his business. "Why are you two here at all?"

"It's a party," Rush said.

"A high school party. Aren't you a little old?"

"At least she's sober enough to insult us," Connor said.

With one of them on either side of me, we walked around the side of the barn toward the highway. We didn't get far before Emily came running up.

"I was looking everywhere for you. What's going on?"

"I don't feel good," I told Emily.

"She's drunk," Rush said.

"No, I'm not."

Emily ignored me and spoke to my brother instead. "Are you taking her home? I'd rather he not do it." She nodded her head in the direction of the party.

"Who?" Rush asked.

"Her date. Enzo Calvetti." At the dry tone of Emily's voice, all my warm feelings for her vanished.

"Don't be like that," I snapped.

"Like what?"

"Judgmental." I pulled away from Rush and reeled for a second before balancing.

"I'm not making a judgment. I'm stating a fact. You came here with him," said Emily.

"And you hate it. You hated him before you even met him."

"Like you were so open-minded about Logan."

"I'm here, aren't I?" I shouted. People around us turned to look.

"Hey," Rush said, "keep it down."

Emily didn't heed my brother's warning either. "You're here, but you brought that creep with you, and you're drunk and making a scene and making this all about you, just like you do with everything!"

"I do not."

"You do! That's how it always is. That's how it's been for the past ten years, Hawthorn. Well, guess what? I'm not a supporting role in your life story."

Then Emily stomped away.

I tried to stay on my feet and puzzle over what she'd said at the same time. Before I made any progress on the latter, Enzo walked up.

"Hawthorn, you OK?" I could tell he was concerned, which made me happy. Even though he'd abandoned me.

"Back off," Rush said to him.

Enzo scowled. "Who the hell are you?"

"I'm her fucking brother, and I'm really not the in the mood for any more bullshit tonight."

Enzo faltered. I sent him a psychic message to save me, to swoop in and whisk me away from the current situation. Even if the whisking would be done on the bus, not a noble steed. And instead of riding into the sunset, we'd go back to his crappy apartment.

"We'll take her home," Connor said quietly.

"She came here with me."

Yes! I would have jumped up and down if not for the risk of throwing up again.

"Yeah, and you ditched her and let her get drunk when she's obviously inexperienced," Rush said.

I cringed. If I hadn't been so out of it, I would have died from embarrassment.

Enzo looked from my brother to Connor and took a step back.

That's when I knew he wasn't going to rescue me. He was going to let himself get bullied by a couple ex-jocks.

"We'll take Hawthorn home," Connor repeated. "Go back to the party or get out of here."

Then Rush and Connor were walking me to the car. It was funny, the way my feet were moving even though I didn't tell them to. Also, the way the ground had turned into one of those fun house floors that tries to throw you off balance. I wanted to tell Enzo about it, but we'd left him behind us. Besides, I hated him for not standing up to my brother.

There was some discussion about which of them would drive me home or if both of them should. Finally, Connor convinced Rush to stay and said he'd meet up with him in an hour. I got the feeling that Rush's new girlfriend was supposed to show up at the Barn and that's why Connor told him to stay. I tried to ask them about it, but I was too tired.

"Let me know if you have to throw up," Connor said when we were on the road.

I nodded and slumped against the window. Watching the trees go by in the glare of the headlights made me light-headed. I closed my eyes, felt sleep trying to take me.

"No one gives Enzo a chance," I slurred.

"You did."

"Yeah. I guess." I risked opening my eyes. The trees were still moving too fast. No, I reminded myself, the trees weren't moving; we were. "He didn't kill Lizzie."

"I never said he did," Connor said as if explaining something to a child.

I meant to tell Connor not to talk to me like that but instead asked, "Do you dislike him?"

"I don't even know him."

"Fair enough."

For a little while, there was silence. I cracked the window, let the chilly air hit my face. The road was smooth, and Connor's car didn't bounce and jerk around like mine did. I was just starting to relax when Connor spoke.

"Your brother has been drunk more times than I can count, but I never thought I'd be the designated driver for the younger Creely."

"Little Creely," I mumbled.

"What?"

"Nothing."

What was I doing in Connor's car? Why had I gone to the party in the first place? I wanted the world to make sense again.

The full moon lit up the road in front of us. Connor could have cut the headlights and still had enough light to see. It made me think of Lizzie, out by herself in the woods. What was she thinking and doing at that moment? Did she feel like she was finally home?

I must have lost the battle and fallen asleep after that. The next thing I was aware of was Connor opening the passenger door.

"Come on," he said, holding out a hand to help me. "You're home."

My eyes didn't want to focus. My mouth had a horrible taste in it, worse than any vegan food my mom had ever made me eat. I tried to get out of the car without any help, but I stood up too fast, and it made my head pound. I took Connor's hand.

"This is the worst night of my life," I mumbled as he helped me across the yard.

"If this is the worst, you should count yourself lucky."

I wasn't lucky though. Lizzie was the lucky one. Lucky Lizzie who always got everything she wanted. She wouldn't have thrown up at the party. And Enzo wouldn't have left her side, not for a minute.

Connor helped me up the stairs and unlocked the front door for me.

"Are you going to make it to your room?" he asked.

"You offering to tuck me in too?"

Connor laughed and shook his head. "Just making sure you're OK, Thorny."

"I am."

"All right. Good night then."

"Night," I said.

I went inside the house and began the monumental task of climbing the stairs. Halfway up, I considered lying down and going to sleep right there but figured that would probably make my mom ask several questions—none of which I wanted to answer. So instead, I very slowly and carefully dragged myself to bed.

CHAPTER 19

PERSPECTIVE

✻ ✻

I would have gladly slept in until noon the next day, but Rush didn't give me the opportunity. I woke up to him shaking me.

"Go away," I moaned, shoving my head under a pillow.

"Come on, get up." He snatched the pillow away. "We need to go back to the Barn."

I squinted up at him, wondering when sunlight had become so painful. "Are you crazy? Why would I ever go back there?"

"To get your car, remember?"

I moaned again.

Rush was obnoxiously perky for so early in the morning. I would have wanted to kill him, except he got me Tylenol and coffee and gave my parents some story about how I'd run out of gas the night before, and he was taking me to fill up the tank.

"Thanks for doing all this," I told him once we were in the car and heading to the Barn.

In response, Rush asked, "What's going on with you and that Enzo guy?"

"You could just say *you're welcome.*"

"And you could just answer the question."

"Enzo and I are friends. That's all."

"Keep it that way."

"You sound like Emily," I grumbled. A phrase I never thought I'd utter.

Rush glanced over at me. I was surprised to see that he actually seemed worried. "There's something not right about Enzo."

"Like he may be a murderer?"

"No, Hawthorn. Like he's a loser who will drag you down with him."

I didn't know how to respond to that, so I didn't. We drove in silence.

Who was Rush to lecture me? Like he was a master of great decisions or something? Like he had *his* life together?

The longer the silence stretched, the more annoyed I got. Finally, I blurted out, "You can't just be my brother when it's convenient for you."

"What?" Rush looked at me sharply.

"You can't sit here and lecture me about how Enzo is bad news, even though most of the time, it's like you forget you even have a sibling. For all you know, I could be hanging out with people who are bad for me every single day. You don't know anything about my life."

"I don't know anything about your life because you don't *tell* me anything about it, Hawthorn."

"I've tried to."

"When have you ever done that?"

I was silent.

"And when have you ever wanted to know about mine?" Rush went on. "I can't say anything without getting insulted by you. Football is stupid; the girls I date are stupid; I'm stupid. If that's how you feel, fine, whatever. But don't sit there and act like I'm a shitty brother, OK?"

"So it's all my fault then? Yeah, right. You've spent half your life making fun of me because I'm not as cool and popular as you."

"Yeah, you're such an outcast. No one understands you. All anyone does is sit around and think about what a loser you are. Grow up, Hawthorn. No one cares."

As if to punctuate his point, Rush turned on the radio, which I pretty much took to mean the conversation was over.

My headache was getting worse by the minute.

When we got to the Barn, there was no sign there'd been a party there the night before. What happened to the beer bottles and Solo cups? Did someone come out early in the morning to clean all the trash? I thought about asking Rush, but a glance at his face convinced me it would be a bad idea.

"Thanks for the ride."

Rush nodded but didn't look at me.

"So…see you later," I said.

"Yeah."

He continued to stare straight ahead. I didn't know what else to say, so I got out of his car and into my own.

✸✸✸

I drove toward my house but couldn't bear the thought of going inside. Not because I was avoiding Rush. He'd gone to coach one of his peewee games after dropping me off. And it wasn't because I was afraid my parents would ask me questions about last night. If anything, they were probably happy I'd gone out and socialized. Besides, a few nights before, I'd caught my mom passing a joint with Sundog. If she was fine smoking pot in our backyard, she could hardly get on my case for underage drinking.

I didn't want to go inside because the house was suffocating. I didn't want to be in my room, alone with my thoughts. All the things I'd accumulated over the past seventeen years trapped me inside of my head, which was the last place I wanted to be. I didn't want to think of what a fool I'd made of myself the night before or how everything Rush said in the car was probably true.

On a normal day, I would have gone to Emily's. But it wasn't a normal day. I couldn't hang out with Emily and pretend our fight hadn't happened. And Enzo was the last person I wanted to see because I still felt like he'd abandoned me. That pretty much summed up my list of friends. For a second, I thought maybe I could call Connor, and he'd hang out with me. But then I dismissed that too. He was my brother's friend, not mine.

With nowhere to go and my head hurting too much to make aimless driving possible, I got out of my car and walked around the side of my house to the backyard. I could at least put off going inside for a while.

Sundog was sitting by his tent, smearing paint on a piece of construction paper with his bare hands.

"Young Hawthorn, how are you on this fine Sunday morning?"

"Hungover."

I sat down next to him and watched him work. The colors on his palette were running together and turning brown. His canvas didn't look much better. Sundog dipped his fingers in a glob of paint at the edge of his paper and used it to draw a long line.

"What's it supposed to be?" I asked.

"It's not what it is; it's how the art makes you feel."

"The painting makes me feel like the artist is confused."

Sundog laughed and scratched the side of his face, leaving a bluish-gray blotch on his cheek. "Confusion is like curiosity—it reminds us we're alive. To not feel confused means we no longer care. Not caring is death."

He reached into the tent behind him, pulled out another large piece of paper, and set it down in front of me. "Try using the paint to express yourself."

I shrugged and pressed my hand onto his palette, then pressed it on the center of my paper. When I pulled away, my handprint looked small, like a child had made it. It made me think of being a little kid and tracing my hand to make turkeys for Thanksgiving.

"What do you see?" Sundog asked.

"My handprint," I said.

"And what do you feel?"

"Nothing. Not everything has meaning, you know."

I got more paint on my hand and ran it across the paper, smearing the handprint and making it into nothing.

"Have you ever felt like you were wrong about everything you thought you knew?" I asked Sundog.

He added some paint to the white parts of my paper. "Growth comes from questioning our own hearts. But unrelenting self-doubt can lead you astray."

I wasn't sure that qualified as an answer. "I don't know what that means."

"Your perception of the world is your own. No one can take it from you. Don't let fear overwhelm what you know to be real."

I thought of Lizzie in the woods, howling at the full moon, learning how to be a werewolf.

"But what if I'm wrong about what I think is real?"

"If you believe it, then it can't be wrong."

"Thanks for the advice." I pushed my piece of paper toward Sundog. "You finish it."

On my way into the house, I passed Timothy Leary curled up in a patch of sunlight. I patted her on the head, forgetting the paint on my hand. She craned her neck toward me for more affection. She didn't mind the streaks of color I'd left on her fur. Unlike me, she didn't see it as a mess.

CHAPTER 20

DAY THIRTY-SEVEN

I was at the sink washing my hands when Mychelle Adler left a bathroom stall, which I thought was pretty awful timing, especially first thing on Monday morning.

"Well, look who it is," Mychelle said. "I'm glad you're not still feeling under the weather."

"And I'm glad you were so concerned about my health."

I finished rinsing my hands quickly so I could get out of there, but Mychelle stepped between me and the paper towels.

"What were you doing at that party? Besides getting sloppy and embarrassing yourself, I mean."

I'd had enough of Mychelle. I was sick of her ruining my days. I was sick of having to dodge her because I didn't know what she'd say and how much it might hurt my feelings. What made her think it was OK to be so horrible to people?

"Wow," I snapped. "I'm being called sloppy by a girl who's gotten wasted at parties and spread her legs for half the football team since eighth grade."

Mychelle looked like I'd slapped her. She took a step toward me, and I took a step back.

"If you want to have a cat fight, wash your hands first. You just came from the toilet, and you've already spread enough diseases to the senior class."

"You can't talk to me like that," Mychelle said, but she didn't step any closer.

"No. It's the other way around. I've spent four years avoiding you in the halls because you only feel good about yourself when you make bitchy remarks to me. But guess what? I don't care anymore. The difference between me and you is that I don't have anything to lose. So say whatever you want to. Just know that you'll be getting a response."

For a moment, the bathroom was dead silent. Then Mychelle said, "Go to hell, Hawthorn."

I laughed. "I'm already in hell. Welcome to Griffin Mills High School."

I pushed past Mychelle and out into the hallway. For a Monday morning, I was feeling pretty OK.

✖✖✖

The feeling only lasted until lunchtime. Up until then, I was so busy replaying my victory over Mychelle that I didn't worry that people were making fun of me for throwing up at the party. I didn't even care about all of the stuff I was hearing about homecoming, because everyone was just concerned with what they were going to wear and where'd they'd have after-parties, and no one was thinking about how I was a loser because I didn't have a date. Maybe. Probably.

My good mood disappeared at lunch when Emily didn't show up behind the gym.

I ate my food slowly, thinking maybe she was late because she got caught talking to her third period teacher or something. It had happened before. But when my food was gone and lunch period was halfway over, I was pretty sure Emily wasn't going to show.

I gathered my stuff and went to the library. Emily wasn't there. I knew she'd never break the rules and leave campus for lunch, which meant she'd done the unthinkable—gone to the cafeteria.

Though I hadn't been there for years, I worked up the nerve to step inside. Sure enough, Emily was sitting at a table with Logan and his musician friends.

I knew I should leave. Emily had made her point. But didn't I deserve an explanation? Couldn't she have given me some warning before deciding to end our tradition of eating behind the gym?

I walked over to the table. Emily was in the middle of a conversation with a girl who had pink-and-green hair. She didn't even notice me.

"Hey. Can I talk to you?"

She looked up with a guilty expression, which somehow made the whole situation worse. "Can it wait until later?"

"No," I said, hopefully sounding more firm than I felt.

Emily excused herself from the table and followed me to the side of the cafeteria, where we were mostly out of everyone's earshot.

"So you're just ditching me at lunch now?" I blurted.

"It's not like that."

"Oh?"

"Look," Emily said. She twirled her necklace around one finger. She bit her lip. "I just think we could use a little space from each other. Just for a little while."

My stomach dropped. "Why?"

"I meant what I said the other night. I feel like our friendship is always about you. You decide what we do and what we talk about and who we dislike. I've spent most of my life being forced to participate in schemes I don't want any part of."

"Like what?"

"Like when you thought the world was going to end and wanted me to steal supplies from my parents' store."

Oh yeah.

"Or when you were convinced that there was a serpent monster in Tappan Lake."

"I was a little kid," I protested.

"You were twelve. And that's not the point."

"What *is* the point?"

"That I'm not like you, and you can't accept that. You want me to help you on your missions and listen to your thoughts, never stopping to think that maybe I have my own."

I could feel my face burning, though I couldn't tell if it was from anger or shame. "I never meant for it to be like that."

"I know you didn't. It probably never even occurred to you. That's the problem, Hawthorn."

"So, are we just not friends anymore?" I sounded pitiful. I *felt* pitiful. "Is this, like, a breakup?"

"We'll always be friends. I just need some space."

"OK," I said. It wasn't OK though. It was one of the most un-OK things that had ever happened to me.

Emily hugged me and walked back to her seat next to Logan. I left the cafeteria and pretty much decided I never wanted to go back there.

✖✖✖

After school, I knocked on the door to Enzo's apartment and shifted back and forth, waiting for him to answer. I started to think he wasn't home, but then the door swung open.

"Hawthorn. Hey."

"Can I come in?"

A record was playing loudly. A man with a deep voice sang about love tearing people apart. Enzo turned the music down, and the lyrics became a whisper.

My eyes went from him to an easel that was set up in the corner. It was turned so I couldn't see the canvas.

"Are you painting again?" I asked.

"Trying."

"Can I look?"

"Not until it's done." Enzo pulled his tobacco from his pocket and rolled a cigarette. I wandered over to the bed and sat down.

"Were you ever going to call me again?"

"What?" Enzo asked with a half laugh.

"You ditched me at the party. It annoyed me. So I decided not to call you."

"What are you doing here then?"

"Don't tease me." I pulled my legs up to my chest and wrapped my arms around them. "I needed a friend and didn't want to wait for you to call me. Which is why I'm wondering if you ever would have."

Enzo took a deep drag from his cigarette and exhaled smoke toward the ceiling. "Don't make our friendship like that. There don't need to be rules."

"Can I have a cigarette?" I'd never smoked before, but at that moment, I wanted to feel like someone other than me.

Enzo raised his eyebrows and passed me his cigarette instead. I took a drag. I could feel the burn all the way down my throat, like inhaling sandpaper. But I didn't cough, so that was something.

Enzo sat on the bed and put an ashtray between us. "I would have called."

"Good."

We passed the cigarette back and forth in silence. I listened to the music. A new song started, just as depressing as the last.

"Saturday was the full moon," I told Enzo.

"I know," he said.

"We should probably check the woods. There might be some new clues."

"I was thinking the same thing."

And just like that, we were OK again.

CHAPTER 21

WELCOME, OCTOBER

* *

L eaves turned gold and orange and red. The air was crisp.
All over the Mills, people started to prepare for Halloween.
Candy appeared in stores, cheesecloth ghosts hung from trees, and
scarecrows stood sentry in front yards. The pumpkin patch was open
for picking, and you could get apple cider there, fresh from the press.

The thing about October is that it makes everyone want to
believe in magic. Sure, it's the spooky kind of magic, but it's better
than nothing. And with everyone planning their costumes, it was
one of the few times a year I felt like I fit in. I wasn't the only one
who wanted to be someone else.

I guess Christmas is a magical time too, maybe even more
magical, but it comes with all kinds of pressure. You have to be
cheerful and jolly and spend time with your family. And then
there's Christmas shopping. Not only is the act itself torture, but
in the end, you have to come up with a super awesome present
that'll wow the recipient, and I've always been really bad at that.
Like the time I got Rush a video called *Overcoming Illiteracy*, which

I thought was really considerate. He disagreed. But it was better than what he got me that year, which was nothing at all.

Halloween doesn't have any strings attached. It's a holiday for hanging out and eating candy and playing pretend. It was the kind of holiday I could get behind.

My mom claimed she celebrated Samhain, not Halloween. It was some kind of Celtic harvest festival or something.

"Halloween *started* as Samhain, Hawthorn," my mom said in early October as she put out decorations.

I raised my eyebrows. "So plastic skeletons were part of Samhain?"

"I have to make do with what's available," she said.

As much as my mom wanted to keep up her New Age facade, the truth was, she loved the Halloween season as much as I did. And if she wanted to call it Samhain, I didn't mind. It was actually pretty cool—the night the boundary between the worlds gets thinner. I was certainly on board with that.

I was also on board with my mom's pumpkin pies. They were made with soy milk, of course, but you almost couldn't tell. I was just happy to have sweets in the house that I didn't have to smuggle in.

The hippies didn't celebrate Halloween *or* Samhain, but they also didn't turn down the pie I took out to their bonfire. I sat down with them and tried to get them to tell ghost stories while they ate. They made an effort but always brought it back to astral projection or past lives, which was not really in the spirit of the season. I wanted stories about vengeful ghosts and witches who ate little kids and creatures that lurked in the dark—the kind of stories that scared me so much, they couldn't help but make me feel alive.

"Tell scarier stories," I urged the hippies.

"Why this fascination with darkness?" Sundog asked.

I shrugged. "The world is dark."

"The world is whatever you want it to be."

"Tell me a scary story," I said to Enzo.

"Real or fake?"

"Real."

It was just before dusk, and we were walking through the woods. It was cold and windy and felt like the start of a horror movie. I loved it.

"Have you ever heard of the brazen bull?" Enzo asked.

"No. But it doesn't sound scary."

"Give me a chance, kid." He stopped to light a cigarette, using his body to block the wind. "It was invented in ancient Greece. A hollow bull, made out of bronze. For kicks, they'd lock people inside and light a fire under them. The person would roast to death, obviously. The creepiest part is, there were tubes inside that turned the person's screams into bull sounds. So these rich assholes would be gathered at a party, and there'd be this bull statue making noises, and everyone would act like it was entertainment, not the sound of someone being tortured."

"OK, you win. That's terrifying."

"Wanna know something else?" Enzo grinned. "The guy who invented it was the first person roasted inside."

"My mom would call that karma," I said.

***

There were no more official searches for Lizzie, just small ones organized by her family. There were no more articles in the paper. No one at school whispered theories about where she'd gone.

"Why'd you stop caring about Lizzie?" I asked Rush.

He was standing at the counter, eating a bowl of cereal. The spoon stopped halfway to his mouth. He seemed thrown by the question, which made me wonder if maybe he hadn't realized he'd stopped caring.

"What? I still care."

"Not like you did when she first went missing."

Rush finished taking his bite and chewed for a long time. "I care. There's just not much to talk about anymore. There's no news. Nothing is changing."

"So out of sight, out of mind?"

"What do you want me to say, Hawthorn? That you were right? That I was upset over a girl I didn't know anymore, then realized I was stupid to care so much?"

"Is that what happened?"

"No. I just got over it."

It was so easy for Rush. Everything had always been easy for him.

I wasn't ready to get over Lizzie. Neither was Enzo. Everyone else might have given up hope, but we kept searching for her. We combed the woods and clipped articles from the newspaper and made lists of any information that might be relevant to the case.

Pretty much, we spent all our free time together.

✶✶✶

"She's spending all her free time with him."

I stopped in my tracks. My dad was speaking. He and my mom were in the kitchen. If I'd been able to find my keys, I'd have already been on my way to Enzo's and wouldn't have overheard my parent's conversation at all. I *really* needed to keep better track of my keys.

"She needs a friend, James."

I crept closer to the kitchen door, unable to stop myself from listening in, even though I didn't think I'd like what I heard.

"There's an entire high school of people she could be friends with" my dad said. "What happened to Emily?"

"Rush says they had a fight."

My insides twisted with anger and embarrassment. I couldn't believe how they were talking about my personal life. It was no one's business but mine.

"I'm sorry, but I'm just not comfortable with their relationship. What do we even know about him? Look what happened to his last girlfriend!"

"She says they're just friends."

"Off in the woods all the time, looking for werewolves. This is your daughter too, Sparrow. How can you sit there like this is normal?"

Even my dad was calling me weird now.

I'd heard enough. I stomped out of the house, slamming the door behind me. I hoped they noticed.

❧❧❧

As the month progressed, I knew I faced a lot of Halloween parties I wouldn't be invited to. I hadn't been invited to a Halloween party since kids had moved from bobbing for apples to spin the bottle—at least, based on what I'd seen in movies, that's what I imagined they were doing.

I was also well aware that homecoming was the weekend before Halloween, which meant another chance for me to be pitifully dateless.

Despite this, I didn't feel like I was missing out. I didn't need loud, obnoxious parties and dances packed with people I hated. I had Enzo. I had his dark, art-filled apartment where I could let down my guard and be myself. I had walks through the woods and werewolf lore, which was worth more than any high school event.

We spent the middle of October watching werewolf movies on TV, making fun of the parts that had been badly edited to take out the gore and sex and cursing. We decided there was no such thing as a great werewolf movie. They always came out cheesy. My favorite was about a teenage girl werewolf, because it reminded me of Lizzie. Enzo's favorite was the original *The Wolf Man* with Lon Chaney Jr. He thought all the old movies were better than any that had been made in the past twenty or thirty years.

"There's a magic to the old films that new movies can't capture. The filmmakers try to hide it with special effects, but no one really buys it."

I disagreed. Movies were movies, whether they were old or new. They always captivated me, pulled me into worlds where anything was possible. Worlds where there were adventures and surprises, and life was never dull.

The only thing I didn't like about movies was when the credits rolled and returned me to real life. At least, that was how I used to feel. Leaving a movie world wasn't so painful anymore. Spending time with Enzo made me realize anything could be an adventure if you looked at it the right way.

One day, when the only horror movies playing were ones we'd already seen, Enzo let me watch a short film he'd made during his brief time in college. It was black and white and tried to imitate a French new wave film. Mostly, it depicted a little boy running through a cornfield with drums beating in the background.

"I don't really get it," I told him when it ended.

"That's why I gave up film," Enzo said. "No one ever got what I was trying to say."

Sometimes, Enzo wrote short stories. One of them was about a man who worked in a fortune cookie factory, whose job was coming up with the fortunes to put on the little slips of paper. One day, he realizes he's spent his whole life telling other people what to expect in their futures without ever thinking about his own. So he sets out to discover his true fortune, which can't be found at the center of a cookie.

"What does he find?" I asked.

Enzo shrugged. "I don't know. That's where the story ends."

"I hate it when you do that to me," I said with a groan.

Enzo thought *ends* were disappointing. He said when you were really immersed in a story, you started to have expectations. And the end was never as great as you imagined it could have been. Even though I mostly agreed with him, I couldn't help wanting to know everything. I was always looking for *more*.

"But *you* must know what happened next," I said about the fortune cookie story. "Even if you didn't write it."

"You'll just have to use your imagination, kid."

Enzo had a lot of stories—and a lot of different ways to tell them. He'd tried writing, painting, filmmaking, playing in a band. I asked him if it was overwhelming to have so many things he wanted to do. He said the storytelling was the important part, not the medium.

I wondered if I had my own story to tell, and if so, what medium I would use. I'd never wanted to be an artist, but I could see the beauty in the idea.

Later that night, I brought it up with Sundog. He said that we're all born with our paths already in place; our job is simply to find them.

I imagined my dad would disagree. When I went to my room, I found a stack of college catalogs on my bed. There was a sticky note on the top one that said, "It's time." I shoved the catalogs under my bed without looking through them.

Unlike the man who worked in the fortune cookie factory, I wasn't ready to find my future. For once, I was enjoying the present.

CHAPTER 22

ON THE THRESHOLD
OF EVERYTHING

Enzo and I went to the thrift store because he liked looking for messages in books. He had a collection. He looked for school books with doodles in the margins. Or inscriptions in books that had been given as gifts. Those were the saddest, because why would someone give something like that away? Enzo had even found one book with a forgotten letter tucked between the pages.

"These notes are little pieces of history no one cares about," Enzo told me. "But they remind you you're not the first person to hold that book. Someone else owned it first and read the exact same words, and one way or another, it impacted them. We're all connected."

"That sounds like something Sundog would say." I liked the sentiment though. It made me want to write messages in my own books.

Dusty Roses was the only secondhand store in Layton, and there were only a few other shoppers that morning. I trailed behind

Enzo, watching him open books and flip through pages, then I got bored and wandered off on my own.

I could see what Enzo meant. It was weird to think about how everything there had once belonged to someone else. Why had they gotten rid of it? Did they ever think about someone else using their dishes or sitting on their couch or wearing their beat-up fedora? It felt like giving away memories.

I walked through the section of women's clothes, running my hands along the racks as I passed. Everything smelled funny. I wondered how many of the people who shopped there didn't have any other choice than to buy something another person considered old or broken. It made me feel a little guilty about my own closet, stuffed with clothes I seldom wore. Though that was largely my mom's fault for continuing to buy me things that were hideous.

Out of the corner of my eye, I got a flash of hot-pink tulle. It was pretty much impossible *not* to see. I parted the hangers to get a better look.

The dress was a monstrosity. It must have been worn to a prom in the 1980s and spent the intervening decades forgotten in someone's attic. In addition to all the tulle, the dress was covered in lace, with a ridiculously poofy skirt that stopped at the knee. It was so absurd that I couldn't help but grin. I had to try it on.

I didn't bother taking off my jeans or tennis shoes—I just pulled on the dress over them. It was a perfect fit. I admired myself in the mirror. I spun, and yards of lace flared up like a tutu.

Enzo was still examining books when I walked up behind him.

"What do you think?" I asked.

He turned, and I did another spin.

Enzo laughed. "Not bad."

"Do you think the first owner had a good prom? I bet she did. She probably had a ton of friends, and they all chewed bubble gum and twirled their hair while talking about if they'd go all the way with their dates."

"I wonder where she is now."

"Maybe she married her high school sweetheart."

"And got divorced ten years later when she realized her husband wasn't a star athlete anymore."

"I can always count on you to look on the bright side," I said dryly.

He laughed. "Come on, can't you see it? They've got, like, five kids, and he's working a dead-end job and spends every night at the bar."

"That does seem to be most people's fate around here," I agreed. "Except they wouldn't get divorced. They'd stay together and make each other miserable forever."

"And you call *me* a pessimist?" he said, grinning.

"Go to homecoming with me," I blurted out.

"What?" Enzo looked baffled by the sudden change in conversation. I was a little surprised myself.

"Please?" I said before I could think about it too much.

"I want to wear this dress somewhere. And it would be fun to go together."

Granted, the last party we'd attended hadn't been a roaring success. But I'd stay away from alcohol, and it wasn't like I could get in another fight with Emily—we weren't even speaking to each other.

"Hawthorn, I didn't even go to my own homecoming dance."

"Exactly. That's why you should make up for it now."

"I'll be the same age as the chaperones."

"Who cares?" I said. "It'll be totally ridiculous. You can wear a suit with a Hawaiian shirt or something, and everyone will probably laugh at us, but it won't matter. Please? I really want to go."

Enzo smiled a little, and I knew I'd won.

"When is homecoming?"

"Next weekend, which I know is super soon, but it's not like we really need to do anything to prepare. It won't be a real date or anything."

"All right. Let's do it."

I laughed and twirled around again. For once, I wasn't going to be the only person in the school who didn't go to a dance. Even if I was just going with Enzo and wouldn't really have anyone else to talk to and would just be annoyed by the bad music, I was still going.

I paid seven dollars for the dress, which was cheap considering it was getting me to the homecoming dance. Enzo bought a fifty-cent book that had a neatly scripted haiku on the inside cover. Then we went werewolf hunting again.

✻ ✻ ✻

The pavement ended a few miles back, but the dirt road was well maintained enough for my little Rabbit to drive down it. I was slightly nervous, because my car was still making chugging noises like a steam engine, but that sort of made the whole experience more adventurous. The road was narrow, and tree branches touched overhead. We were deeper in the woods than we normally went and much deeper than the search parties had looked those first few days, since Lizzie was on foot. But Lizzie had nothing but time. She could be anywhere.

Enzo was in the passenger seat, frowning at a map like it was a book written in a foreign language.

"What happens if a car comes from the other direction?" I asked. "There's not enough space for them to pass."

"I don't think many people drive out here."

"Then why is there a road and not a trail?"

Enzo shrugged.

But that was OK too. I wasn't really worried, just making conversation. How could I be worried on a perfect fall day when I had nothing to do but wander through the woods with my friend and think about mysteries and dances? I rolled down my window and let the cool afternoon air hit my face.

A few minutes later, the road split. I stopped the car and looked at Enzo.

"It's not on the map. At least, I don't think it is." He spread the map on the dashboard and pointed out where he thought we were. We both leaned in to get a closer look, and I could feel the soft sleeve of his leather jacket brushing against my arm.

"Look at how the road is kind of squiggly," I said, tracing our path on the map. "I think that's the right fork."

"I think so too."

I shivered with excitement. "I wonder why the left road isn't marked."

"Probably because it's not a real road anymore. Look at it."

I followed Enzo's gaze. The right fork continued on in pretty much the same condition as it had been. The left side was more overgrown. Grass grew around the wheel ruts, and bushes lined the sides of the path. The woods were trying to take back the road.

"I think we should go left," I said.

"I don't know if your car can make it."

"That's OK. I don't care if the sides get scratched up."

"It's not that," Enzo said. "Look at how uneven the ground is. We don't have a lot of clearance in this thing. It's a Volkswagen, not a Jeep."

"No adventure ever started with someone turning back because they weren't in the ideal vehicle."

"You're crazy, kid," Enzo said, but he was smiling, and I knew he meant it in a good way, not like how the kids at school said it.

"So left?"

"Yeah. Left."

The road was a little worse than I thought it would be. I had to drive really slowly, and at one really big dip, the front of my car thumped against the ground. I rolled up the window, because the bushes and trees were so close that I felt like something could be waiting in the shadows to reach inside and pull me out. A couple times, a branch scraped the side of the car, making a nails on a chalkboard screech. Enzo seemed tense, but I thought the whole thing was fantastic.

I turned the radio to an AM station that was mostly just static and a few garbled words.

"What are you doing?" Enzo asked.

"Setting the mood. Now it's *really* like we're in a horror movie."

After a while, the road widened a little, and we came to a gate. It was made of rotting wood and closed but not latched. I stopped the car. Enzo and I looked at the old gate through the windshield.

"I suppose there's no way you're turning back now," he said.

"Go open it," I replied.

Enzo didn't move, so I got out of the car. From what I could see, the road continued on for a short distance, then opened into some sort of clearing.

I grabbed the wooden gate and pulled. Rusty hinges groaned, and the rotted wood started to collapse. I jumped back with a squeal.

Enzo finally got out of the car and looked at the pile of wood at my feet. "Well, your car certainly isn't getting over that."

"We'll have to walk the rest of the way," I said.

"What do you think is back there?" Enzo asked, peering down the dirt road. He sounded a little too hesitant for my liking.

"I think someone used to live here."

"Maybe we should go back."

"Are you kidding? We got this far. Aren't you even a little bit curious?"

I could tell he was.

"Let me just turn my car around first," I said.

"Why?"

"Haven't you been paying attention to all those horror movies? If there's a demon back there waiting to eat us, we'll need to get away fast. Do you really want to take the time to make a U-turn?"

"How often have you been in situations like this?"

"Well, never. But I've thought about them a lot."

After I had the car situated, Enzo and I started down the path. The woods around us were quiet except for our footsteps and the papery sound of dry leaves rubbing against each other.

Enzo and I didn't talk much while we walked. He smoked a cigarette and glanced back every few feet, as if he wanted to make sure the car was still there. In all the time we'd spent looking for

Lizzie, I'd never noticed how out of place he seemed in the woods. Enzo lived his life in dark rooms, making art that only he understood. The camping trip must have been Lizzie's idea. Was she the one who got the fire going and set up the tent? Enzo could sculpt and draw and write music, but I couldn't imagine him using his hands to drive a stake into the ground. He wouldn't know what berries you shouldn't eat or how to use the sun to figure out where you were. I wondered if he even knew how to use a compass.

There was a time when I thought Lizzie was the same way, that she wouldn't have survived a weekend without a hair dryer. But Lizzie had changed. Or maybe I just never understood who she really was. Maybe a person could be equally comfortable out in the woods and at the top of a cheerleading pyramid. Just like Emily could be as comfortable playing a classical piece on the piano as she was swaying in the audience at sweaty rock concert. I used to think there were so many rules about how people could be. Maybe I was wrong.

Enzo and I reached a clearing and stopped short. It was like something from my imagination had come to life.

The farmhouse had seen better days, but it was still standing. It was possibly in better shape than some of the houses in downtown Griffin Mills. The paint was mostly gone, but the clapboard siding was intact. Same with the windows. I only saw two that were broken, both on the second floor. The steeply pitched roof was covered in moss, and a lot of shingles were missing, but it wasn't sagging.

A sea of tall weeds separated us from the house. I could see where there had once been a path leading to the front porch, and I started in that direction. I couldn't wait to get inside. It was like getting a second chance to explore the Griffin Mansion. This time, I wasn't letting the opportunity pass.

"Wait," Enzo said. "The whole place will probably collapse if we go inside."

"Old houses were built with solid materials," I told him.

"I hardly count you as an architectural expert, Hawthorn. This place has probably been here for a hundred years."

"No way." I pointed toward the front door. "There's a porch light. It can't be that old if they had a generator out here."

"Well, what if there's someone in there?" Enzo asked.

"That's sort of the point. What if *Lizzie* is in there? She's been gone for almost two months now. She must have found some kind of shelter. Maybe a cave or old mine or something. Why not an abandoned house?"

Enzo frowned and looked at the house more thoughtfully.

"I'm going in," I told him. "You can wait out here if you want."

This time when I started through the weeds, Enzo followed.

I tested my weight on the first two porch steps before climbing up them. They creaked, but the wood didn't give. I stopped and waited for Enzo to catch up.

My heart pounded, and my fingertips tingled with anticipation.

"Are you scared?" he asked, dropping his voice to a whisper as he joined me on the porch.

"I feel alive."

When we walked through the door, anything could happen. Anything at all. Maybe we would find Lizzie sleeping in an upstairs bedroom like a werewolf Goldilocks. Maybe this was the secret hideout of some serial killer, and my life was about to turn into a scene from *The Texas Chainsaw Massacre*. Maybe we would find skeletons of a family who'd mysteriously died there. Or maybe we wouldn't find anything at all. It didn't matter. The important thing was that, unlike my daydreams, the house was real. I could reach out and touch it. It had a story to tell that I didn't know the ending to. And no matter what happened when I went inside, I would always have that one perfect moment standing on the threshold when anything was possible.

Enzo was the one who finally reached out and turned the knob. The door wasn't locked. He pushed it open, revealing a dusty corridor with rooms branching out on both sides. A staircase with a thick wooden bannister hugged one wall. We couldn't see much else through the gloom from where we stood.

Then something really weird happened, which was that Enzo reached down and grabbed my hand. I was startled and glanced at him, but he was already stepping into the house and pulling me behind him.

It was dim inside. None of the windows had curtains, but they were so dirty, they filtered the afternoon light. Enzo and I walked slowly from room to room, and I didn't know if my hands were sweaty because I was nervous or if it was because one of them was clasped in his.

The floorboards were covered with dirt, and I looked for footprints that didn't match ours, but it was too hard to tell in the low light. There were a few small pieces of leftover furniture and bits of trash, but mostly there was dust. The wallpaper was peeling, the pattern so faded that I could barely see there had been a pattern to start with.

"Nothing," Enzo whispered after we'd explored the first floor.

"Let's go up then."

I expected him to argue with me, but he just nodded and started up the stairs, still gripping my hand.

There was more light on the second floor, because of the broken windows. The stairs led to a long hallway, which was empty and in pretty much the same state as the rest of the house. The first room we found was a bathroom with cracked tile and a toilet filled with dark-brown water.

"Ew. Next room." I tugged Enzo's hand, and he followed me down the hall.

The bedroom was empty except for an ancient-looking sheet balled up in one corner.

"Who do you think lived here?" I asked.

"I have no idea," Enzo said.

"Pretend you do. Come on. You love to tell stories."

"OK." Enzo took a deep breath and thought for a moment. "It was probably some guy who went nuts after the war. He didn't

THE HUNDRED LIES OF LIZZIE LOVETT   215

trust the government, so he moved his family out here where they could live off the land and have peace and be happy."

"And *were* they happy?"

"For a while. But you know happiness never lasts forever."

"Whose room was this?" I urged, ready to get lost in his story.

"A little boy's," Enzo said. He pointed to the far corner. "His bed was over there. And his desk was in that corner, and he had a toy box right where we're standing. He wanted to play with army men, but his dad wouldn't let him, so he played cowboys and Indians instead."

"Tell me about the rest of the family."

Enzo laughed, and it echoed in the empty room. "Come on."

He pulled me to the next bedroom, which was pretty much the same as the first, except for some leaves that had blown in through the broken window.

"This was the girls' room. There were two of them. Twins."

"And?"

"And they were afraid of the woods at night," Enzo said, not trying to keep his voice low anymore. "They said they could feel creatures watching them. That's why they got a room at the front of the house. Their window faced the field instead of being close to the trees."

"Were they right? Were they being watched?"

Enzo looked at me. "What do you think?"

"Yes. Of course they were. The twins were probably out

playing one day and saw something, a beast. Maybe it lunged at one of them, but they managed to get away. And that's what started the haunting. Every day, something strange and scary happened until it became too much, and the family abandoned the house."

I was out of breath by the time I finished talking. I was excited and scared and, well, *happy*. I'd been waiting forever to find someone who'd tell stories with me the way Enzo did.

Enzo grinned, and I smiled back at him. My heart was pounding even more than before. We were both suddenly very quiet, and Enzo looked at me, and everything felt different and strange.

"Come on," Enzo said. "Let's go see where the parents slept."

Enzo pulled me toward the next room, and I let him, laughing. He reached the doorway first and stopped short. He dropped my hand.

"Shit."

"What?" I pushed ahead of him then stopped too. "Oh."

Unlike the other rooms, this one had been occupied recently. A mattress piled with blankets was pushed up against one wall. There was a gallon water jug and a flashlight on the floor next to the mattress. And a book, laid open to mark a page. I tried to see the title and take in the other stuff in the room—newspapers, food wrappers, a pair of boots—but Enzo pulled me back and whispered that we had to leave, and he didn't sound happy anymore.

I pulled away from him. "Enzo, it could be Lizzie."

"It's not."

"You don't know that."

I moved toward the mattress. Enzo grabbed my shoulder hard enough to hurt.

"Hawthorn, it's not Lizzie."

I turned to look at him. His face was pale.

"We spend all this time looking for her, and now that we finally have a real lead, you don't even want to check it out?"

"Stop it," Enzo said. "This isn't pretend. Someone has been squatting in this house. Not Lizzie. Not a werewolf. We need to get the fuck out before whoever it is comes back and finds us here. So let's go."

I still hesitated, glancing back at the bedroom. My eyes landed on boots. Men's boots.

My stomach sank. It was suddenly hard to breathe. I imagined every killer from every horror movie I'd ever seen, waiting downstairs for us with a knife or machete or chainsaw. Probably not a gun. That would be too easy. Our death would be too quick.

"Let's go," I agreed in a whisper.

Enzo nodded and started down the hallway. I followed. I wanted to reach out and grab his hand again, but I didn't.

We were halfway down the stairs when I heard the noise, a creaking sound from somewhere below us. Enzo and I froze. I put my hand over my heart, which felt like it was going to pound right out of my chest.

We waited.

There was nothing but silence.

I opened my mouth to ask Enzo if he thought it was clear when there was another sound. Someone—something—other than us was moving around in the house.

"Enzo."

"Shhh."

We listened. There was definitely something in the house with us. Something that was trying to be quiet. Maybe something that was listening for us the same way we were listening for it.

"We can't stay here forever," I whispered.

Enzo nodded and slowly began making his way down the stairs. He winced every time a riser creaked.

We hesitated again at the bottom of the steps. The hallway was empty. The front door was still ajar, like we'd left it. We could run for it and be outside in a moment. Unless the *something* in the house was crouched in one of the shadowy doorways between us and the front door, waiting to grab us as we passed.

I stepped out and looked back toward the kitchen. There was a door at the end of the hallway we hadn't opened when we were exploring the first floor. It was smaller than the others, more like a coat closet than the doorway to a room. But I was pretty sure it wasn't a closet. I was especially sure of it when I heard another shuffling sound.

"It's in the basement."

Enzo nodded. He made a beeline for the front door. But I stayed. There was something below us, maybe a monster, maybe a man, and maybe even Lizzie Lovett. My imagination wasn't playing tricks on me. This wasn't me being weird or wishing for something crazy to happen. There was *really* something moving around downstairs.

"Hawthorn," Enzo hissed.

I didn't take my eyes off the basement door. I wanted to know what was behind it. I *needed* to know.

"Hawthorn, let's go!"

Enzo was getting frantic. The footsteps were coming up the basement stairs. I couldn't look away.

"Hawthorn!"

I could hear a doorknob rattling, a rusty hinge whining as a door swung open.

Or maybe it was just my imagination. Either way, I bolted.

Enzo and I ran down the porch steps and raced across the field toward the trail and my car. I was pretty sure I'd never moved so fast in my life. I wondered if the rush was anything like what my brother had felt while running across a football field to score a touchdown.

Enzo and I got to the broken gate and hurdled over the debris. I dug in my pocket for my car keys. For a brief moment, I wondered if this would be the time my car didn't start, if all the months of putting off taking it into the shop would finally catch up with me. The thought was scary but also exciting. The whole situation was scary and exciting.

The adrenaline rush gave me clarity. It was as if I were watching myself in a movie instead of actively participating. I was fully in the moment, aware of everything around me at once.

My car started on the first try. I drove, bumping down the dirt road faster than was reasonable in a Volkswagen. Enzo twisted in his seat and watched out the back window.

When I got to the fork in the road, I slowed.

"Is it following us?"

Enzo shook his head.

For a second, we just looked at each other. Then we started laughing. The tension left my body. I stopped the car and leaned my forehead against the steering wheel, giggling. I could feel Enzo shaking with laughter next to me.

"What *was* that?" I asked a little bit later when I caught my breath.

"I don't know. Maybe we imagined it," Enzo said.

"Something was totally there."

"It could have been a squatter. Who was probably as scared of us as we were of him."

"Did you see the book he was reading?" I asked.

"No."

"I'm not positive, but I think it was *Macbeth*."

Something about a basement monster reading Shakespeare made us laugh all over again.

If there *was* a monster, and it suddenly sprang up behind my car to get revenge on us for infiltrating its lair, I didn't think I would mind. Even if the monster killed me, at least I would die having the best day of my life.

CHAPTER 23

SHEDDING SKIN

M y house was empty when I woke up on Sunday morning. Rush's peewee football team had a game, and my parents went to see it, like his coaching was some big accomplishment. I stayed home and hung out with the hippies.

"Free associate it, man," said the guy who called himself CJ, which was short for Castaway Jesus, which I wasn't going to question.

"I don't know what you mean," I said. Timothy Leary was curled up in my lap while I worked dry shampoo through her fur. Sundog lay next to us on an Indian blanket with his eyes closed and his hands folded over his chest.

"Free association is the pathway to embracing your own naturality," CJ said.

I looked at Sundog. "Translation?"

"It's a way to look inside yourself for answers," Sundog said.

"But how can the answer be inside me? I mean, there was either something in the house with us or there wasn't. If I knew the answer, it wouldn't be driving me crazy."

CJ held up a hand as if to stop my train of thought. "Your consciousness isn't limited to your body. Yesterday, you saw and felt things your brain couldn't register, because it's just too much for an unexercised mind. But it's all here." He leaned over and lightly tapped my temple. "Get it?"

"So I can free associate and, uh, unlock the answers or something?"

"Let me show you." CJ closed his eyes, straightened his back, and put his hands on his knees, almost like he was meditating. "Basement. Tablecloth. Vicodin. Argyle. Mother. Pain. Supernova."

CJ fell silent. I glanced at Sundog and was relieved to see that he looked amused and wasn't taking the whole thing super seriously.

After what seemed like an uncomfortably long time, CJ opened his eyes. "Whoa. That was intense." He shook his head as if to clear it. "Your turn now."

I shrugged and closed my eyes. "Basement. Dark. Damp. Cold. Silent. Stagn—"

"No," CJ interrupted. "That's not how you do it. You just described a basement. That's not the point, man."

"Oh. Sorry. I guess I'm not, you know, enlightened yet."

CJ sighed, clearly frustrated by my ignorance. "Whatever. I need to recharge."

After CJ wandered away, Sundog sat up and stretched. "The question is, Hawthorn, did you *want* someone to be in the basement?"

"I think so."

"Why?"

I shrugged. "Because it would've been interesting."

"The world is always interesting."

"Not really."

"You need to open your eyes and experience the glory of being alive and part of this universe."

Sundog wasn't really making a ton of sense, but compared to CJ, he sounded like the most rational person who'd ever lived. And I didn't really care what was or wasn't in the basement. It had mostly been something to talk about.

I changed the subject. "What's it like to not have a real home?" I asked Sundog.

He looked surprised. "I have a home. I don't have a house, but these people are my home."

"Well, what's that like then?"

"It's the same as your home is to you. Happiness, love, comfort."

Sundog obviously wasn't familiar with my and Rush's relationship.

"Doesn't all the traveling get old?" I asked.

"I didn't always travel. I had a house once. That was before the war. I had a wife too and a well-paying job."

I must have looked surprised, because Sundog laughed.

"Some people are born knowing their paths from the start," he said. "The rest of us take a while to get there."

"I wish you'd tell my dad that. All he wants to talk about is what I'm going to do with my life."

"He means well. He wants you to be happy."

"Well, maybe happiness isn't randomly picking a life path from a course catalog."

"What is happiness then?"

I thought for a moment. "Happiness is living in the moment and not thinking of the future at all. It's learning new things and having adventures and solving mysteries."

"Then you're in luck," Sundog said. "Life is the biggest mystery of all."

Timothy Leary stood up and stretched. I imagined how simple life must be for her. If Lizzie was a werewolf, no wonder she wasn't coming back. It must be nice to not have to think about school and work and what you're doing with the rest of your life.

Though I guess even animals have fears and worries. Maybe there was no avoiding that.

"So what happened to you?" I asked Sundog. "To your wife and job?"

"My previous life was withering my chakra. I was in a cage, and the corporate world was draining me. You believe in werewolves, Hawthorn. There are vampires too."

"So you ran away?"

"And never looked back." He said it without any shame but without pride either. It was just a simple fact to him. The way it had to be.

"What about your wife? Did you ever talk to her again?"

"She thinks I'm dead. Which in a way is true. I was reborn and given a new name. She wouldn't know me anymore."

It was sort of terrible but also sort of brave and amazing. I would never have the guts to walk away from everything and everyone I knew. I thought of Lizzie, of course. Like Sundog, she shed her old skin and became someone new, started over from scratch. I wished I had their courage.

At work later that evening, I tried to ask Vernon his opinion on my conversation with Sundog, but he wasn't in the mood to talk. I helped him with a seek-and-find puzzle instead and wondered if there'd ever been a point in his life when he started over. That's when I noticed that Vernon and Sundog weren't that far apart in age.

How could Sundog be traveling around the country, getting high with a band of young people and preaching about the dangers of chemtrails and fluoride, while Vernon's hands shook while he drank coffee, and I was never sure if he heard the things I said to him while he worked on his puzzles.

Why do some people get old faster than others? Is it just luck? Like how some people are lucky enough to be born as one of the Lizzie Lovetts of the world?

"Deep thoughts?" Christa asked me, coming out of the kitchen.

I shook my head. "Sort of zoning out."

She poured a cup of coffee for herself and leaned conspiratorially over the counter. "Daydreaming about Enzo?"

"What? No."

"He likes you. I can tell."

"How?" I asked, not that I was interested. Maybe. Probably.

"The way he looks at you."

"He looks at me like he's anxious for my shift to end so we can look for his girlfriend."

"I think you like him too," Christa said. She was teasing me, and I knew it, but I could still feel my face getting red.

"Weren't you the one who called him weird and creepy?"

"Well, maybe I was wrong. You wouldn't hang out with him if he seemed messed up, would you?"

I didn't know how to tell Christa that being a little *messed up* was exactly what would make me interested in a person.

"He's taking me to the homecoming dance," I admitted.

Christa squealed.

Vernon looked up and shouted, "Homecoming dance!"

"I knew it," Christa said, not even blinking at Vernon's outburst.

"It's not a date. I just found this ridiculous 1980s dress that I want to wear."

"Hawthorn, it's a date," Christa said.

I bit my lip and stacked the coffee creamers in front of me, one on top of the other, until the tower fell down.

"It's just…isn't it too soon?"

"Because of Lizzie, you mean?" Christa asked.

I nodded. I didn't imagine going on dates while Lizzie was still missing would do much for Enzo's reputation. Or that anyone would be thrilled I was the one he was going on dates *with*.

Christa thought about it. "It's been a few months."

"Barely two."

"It's not like she died."

"We don't know that," I said. "Not for sure."

"If she were dead, someone would have found the body by now. Lizzie walked off. She left Enzo, not the other way around. If he's found someone to help him get over his loss quickly, there's nothing wrong with that."

"Yeah, I guess so," I said, but I was still dubious.

"Besides, I doubt he was very happy with her."

I looked up sharply. "Why not?"

Christa shrugged and looked away. She checked to make sure the tops were secure on the salt and pepper shakers. She lined up the ketchup and mustard and Tabasco in a neat row. But she didn't make eye contact or answer my question.

"Oh, come on," I said. "I know you want to tell me."

"She was standoffish," Christa said finally.

"That's all?"

"She hated being here. Hated everyone who worked here. Like she thought we were all beneath her, you know?"

I raised my eyebrows. Maybe Lizzie *hadn't* changed after high school. Of course, that didn't fit with Enzo's version of her.

"Enzo told me Lizzie always saw the best in everyone."

Christa snorted. "Yeah. When she wanted tips. She sure knew how to turn on the charm for customers, but the second her back was turned, it was a different story. I always figured she must be like that with Enzo too."

"He never said anything like that about Lizzie."

"Well, of course not," Christa said. She fiddled with the sugar packets. She sighed. "Maybe I'm totally off base. I didn't know her well, but I got a bad vibe."

Every new piece of information I learned about Lizzie muddled my idea of her more. It was as if she was a different person every day. Like she woke up in the morning and decided which mask to put on. It sounded exhausting.

"Enough about that," Christa said. "Tell me about this ridiculous dress of yours."

So Christa and I talked about girlie homecoming things, and she squealed a lot. It was probably a conversation I should have been having with girls my own age, who were getting ready to attend the same dance, but I guess life would never work like that for me.

Christa launched into a story about when she went to homecoming in high school, but my mind drifted to what she'd said about Lizzie being hateful and if there was any truth in it. And I thought about the other thing she said, about there being chemistry between me and Enzo. Maybe she was right. On the other hand, maybe I was just doing that thing my mom and Emily said I did, where I made everything into a bigger deal than it actually is.

It was all too confusing to think about right then, so instead, I asked Christa if I should wear my hair up or down. But as hard as I tried to stop them, thoughts of Enzo kept creeping into my mind.

Christa said she knew Enzo liked me because of the way he looked at me. What way was that? Could it possibly be the same way he used to look at Lizzie?

CHAPTER 24

THE ALMOST MOMENT

✳ ✳

I'd gone an entire week without anyone in school making werewolf jokes. Mostly because there was a sophomore who was pregnant, and no one knew who the father was, and all the gossips at Griffin Mills High School were focused on her. So on the Thursday before homecoming, I was in the bathroom because I was actually using it, not because I was hiding from anyone.

I was washing my hands when there was a flush from one of the stalls, and Emily emerged.

Our eyes met in the mirror, and it was silent except for the running water. Then the automatic sink turned off, and I turned my attention to it, waving my hands under the sensor. The thing about automatic sinks is that most people seem totally fine with them, but for some reason, I can hardly get them to work, and a lot of the time, I end up just trying to wipe soap residue off my hands with a paper towel.

Emily came up next to me and flicked her hand in front of the sensor. The water turned on.

"Thanks," I said.

"No problem."

She started washing her own hands, and there was that strange silence again. We weren't angry or anything like that—we just didn't know what to say to each other, and in some ways, that was even worse.

"How have you been?" I asked finally.

"Pretty good. You?"

"The same."

For a second, I thought Emily would leave the bathroom, and that would be the extent of our conversation. But then she said, "I got into that summer program. The letter came yesterday."

"The composition program? That's great, Em."

She nodded, and I could see how proud she was. Emily was probably going to be a famous pianist one day, and it wouldn't matter how unpopular she'd been in high school, because she would have finally found a place where she was appreciated. I was envious, but not in a bitter way. I wished I had something equally awesome to tell her.

"I'm going to homecoming," I blurted out.

Emily looked surprised. "Really?"

I nodded. "Are you and Logan going?"

"For a little bit, but his band is playing one of the after-parties, so we'll have to leave early to set up." Emily dug through her messenger bag and pulled out a flier. "Here. The address is on there. If you want to stop by."

The enormity of her peace offering made me dizzy with happiness and relief and a million other emotions that I couldn't even name.

"Cool, thanks," I told her.

Then the bell rang, and we went to class. I kept the flier folded in my pocket, and for the rest of the day, I occasionally took it out and looked at it, just to make sure the bathroom encounter and Emily's forgiveness hadn't been in my head.

✖✖✖

"I guess I don't get it," Enzo said later that night.

He stood at his easel, which was facing the wall so I couldn't see the canvas he was working on. I was lounging on his bed.

"Which part?"

Enzo shrugged his bony shoulders and kept painting. "You've spent, like, two weeks talking about how much Emily has changed. Now you're psyched because she gave you a flier to some shitty party. For all you know, she was only trying to promote her boyfriend's band."

"It wasn't like that," I said, but I didn't know how to explain exactly what it *was* like, so I let the subject drop. "When are you going to tell me what you're painting?"

"When it's finished."

I rolled my eyes. "Fine. Have your secrets."

I wanted to ask Enzo a million questions about the dance,

because it was only a couple days away, but there was this part of me that thought it would remind him of all the reasons he hated high school events and scare him off.

I also wanted him to stop painting and look at me, but I didn't dare tell him that either. Instead, I studied the portrait of Lizzie, her beautiful face turned up to the sun.

"Did Lizzie pose for this painting?" I asked Enzo. I liked to think of him painting it. Them out in that field together, him looking at her face, tracing the outline of her jaw, the curl of her lips, onto his canvas. I imagined that she could feel it, feel how all of his concentration was on her and nothing else. Feel which part of her body he was painting as it was happening.

But Enzo said she hadn't. He left his current work-in-progress for the first time that night and crossed to his desk. He sifted through one of the drawers for a moment before handing me a stack of photographs.

The top photo was similar to the painting on Enzo's wall, taken in the same field. Except in it, Lizzie had her pretty, blue eyes open and was looking straight at the camera. The next picture looked to be the one the painting was based on. I quickly flipped through the rest of the photos, Lizzie in different outfits and different poses, sometimes serious, sometimes grinning, always gorgeous.

"I wanted to turn them all into portraits eventually," Enzo said. "You know. Before."

Before what? Before she disappeared? Before he thought she was a werewolf? Before he met me? There were so many befores.

"I had this idea for a series that would compare paintings to the photos they were based on. Like, which one seems more real?"

"Isn't a photo always more real?" I asked.

"That's the question. How much truth does an artist bring to a painting? Beyond what a photograph can capture?"

"I guess that is a good question."

Enzo went back to his canvas, and I looked through the photos a second time, starting at the beginning and studying each one. Lizzie on a tire swing. Lizzie at the lake. Lizzie leaning up against a rusted old car. Lizzie, Lizzie, Lizzie. Everywhere. Commanding attention, no matter what the location. No matter how beautiful or ugly the setting, Lizzie was always shining.

Then there was Lizzie sitting in a ratty armchair, her feet tucked under her, her shirt unbuttoned to reveal the curves of her perfect breasts, an eyebrow arched suggestively at the person taking the picture—at Enzo. He was the one she was looking at.

Suddenly, my chest felt tight. Looking at the next picture didn't help either. Lizzie was fully clothed, but she was sprawled out on a bed, laughing like someone had just told the best joke ever. Not on *a* bed. On *the* bed. Enzo's bed. Right where I was sitting.

It was sort of a jolt, a revelation, even though I'd known they'd been together from the start. I set the two pictures on the bed, the bed where Lizzie once threw back her head in laughter, and looked from one to the other. Lizzie on the bed. The bedspread was the same; the room was the same; the boy who lived there was the same. Then there was the photo of Lizzie with her shirt open. The look on her face said she knew she looked good; she knew how much the boy behind the camera wanted her. What had happened after he took the photo? Did she grab his shirt and pull him toward her? Did he kiss her deeply, pick her up, and carry her to bed?

How many times had Lizzie sat in the exact same spot I was in? How many times did they have sex right there, right where Enzo and I lounged around, watching stupid horror movies?

Lizzie and Enzo. Enzo and Lizzie. They were together. Like, *really* together.

It probably seems stupid that I'd never all-the-way thought about it. I'd thought about it *before* I met Enzo. But then we talked, and I got to know him, and he became real to me. He wasn't the same Enzo I'd read about in the paper. Sure, we were searching for his missing girlfriend, but Lizzie was more of an idea than a reality. I never thought of them together in *that* way, in a suggestive-look-leading-to-removed-clothing-leading-to-him-on-the-bed-on-top-of-her-right-in-the-spot-where-I-was-sitting kind of way. Not even a him-reaching-out-to-hold-her-hand way. I felt like someone was squeezing my insides, turning my organs to mush.

"Did you have sex a lot?" I asked.

"What?" Enzo looked up from his painting.

"You and Lizzie. Did you have sex a lot?" I repeated.

"I guess. I don't know. What's a lot?"

Anything was a lot to me. I looked down at the pictures again. Lizzie was perfect. She was beautiful. I had envied her and hated her for so many years. And Enzo was the person she ended up with. He was across the room, covered in paint, looking at me quizzically. He knew me. In the recent weeks, he'd gotten to know me better than anyone else, and I knew him too, but once upon a time, not that long ago, he had belonged to Lizzie Lovett.

"What was it like?"

"What was what like?" Enzo asked.

"Being with her. Being intimate, I mean."

"Jesus, Hawthorn."

He sounded annoyed, but he put down his paints. He wiped his hands on his jeans and crossed the room and sat on the bed next to me. My heart started pounding like it did when he held my hand in the abandoned house.

Enzo looked down at the two pictures. For a moment, I thought he would get weird or annoyed or something. But he didn't. He looked back and forth between the photos like I had.

"Well?"

"Well. It was good. Great. Lizzie liked sex."

"Doesn't everyone?"

"Not everyone. Do you?"

What I wanted to do was smirk the way Lizzie would have. Tilt my head back a little, arch an eyebrow. I wanted to say something like *Do you want to find out?* And I wanted to say it in a way that left him wondering if I was joking or not.

Instead, I said pretty much the worst possible thing, which was, "Uh, I don't know. I guess. I mean, I don't really have that much experience. Not that I have *no* experience. Just not the same as Lizzie or whatever. Not that I'm saying she was a slut or anything. I didn't mean it that way."

As soon it was out of my mouth, I regretted it and wanted to disappear, which was something *else* that Lizzie had perfected.

But Enzo smiled. "Hey, no one's judging you. You're seventeen. You have plenty of time for sex."

While he was talking, something really weird happened. He put his hand on my knee. I looked at his hand, then looked up and met his gaze. He seemed to be asking me if that was OK, and I hoped my smile let him know that it was. I could feel the warmth of his palm, our electricity, running through my entire body.

I thought he was going to kiss me. He looked like he wanted to. I think I probably wanted the same thing.

Then I ruined it.

"Did you and Lizzie have sex the night she disappeared?"

Enzo jerked his hand back and sort of leaned away from me, and I knew that what had maybe almost happened between us was probably, for sure, over. When he spoke, his voice was clipped.

"We didn't."

I couldn't stop myself. "Why?"

"I don't know. She didn't want to. Maybe neither of us wanted to."

Enzo walked back to his canvas, and I knew he'd be there for the rest of the night. Our moment had definitely passed. If there had even been a moment. Suddenly, I doubted myself, thinking maybe looking at those pictures of Lizzie had distorted my perception of what had just happened. Maybe I had turned a friendly pat on the leg into something much, much more.

"Why didn't you want to?" I prodded.

"You have too many questions, kid."

"You never have enough answers," I replied.

Then the conversation dried up, and for a while, I watched Enzo paint while mulling over all sorts of thoughts, like maybe he and Lizzie were losing interest in each other even before she disappeared, and maybe they weren't really meant to be together, and if Enzo had actually been thinking about kissing me and if that was something I wanted.

After an hour of sitting alone with my thoughts, I decided to go home. I gathered up my things and told Enzo good-bye. He was so focused on his painting that he didn't notice me slip the stack of Lizzie photos into my bag.

✱✱✱

I couldn't get that moment with Enzo out of my head. The almost-moment. It played out in my mind over and over again while I was lying in bed, and the next morning while I was eating breakfast, and later still while I was trying not to doze off during a lecture in history class.

Then it was evening again, and I was still thinking about the almost-moment, which had happened—or *almost* happened— twenty-four hours earlier. I thought about it during dinner with my family and was so distracted I agreed to do the dishes for Rush. I hung out at Sundog's campfire for a little bit, and I thought about it there. Then I moved to the swing on the front porch, then later to my bed, and the whole time, I thought about Enzo sitting next to me on his bed and if there had been a moment or an almost-moment or a non-moment and what it all meant.

Of course, I also thought about how it could have played out differently if I'd kept my mouth shut. I imagined Enzo's hand continuing to move up my leg, both of our hearts pounding. I imagined him leaning over, slowly and cautiously, the whole time keeping his gaze on me, silently asking, *Is this OK? Do you want this?* And in return, my eyes would say, *Yes, yes, yes.* Then his lips would be on mine, soft at first, but then pressing harder, more aggressively, and his arms would wrap around me, and he'd push me back on the bed, and there I would be, in the same spot where Lizzie Lovett had once been, kissing the same mouth she had kissed.

I wasn't sure when our friendship had changed, but I wanted that kiss. I wanted the scenario that real-life me had totally screwed up. I liked Enzo. He wasn't just a friend or a partner in crime. I liked him a lot. I liked him the way Lizzie had once liked him. And I wanted him to like me too.

Which pretty much seemed impossible, since, you know, he had dated Lizzie Lovett. Lizzie had blond hair and a perfect body and always knew the right thing to say and the right way to act. I was just me. Hawthorn Creely. I didn't turn heads. I was awkward and weird and could barely communicate with the few friends I had, let alone make everyone I talked to fall in love with me. I was nothing special, which made it hard to believe that Enzo would like me after being with a girl who was the *most* special.

But there was still a part of me that hoped.

Sometimes, I'm really good at ignoring the things I don't want to think about, so I kept pushing all the bad stuff out of my mind and focused on what could have happened at Enzo's and what could still happen there in the future.

And I thought about the homecoming dance, which was only one night away. I thought about that a lot.

CHAPTER 25

HOMECOMING DANCE

I possibly spent more time getting ready for the dance than I'd spent getting ready for anything else, ever. That was probably still less time than Lizzie spent on her appearance every single day in high school.

I painted my nails, and while I was doing it, I thought about what a waste of time it was. Enzo wouldn't even notice something like that, and I didn't care to be with a guy who noticed that sort of stuff. And anyway, as far as Enzo was concerned, it wasn't a date. Going to the dance with me was more like a favor. So the sparkly silver nail polish didn't matter. The whole thing was actually super dumb. But I painted my nails anyway.

I had similar thoughts while I was using the exfoliating body scrub that promised silky, super-touchable skin. Wasn't it sort of presumptuous of me, thinking that my skin was going to be touched?

I curled my hair and had my mom help me pull some of it back off my face. When it was done, I felt like I was wearing a crown of bobby pins and hairspray, but it looked nice; it looked like the hair of a girl who was about to go to a dance. And I wondered if Enzo would notice how much effort I put into my appearance, how much I wanted to be a different girl, one like Lizzie had been in high school, just for one night.

After securing the final bobby pin in my hair, my mom started getting sentimental. She said she'd be right back, and I was so caught up in my own thoughts, it didn't even occur to me that she was getting the camera, which was exactly what I didn't want her to do.

The next thing I knew, my mom was in my bedroom doorway, snapping pictures of me in front of the mirror. My hair looked ready for the dance, but that was it. I was wearing boxers and one of Rush's old jerseys, and I hadn't even begun the monumental task of putting on makeup.

"Mom! What are you doing?"

"This is a big moment, Hawthorn. You'll want to remember it."

She kept snapping photos, and the rest of my family heard the commotion and decided to see what it was all about, which is how my dad and Rush ended up in my doorway too. They all gushed about my hair and acted happy that I was participating in a school activity of my own free will, and I acted put out and embarrassed and tried to block myself from the camera, but the truth was that I was enjoying the whole thing.

I waited for Rush to make a comment about Enzo, about how he was a loser and didn't deserve to take me to homecoming, but he kept his mouth shut, which I thought was really cool of him. I looked for signs of disapproval on my dad's face, because I hadn't forgotten his conversation with my mom that I'd overheard. But if he was unhappy, he hid it really well.

I swiped blush on my cheeks and applied mascara to my eyelashes and put on a peachy pink shade of lipstick. Yes, I was carefully putting on lipstick and blotting it, like a girl who went to dances on a regular basis. I was a girl who had exfoliated and plucked and perfumed and all the other things you were supposed to do before a date. I was a girl who was going to a dance, a girl who had a loving family that hovered, offering encouragement and good-natured teasing.

That wasn't the girl I normally was. I liked it. I felt as if I'd slipped into someone else's skin, and I wasn't ready to go back to being me.

But I made my family leave the room while I changed into my dress because, you know, there's such thing as being *too* close.

I put on my crazy eighties dress. Then came the shoes, silver heels that added at least three inches to my height and made my ability to walk questionable. Then I went to the full-length mirror, braced myself, and looked.

I was actually pleasantly surprised. The poofy dress *was* absurd. It fit me just right though, and that made it look less strange than it actually was. I didn't look like Lizzie—I wasn't golden and blond and curvy—but there are a bunch of girls at my school who are pretty even though they don't have those qualities. Maybe I could be one of them or enough of one of them to get Enzo to notice me, like he had for that half second in his room while his hand was on my knee.

That's when the enormity of the situation hit me. I sat down heavily on my desk chair. I'd just spent half the day getting ready to go to a high school dance, which was weird and unfamiliar in itself. And I was going to that dance with the boyfriend of a girl who was missing, probably a werewolf but possibly killed by said boyfriend. And the girl in question was none other than the cheerleader dream queen who I'd spent years resenting.

It was all bizarre and crazy, and I felt lost. What was I doing? What did I want?

I wanted Enzo to see me how he saw Lizzie. I wanted him to like me because I was different from Lizzie. I wanted Lizzie to be alive, but I also wanted her to stay away forever. I wanted my life to be interesting and complicated.

I could have sat at my desk thinking all night, but there was a knock on my door.

"Are you done yet? Mom wants more pictures before you go."

"Just a second," I shouted back at my brother.

I turned to the mirror and gazed at my reflection. I was a different person. Just for one night. That's what I had been telling myself. Which meant I should try to shut off my mind. I needed to stop spurting out worries and questions. I needed to just *be*.

That was my goal on the night of the homecoming dance. For

once, I was going to stop worrying about my motivations and just do what felt right.

✖✖✖

There were so many pictures. Too many. My mom made me pose with my brother and my dad. Then the hippies saw what we were doing and wandered over, and Mom had me take a few photos with them. Sundog told me I looked beautiful and gave me some sort of blessing that was probably really nice but sounded like gibberish to me. The whole thing was super overwhelming, but I was trying not to be the kind of girl who got overwhelmed.

"I'll want pictures of you and Enzo when he gets here," my mom said after snapping a photo of me standing in front of the house.

"Mom, no. It's not like that. We're just friends."

"You can't take pictures with your friends?"

"How's he getting here anyway?" Rush asked. "I thought he was too artistic to drive."

There it was. I knew my brother couldn't make it through the entire evening without taking a jab at Enzo.

"He's taking the bus here. Then I'll drive us to the dance."

"Chivalrous," Rush said. He said it dryly, obviously as an insult. But I actually thought it was kind of a nice gesture. Usually, I picked Enzo up. He couldn't drive me to the dance, but he was meeting me at my house. He was doing his best.

"Be nice to your sister," my dad said, but he frowned a little, and I knew he was secretly on Rush's side.

"It doesn't matter anyway," I said. "This isn't a date. We're just going to the dance."

No one believed me though, and I sort of didn't mind.

"Can you guys, like, give me some space? I swear I'll let you know when Enzo's here."

I made my way over to the porch swing to wait for Enzo. My mom wanted to sit with me, but my dad dragged her inside, which I appreciated. Having my family around while I was getting ready was one thing, but when Enzo arrived, I wanted the moment all to myself.

★★★

I waited a long time. Then I waited some more.

I tried to look straight ahead or down at my feet or anywhere that could distract me. The goal was not to look down the street in the direction of the closest bus stop, the direction that Enzo would be coming from. I didn't want him to find me like that, hunched over on the front porch, eagerly waiting for his slouchy, shuffling arrival at my house.

So instead, I attempted to focus on other things, because it wasn't so much like I was waiting for him that way. I was just looking at where the porch railing was scratched or how the poppies in the flowerbed were starting to die or the way our mailbox tilted very slightly to the left. I told myself to concentrate on those details, and eventually, I would glance casually up the street only to find Enzo, standing on the edge of the lawn, a sheepish look on his face and some story about how the bus had broken down or the homeless man who always rides in the back row pulled out a machete and held everyone hostage or something. Anything.

But every time I glanced up, I was still alone, and eventually, I stopped pretending and just watched the road. What did it matter if Enzo saw me sitting patiently, desperately waiting for him to arrive?

More time passed, and I became positive that looking for Enzo *really* didn't matter. I could watch the road or run out into the middle of it if I wanted. I could kneel down on the front lawn and scream at the sky. I could cry and rage and do whatever I wanted without worrying about Enzo finding me that way, because Enzo was not going to show up.

It was getting dark when my mom opened the door and poked her head out.

"Everything OK?"

"Yeah."

"Maybe you should give him a call?"

"Maybe later."

"All right," my mom said, though I knew she was hesitant to leave me sitting by myself without first bestowing hippie wisdom about how we all need space to uncover our true emotions or something. "Just let me know if you need anything, OK?"

What I needed was someone to shake me and tell me I should have expected this. Enzo was unreliable. Enzo didn't care about a high school dance. Enzo didn't really care about me, not the way he cared about Lizzie. What did I *think* was going to happen? He was going to wander off the bus, still smelling like diesel fumes, and whisk me away to a magical homecoming event? Enzo, with his cigarettes and messy hair and ratty sweaters, was going to suddenly turn into some 1950s superjock stereotype, and I would be pretty in pink, and we'd go to the dance, and all the other kids there would somehow forget that they'd spent the last four years hating me? More likely, I would have ended up covered in pig's blood.

I watched the neighborhood get dark. Crickets chirped. Lightning bugs came out. A few miles away, there was a dance just getting into full swing. It would be just like the movies, with kids laughing and dancing and judging what other kids were wearing and who they'd shown up with. Chaperones would pretend not to see alcohol being passed around. There would be talk about who was having the best after-party and who would be getting laid that night and, of course, who the homecoming queen and king would be. No one would notice that I wasn't there.

The next time the front door opened, it was Rush. He ventured out and sat next to me on the swing.

"Did Mom tell you to check on me?"

"No. I just thought you could use some company while you waited."

"I'm not waiting," I said.

"What are you doing then?"

"Nothing. Just sitting. He's not going to show." I tried to play it off like it didn't matter, like I hadn't spent half the day preparing for the dance.

"Maybe he's just running really late. He could have fallen asleep or something. You should call," Rush said.

"I appreciate the optimism, but he's not coming."

"Is there anything I can do?"

It would have been easier if he mocked me or said, "I told you so." Rush's concern made me feel like crying, which would be especially unfortunate, considering the mascara I'd put on.

"Just give me some space?" I asked. "And let Mom know I'm OK so she stops peeking out the window every two minutes?"

"Sure thing." Rush squeezed my shoulder as he stood up, just a simple gesture to let me know he loved me, and my eyes stung, and my lips trembled. I took a deep breath. I was *not* going to cry.

I rocked on the porch swing and thought about Enzo until I was shivering in the cool October night. I considered going in and getting a sweater or just climbing into bed in my dress and heels and bobby pins. I also thought about walking to the back of the house to get warm around Sundog's fire. But I didn't do any of those things. It would have taken too much energy. So instead, I just sat and felt sorry for myself.

When the headlights swept across my front lawn, my heart

leaped. Enzo. Maybe something happened with the bus and he'd had to find a ride to my house? I held up my hand, trying to shield my eyes, but couldn't see anything in the glare. Then the headlights were turned off, and the yard plunged into darkness. Before my eyes could readjust, I heard a car door slam and an incredulous voice.

"Thorny? What the hell are you wearing?"

Not Enzo.

Connor plodded up the porch steps, grinning. He stopped when he saw my glowering face.

"What's going on?"

"I'm supposed to be at the homecoming dance," I said. "Clearly, that didn't work out."

"Was the dance taking place in 1985?"

I gathered a handful of my pink skirt and examined it. "I thought it would be a funny thing to wear. It's not."

"So why are you sitting here like the rest of *The Breakfast Club* went out partying and forgot to take you along?"

I kept looking at my dress, because I couldn't bear to meet Connor's gaze. "That's not so far off, I guess. Enzo was supposed to take me to the dance. He must have found a better party."

"He's a dick," Connor said.

I expected for us to exchange small talk for a few more minutes, then for Connor to excuse himself to see Rush. A little while later, they'd come out of the house together and leave for some college party, passing by me, sitting there in my pathetic pink dress with only the slightest acknowledgment.

What actually happened next was Connor held out his hand and said, "Come on."

I stared at him. "What? Are you going to, like, take me to the dance as a pity date or something? This really is an eighties teen movie."

Connor laughed. "I'm not exactly dressed for a formal dance. But I can get you off the front porch at least."

He was still holding out his hand. It's not like I had anything better going on, so I reached out and took it.

✻ ✻ ✻

It was the second time in the past month I'd been in Connor's car, which was pretty weird.

I leaned over and scanned the radio stations, finally settling for an oldies channel. Boys and girls from another lifetime sang about how breaking up was hard to do and how words of love weren't enough to win a girl's heart.

"I feel like I'm in a horror movie," I told Connor.

"You what?"

"You know, it's dark, and we're driving through the woods, and there are scratchy-sounding old songs on the radio, and I'm in this stupid dress."

"I'm still not getting the horror movie part."

"Like, any moment now, a shadowy figure is going to dart

in front of the car, and you'll slam on the brakes, and there will be a girl standing on the side of the road, wearing some white 1950s dress."

Connor laughed, getting what I meant. "And she'll ask us for a ride home, right?"

"Yep. And then somehow, we'll find out she died sixty years ago in a car accident on this very stretch of road."

I sighed and rested my head on the back of the passenger seat, imagining a situation like that actually happening. I liked the idea that Enzo standing me up could be a good thing because I would end up doing something way more fascinating than going to a stupid dance.

Connor glanced at me and reached into his backseat, fumbling for a moment before pulling out a sweater.

"Here. You must be freezing."

Being cold was the last thing on my mind, but I pulled the sweater over my head anyway. What did it matter if I was wearing a poofy dress and a men's pullover? It's not like I was going to homecoming.

The sweater smelled like boy, that earthy, almost dirty smell, like trees and beer. If it was Enzo's sweater, it would have smelled like cigarettes too. I'd put his leather jacket on once when I was cold, and even after I took it off, the scent of tobacco clung to my skin.

For a while, we drove and listened to music and didn't say much to each other. Then Connor asked if I was hungry. I hadn't realized I was it until he asked. He pulled into the parking lot of DiCarlo's, where you ordered pizza by the slice, and it came topped with a layer of unmelted cheese.

There wasn't a dining room, so we took our food outside and sat on the hood of Connor's car, eating quickly and shivering. The air felt heavy, like a storm was coming.

"So," Connor said eventually. "What happened tonight?"

I shrugged. "Nothing. We were supposed to go to the dance. Enzo didn't show. There's not, like, a big story or anything."

"So are you and Enzo together now?"

"No," I said, focusing on my pizza.

"But you like him?"

"I don't know."

I pulled the sweater around me more tightly, wishing I had jeans covering my legs and tennis shoes on my feet instead of my embarrassingly optimistic high heels.

"It wasn't like that," I said. "Before, anyway. We were just trying to find his girlfriend. But then we were spending all this time together, and I started wondering if it meant something, you know?"

"Maybe you just feel like you're supposed to like him," Connor said nonchalantly. "Or you like him because he's around. It happens."

"Maybe."

"Or maybe you like him just because he belonged to Lizzie."

I scowled. "You think I'm that shallow? Like, I've spent all this time wanting to be Lizzie or something, so I end up taking her boyfriend?"

"Stranger things have happened. I'd think a girl who believes in werewolves would be open to any possibility."

He had a point.

"I just kind of wanted to go to homecoming."

"Why? Since when do you care?"

"I guess I just wanted to feel normal for once."

Connor laughed. "What does that even mean?"

"I don't know. There're all these things happening, all this *life* happening around me. And I'm always on the outside, watching. For once, I wanted to experience it."

"I went to all the high school dances," Connor said after a moment.

"You don't need to rub it in."

"I'm not, believe me. I always felt out of place at them. Like it was some ritual we all needed to go through but no one really enjoyed, and I never knew how to pretend as well as everyone else."

Connor finished a slice of pizza and wiped his greasy fingers on his jeans. We'd forgotten to ask for napkins, which was fine, because the thought of getting sauce on my dress and ruining it forever appealed to me.

"I went to senior prom with this girl Alyssa," Connor said. "Do you remember her? Tall, dark hair, had a different designer purse for every season?"

I shook my head, and he went on.

"Anyway, the whole night was a mess. I didn't even want to go with her, but neither of us had dates, and some of my friends were going with some of her friends, so it seemed like the right thing to do. A bunch of us went to this nice Italian place for dinner. I spent an entire paycheck on that meal, and she got pissed at me because I ordered pizza. Said you didn't order pizza at a place like that. It was on the menu though. Why put it on the menu if you aren't supposed to actually eat it? She spent the entire night bitching. I ended up ditching her at the dance and hanging out with a different group of people. And she bitched about that too. That's what high school dances were like for me."

"Not for everyone though," I protested. "There are people who have normal high school experiences. I bet Rush had a good time at that dance. I'm sure Lizzie did."

"There's no such thing as a normal high school experience, Thorny. You assume everyone else is happy all the time and living an ideal life. You don't get that other people are pretending too."

I finished my pizza and leaned back on the hood of the car to look at the stars. "Maybe. But it's still easier for some people than it is for others."

"Only for a while," he said. "Look at Lizzie. She might have been a star in high school, but what then? Living in some shitty apartment, working as a waitress, and then one day disappearing. Her life peaked when everyone else's was just getting started."

"Unless she *meant* to disappear," I said.

"What if she didn't? What if she was killed? I know you don't think she was, but she's been missing for a long time without a trace." Connor's tone had turned serious. "You know how these things usually work out, Thorny."

"I guess so."

Connor lay down next to me. I thought he would keep trying to lecture me about Lizzie and then we'd argue, and then the night would be an even worse disaster. Instead, he looked up at the sky and said, "Do you know much about astronomy?"

"Not really."

"Me either."

"For a minute there, I thought we were going to have some cliché moment where you told me all about the stars," I said, but I was happy he'd changed the conversation.

Connor laughed. "Not quite."

"You could make up some stories about constellations, and I'll pretend to believe them."

"I'm an engineer, not a novelist."

"Tell me something as an engineer then."

He thought for a moment. "Want to hear a joke?"

I nodded.

"A woman asks her husband, an engineer, 'Could you please go buy me a gallon of milk at the supermarket, and while you're there, get some eggs?' He never came home."

There was a long moment of silence.

"I don't get it."

"Ah, well, *while you're there* is an infinite loop. There's no exit statement. So he's forever at the supermarket getting... You know what? Never mind."

I looked over at Connor. "You're kind of a nerd, aren't you?"

"Me? Look at what you're wearing."

I tried to keep a straight face, but that only lasted for about two seconds. I started laughing, and Connor did too.

And for a little while, that was enough to make me forget getting stood up.

✻✻✻

It was late when Connor took me home. He insisted on walking me to the door, and I grabbed on to his arm as I stumbled up the driveway, my fancy shoes hurting my feet. I wondered how we would look to someone who didn't know us. Like a couple coming back from a party, I guess. Like normal people.

We were a few feet from the porch steps when I saw Enzo sitting there in the dark, hunched over in his thrift-store suit.

I stopped abruptly and dropped my hand from Connor's arm. "Enzo."

"Hey." He stood up and looked at Connor, then back to me. "Your brother said he didn't know how long you'd be gone, but I waited anyway."

Was I supposed to give him an award or something? *Wow, Enzo, so great of you to wait around for a bit after totally ditching me.*

"Did he tell you how long *I* waited?" I asked coolly.

"Yeah. He did."

There was a long silence, and Connor stared at Enzo, and Enzo looked at me apologetically, and I just wanted to take off my shoes and change into comfortable clothes.

"Are you going to give me some sort of excuse?" I asked.

Enzo glanced at Connor. "You think you can give us a minute alone?"

"Ask Hawthorn, not me," he said, and I was surprised by how annoyed he sounded.

Two sets of eyes stared at me. I felt like I was onstage, in the spotlight, and they were waiting for me to say my lines, only I couldn't remember them.

"Uh, yeah, I guess that's OK," I finally said to Connor. "You don't need to stick around."

Connor hesitated. He looked like he had something to say but then thought better of it. He stuck his hands in his pockets and started to back away.

"OK. Well. Have a good night, Thorny." He nodded curtly at Enzo, then took off toward his car.

The moment he left my side, I wanted to shout for him to come back. Or even better, I wanted to jump back in the passenger seat of his car and speed away from my house. My life. At the very least, I wanted to thank him for the pizza and for saving me from pathetically sitting on the porch like I had nothing better to do when Enzo showed up.

But I didn't do any of those things, because acting so gushy would have embarrassed me, and besides, I had to deal with Enzo.

"Who was that?" Enzo asked.

"Why? Are you jealous?" I regretted it the second the words were out of my mouth, because he probably wasn't jealous, just making conversation, and I sounded presumptuous, as if I was expecting him to get jealous over me, which was silly, given he'd totally ditched me earlier.

"You're angry," Enzo said.

"Well, *yeah*. You could have called. Or just not said you'd go to the dance with me in the first place."

"I wanted to go to the dance. Really. I was planning on it. But then I was painting and lost track of time, and then I had to wait for the late bus." He held up his hands in an *I tried, but what can you do?* gesture.

"You still could have called. I don't care about the dance, but it wasn't cool to leave me waiting like an idiot."

"Looks like you found something else to do anyway," Enzo said. I listened for bitterness in his tone and was disappointed there wasn't any.

"This whole conversation is stupid. I'm going to bed now."

I clumsily pushed past Enzo and up the porch steps, cursing myself again for wearing heels.

"Hawthorn, wait," Enzo said as I opened the front door.

I turned back to him. Our eyes met. I held my breath, hoping that he could say something to magically fix the tension between us, to make me forget all about the dance.

"The, uh, the buses don't run this late."

"So?" I said. The buses were pretty much last on the list of things I cared about right then.

"Do you think you could give me a ride home?"

His request was so absurd that I thought he must be kidding. He wasn't.

"No," I said. Just no. No apology or explanation. It wasn't the response that Enzo expected.

I went inside and shut the door behind me, feeling the tiniest bit of satisfaction.

CHAPTER 26

HOWL

✻ ✻

I used to think not being asked to dances made me a social outcast loser. That was before I'd been *stood up* for a dance. It was pretty much the most humiliating thing that had ever happened to me.

I was an idiot.

I should never have gotten my hopes up.

I shouldn't have let myself think my friendship with Enzo was anything more than that.

A guy held my hand, and I decided it meant something, that he must like me, that there must be chemistry between us, that I must like him too, that a relationship was pending. Really, he'd just been scared.

I had turned into one of those stupid girls. A girl who obsessed over every little thing a guy did and thought it was all about her.

"Do you think I'm self-centered?" I asked Sundog.

He laughed. "Every teenager is self-centered."

"Some of them don't grow out of it," I said, thinking about Enzo. Thinking about the promises he couldn't keep, because his stupid art was all that mattered to him.

I wondered if he'd ever stood up Lizzie.

What had *she* seen in him?

At first, I'd wanted to find Lizzie to prove that werewolves were real. I didn't realize how many more questions I'd eventually have for her. If I could sit down and talk to her, just for an hour, my problems might be solved. If I knew what Lizzie really felt about Enzo, maybe I could figure out what I felt too.

The thing was, I had *really* wanted to go to the dance.

"Why couldn't he just be on time?" I asked Sundog. "Is that really a lot to ask?"

"That all depends on the person. What's simple to one person might be inherently challenging to someone else."

"Are you saying it's just *too much* for some people to be punctual? So, what, they just get a free pass?"

"It's not the lack of punctuality that weighs on you; it's what it means."

I decided I'd gotten enough advice from Sundog for the day. I didn't need him to remind me that Enzo was late because I wasn't a person worth being on time for.

"At least I have you," I told Timothy Leary, who was sleeping in my lap. "You're always here for me."

Sundog sighed. "Oh, Hawthorn."

I looked at him, bracing myself for more bad news.

"The weather's turning," Sundog said. "We'll be moving on soon."

Of course they would be. If I'd taken time to think about it, I'd have realized it was getting too cold for them to sleep outside. But I'd gotten so used to having them in my backyard during the past two months, part of me felt like they were going to be there forever.

"Where will you go?"

"West. Nevada maybe. We haven't been there for a while."

"Nevada? What's there besides casinos?" I asked.

"The Mojave Desert. You owe it to yourself to see it one day," Sundog said.

I imagined Sundog sleeping in a teepee and skinning rattlesnakes and cracking open cacti for a few precious drops of water. I'd never been to the desert, but from what I'd seen in movies, it was a bleak, unforgiving place. It seemed too harsh for CJ, with his free association exercises, or Marigold, who offered light healing sessions in exchange for donations. The Mojave would suck the life from them. They'd wither in the desert, same as I'd wither in the Ohio snow.

"You're, like, the only person I have to talk to anymore," I told Sundog.

"You have yourself. You look to me for guidance when you already have the answers."

"Well, I'm not going to sit here and talk to myself."

"Don't talk then. Paint. Dance. Write. Just don't hold your feelings inside. The longer we let pain hide in our hearts, the more it turns to poison."

In the time I'd known him, Sundog had never really made sense. But I was still going to miss him. He'd become a friend. Another friend who was ditching me.

I knew life was full of people coming and going. It was sad, but you dealt with it. You made new friends and moved on. Except for me. I only excelled at the part where you lost people.

✹✹✹

The days after the dance were filled with awkward encounters.

I ran into Emily on the way to third period.

"Hey, I didn't see you at the dance. Did you have a good time?"

"Actually, I didn't end up going," I said, feeling my face heat up.

"Why not?"

I shrugged. "It's just not really my thing. I thought I'd give it a shot but decided it was kind of a waste of time."

I could tell from Emily's expression that she didn't believe me, not even a little bit.

Connor picked up Rush for some concert, and before they left, he asked me how I was doing and if the situation with Enzo had worked out OK. Like he thought I was super pathetic and would be all broken up about missing the dance. Which I wasn't. Mostly. I tried laughing so he could see how trivial it was to be left sitting on the porch, how little I cared about homecoming or Enzo or any of it. It wasn't Connor's business anyway. Or Emily's. Or anyone's.

The other awkward thing had to do with the phone ringing. A lot.

Enzo kept calling, and I kept ignoring him. He left messages, and I deleted them.

I didn't want to hear what he had to say. I didn't want to think about Enzo at all. But to stop thinking about him, I had to stop thinking about Lizzie. So for the first time in months, I had nothing to think about at all.

The truth was, I couldn't *completely* push Lizzie from my mind. One night when I was taking out the trash, I thought I heard a wolf howl, and my whole body tensed. I stood there—the lid to the trash can in one hand, the trash bag in the other.

I froze and listened, straining to hear. I shut my eyes to try to make my ears work better. The sound came again. Definitely a howl. Long and low and melancholy. It could have been dog, but it was different—more primal—than a dog's howl. And there are no wolves in Ohio. *It was Lizzie.*

My heart pounded. My mouth went dry. I felt a shiver of excitement wind down my spine. In that moment, I was transported back to the abandoned house. Back to Enzo holding my hand and looking into my eyes while the world around us was super still and time sped up. When everything felt like magic.

I stood outside for a while, waiting to see if I would hear it again, but the night went back to making its normal sounds. Crickets chirped, and wind rustled dry leaves, and a voice drifted from my backyard where the hippies were gathered around their fire.

I threw away the trash bag and closed the lid, making sure it was shut tightly so the raccoons couldn't get it. As I trudged back into the house, the world around me brightened. I looked up at the sky and saw that the moon had emerged from behind clouds.

No matter how much I vowed to push Lizzie from my mind, the moon always drew me back. My nightly reminder that regardless of what happened between Enzo and me, Lizzie Lovett was still out there. It the moon could talk, it would scold me for giving up.

That night, I tossed and turned while dreaming of being chased through the forest.

CHAPTER 27

TRICK OR TREAT

✳ ✳

Sometimes, when I'm upset with people, I pretend they don't exist, because that's easier than dealing with the problem. Then, eventually, I've pretended for so long that it sort of becomes true, and it's like that person isn't real to me anymore. Maybe that would have happened with Enzo after our fight. If things had gone a little differently, a few years down the line, someone might've said, *Remember that guy, Enzo Calvetti?* and I'd be like, *Enzo who?* and even though it might seem like I was faking, I wouldn't be. It would for real take me a second to remember that—for a little while—he'd been important to me.

That didn't happen though. I wanted to believe it was because there was something special about Enzo, but I probably just forgave him because he showed up at the diner on Halloween.

I was already feeling sorry for myself, which I'd mentioned to Vernon, like, eighteen times.

"Only because it's my favorite holiday," I said again.

Vernon didn't get mad or tell me I was boring him. He was

doing a Sudoku puzzle and pretty much ignoring me. Every once in a while, he'd start to bob his head up and down like a chicken, and I thought maybe that was his old-man version of indicating he agreed with everything I said.

"Do you know how many kids at my school don't care about Halloween?" I asked, wiping down the counter for about the fifth time that hour. "But they still have parties to go to tonight. How is that fair?"

Vernon bobbed his head.

I threw down the dish rag and poured myself a cup of coffee. Last month, I'd started to drink my coffee black because that's how Enzo drank it. He said anyone who used cream and sugar probably didn't like the taste of coffee, so what was the point of drinking it? I wanted him to think I was cool, that I was artsy like him, that I was a person who *got* coffee. So I swore off cream and sugar and tried not to wince at the bitterness when I took a sip, as if I were doing a shot of whiskey or something. That night, on Halloween, the bitterness tasted good. The coffee was too hot—it burned my throat all the way down, and that was good too.

Mr. Walczak was hardly ever around. He owned the Sunshine Café, but he didn't know what it was like to spend all day there. That's why he thought some ideas were good, even though they weren't. Like the Halloween mix CD that we'd been playing all month. Really, it was just horror movie music, "Monster Mash," and a few tracks of spooky sounds like chains rattling and owls hooting. The first time I heard it at the beginning of October, I thought it was kind of cool and festive, which was probably what Mr. Walczak intended. But when I realized there were only about ten songs on the CD, not even an hour of music, it lost its charm.

I felt like maybe, probably, I was about to go crazy.

Particularly when on Halloween, my favorite night, instead of doing something scary and fun and adventurous, I was working in a crappy diner, listening to stupid ghosts *whooooing* on repeat, drinking black coffee that I didn't even like, and feeling pathetic and unappreciated in my hippie costume. The costume had been inspired by Sundog and put together mostly from my mom's closet, except for the beads, which I'd borrowed from Marigold. Sundog had laughed when he saw my outfit, but not like he was making fun of me. He said soon enough, I'd be joining their prayer circle.

My hair was parted in the middle, and I was wearing Mom's old jeans that were only a little too big and had patches sewn all over them. I had moccasins on my feet, because my mom said that's pretty much all she wore when she was my age. They were real moccasins with leather bottoms, and I liked how silently I could creep around in them.

The truth was, I was pretty pleased with my costume. I felt authentic. Totally more awesome than anyone walking around in a mass-produced, tie-dyed hippie costume bought from the drug store. My outfit came from real hippies after all. But what did it matter that I had a cool costume if only Vernon saw it? He didn't really notice it anyway.

I pouted and drank coffee, and the theme from *The Exorcist* was playing, and that's when the chime on the door rang. I looked up to see who'd come in. It was Enzo.

He wasn't wearing a costume. He was just dressed as himself, looking nervous, carrying a large, flat package wrapped in newspaper under one arm.

"Hey," he said, pushing his hair from his eyes with his free hand. "I called your house, and your dad said you were working."

"He was right. Here I am."

"I can see that."

We stood awkwardly on opposite sides of the diner like there was a line drawn on the ground that neither of us could step over. The horror movie music wasn't helping the tension between us. I wanted to know what Enzo was doing there. I wanted him to leave. I wanted him to know I wanted him to leave. But I also wanted him to stay.

"So, uh, I like your costume," he said, walking over to me.

"Thanks," I said.

"Lizzie used to wear a headband like that all the time."

The headband, a scarf really, had been my own touch, not an accessory from my mom or Sundog or the rest of the hippie crew. I wondered if I'd become so connected with Lizzie in the recent months that I instinctively made the same choices she did and if that would bring me closer to her, maybe close enough to find her.

"Look," Enzo said after another long pause. "I know I shouldn't have left you hanging the other night. It's not because I don't care about you. I do. More than anyone else in my life right now, if you want to know the truth."

He was saying all the right things. And I really didn't want to go home after my shift and sit alone in my room. Not on Halloween, when it felt like magic could be willed into existence. The one night of the year witches and goblins and ghosts come to life. You could practically feel the air crackling with magic, with everyone's desire for something extraordinary to happen— not just me.

So that's why I forgave Enzo. I didn't push him to the back of my mind until he disappeared. He apologized, and I accepted, and just like that, everything was OK again.

"I have something for you," Enzo said. He slid the package he was holding onto the nearest table.

"What is it?"

"Well, kid, the way this usually works is you unwrap the gift and find out."

I laughed, and Enzo smiled, and we made peace, the way other people might signal a truce with a handshake.

Then my curiosity got the best of me, and I moved over to the table to open the present. Enzo hovered anxiously behind me as I peeled back layers of paper, one after another. The gift seemed to be fragile.

Eventually, I got to the final layer of paper and carefully pulled it away.

"Oh." I couldn't think of more to say. A million thoughts and feelings crashed around inside my head, and I opened my mouth to speak, but nothing came out.

"Do you like it?" Enzo asked, looking over my shoulder.

It was a painting. *His* painting, the one he'd been working on for weeks, the one he told me I couldn't see until it was finished. And it was perfect. As good as the painting of Lizzie that hung by his bed, maybe better, because this one was so intricate and detailed, like a puzzle. No matter where I looked, I saw something new.

The painting showed Griffin Mills almost like it was in real life. But the perspective was distorted. A building leaned slightly to the left. The road was bumpier than it should have been. The colors were wrong, bright and cheerful in some places, washed out in others, the way the horizon looks when you've been out in the sun too long and all the shapes start to bleed together. Enzo's painting made me question if I was really seeing the canvas right, if the issue was with the painting or with my eyes.

The main street meandered out of the town and into the woods, up to a hill with a tiny version of the Griffin Mansion. Only it wasn't Griffin Mansion exactly. It also resembled the farmhouse that Enzo and I found in the woods. The door of the mansion was open, and I could just make out a shadowy figure in the doorway, looking out over the town below him.

The more I looked, the more other details jumped out at me. Two ghost suns flanked the real sun, a sundog, just like Edward the IV supposedly saw on the battlefield. A hand, humanoid except for the hair and claws, reached out of a coffee shop.

There was something dreamlike about the painting but the sort of dream that can quickly turn to a nightmare.

"It's, ah, about you. How you see the world," Enzo said.

I didn't know what to say, so I kept staring at the painting. There were references to all sorts of things I'd told Enzo, never really thinking he was listening to me. For the first time in my life, someone really understood me.

"It's meant as a compliment," Enzo said. "I'd climb in your head if I could. Painting the way you talk about the world was as close as I could get though. I wanted you to have it so, you know, if you're feeling down about being different, you can look at this and remember that being different is good. My whole life, all I ever wanted was to be unique, but you never had to try."

I finally tore my gaze away from the painting and looked into Enzo's dark-blue eyes, eyes that really *saw* me. Not because he missed his girlfriend and needed a distraction but because of who I was. Just the thought made me feel like I could float away.

"This is the best gift I've ever gotten."

Enzo's grin lit up his face. We stood there like that, looking at each other all dopey, until Vernon cleared his throat and spoke up from his place at the counter.

"Can yinz turn off this jaggin' music?"

The spell was broken. I laughed and rolled my eyes.

"Can we hang out when you get off work?" Enzo asked. "It's been weird not seeing you this week."

I told him we could. Of course we could.

***

An hour later, Vernon wandered out of the diner without saying good-bye. I didn't know where he went when he left the Sunshine Café or whether he went by car or bus or on foot. For all I knew, he stepped out the door at ten thirty every night and simply disappeared into thin air. If I'd learned anything in the past few months, it was that disappearing is very possible.

With Vernon gone, I quickly closed up the diner, even though we were supposed to stay open for another half an hour. We wouldn't be getting any other customers. It was Halloween. And if I had to listen to "Monster Mash" one more time, my head would explode.

"Where do you want to go?" Enzo asked while I carefully secured his painting in my trunk.

"It doesn't matter. Anywhere."

For a while, we just drove around. I turned on the heat as high as my beat-up little car could pump it out, and we rolled down the windows. I wanted to feel the air on my face, wanted to feel like I was part of the night around me. Angsty British rock music, Enzo's favorite kind, blasted from the stereo. Enzo rolled cigarette after cigarette, occasionally passing them to me so I could fill my lungs with smoke. Every drag burned more than the last but made me feel free, like rules had stopped applying to my life.

We passed a few straggling groups of trick-or-treaters, their costumes in disarray, lugging overstuffed sacks of candy home to inventory their loot. On other Halloweens, I would have envied them, soaking up the last bit of magic before the world went back to normal. But not that night. That night, I was with Enzo, exactly where I wanted to be. Our night had a magic of its own.

"What was your best costume?" I asked Enzo, shouting over the music.

"Seventh grade. Edgar Allan Poe. I don't think anyone knew who I was supposed to be. But I loved that costume so much that it didn't matter."

"I was Hester Prynne once. I don't even like *The Scarlet Letter* that much. I just felt like I should, since everyone always thought I was named for Nathaniel Hawthorne."

With the music so loud, Enzo probably wasn't getting every word I said. It didn't matter though, because after seeing his painting, I was sure he could read my mind. We understood each other without ever having to speak. We were in sync; we wanted all the same things. When I was hit with the urge to stop driving and go into the woods, I knew without asking that Enzo felt the same way.

I drove to Wolf Creek Road, to where it all started, where Lizzie disappeared and our lives started spinning in new directions, hers and mine and Enzo's. I thought about the first time Enzo and I had gone to the campsite together, the night I told him Lizzie was a werewolf. That night was normal, ordinary, but it actually meant everything. And that made me think, do you ever know a moment is important as it's happening, or is it only when you look back that you can see your life changed?

We got out of the car and walked around the old campsite again, stumbling until our eyes adjusted to the dark. I knew that Lizzie and Enzo had memories there. But I had memories of being there with Enzo too, and mine were more recent. I sat down on the flat rock by the edge of the clearing, shivering a bit from the chill. After a minute, Enzo joined me. We were close but not touching. I imagined leaning against him, grabbing his hand, stealing his warmth.

"Do you remember the first time we came here?" I asked.

Enzo smiled. "I thought you were crazy."

"Not too crazy, I guess. You came back."

"Yeah, well. Maybe I'm crazy too."

We looked at each other, and it made me dizzy, like I was looking over the edge of a cliff. My heart pounded, my stomach did flips, and I thought the excitement and anxiety would make me explode.

"Hawthorn," Enzo said softly. "What are we doing?"

"Sitting in the woods."

"That's not what I mean."

I knew that; I just didn't know how to answer. "What do you want us to be doing?"

Enzo stood up and walked away from me, blending into the dark trees on the other side of the clearing. "I don't know, Hawthorn. I really don't."

I stood too, because I had too much nervous energy to keep still for a moment longer. I stepped toward Enzo and watched him roll a cigarette, his hands shaky. For the first time since we'd met, he didn't get it right on the first try.

Still, I pushed for an answer. "Because of Lizzie, you mean?"

"Yeah. But not just that." He lit the cigarette, the flame from his lighter momentarily illuminating the clearing, and looked at me. "You're so young."

"I'm not that young."

"You are. Jesus. You're not even eighteen yet. You still care about things like prom."

"It was homecoming," I said, not bothering to hide my annoyance.

"Whatever. That's not the point."

"What is?" I pressed.

Enzo crushed out his cigarette after just two drags. He stepped closer to me, then caught himself and pulled back. "The point is that it's fucked up to feel this way about you."

"What way?"

"You going to make me spell it out?"

A long moment passed, and we simply stared at each other. The shadowy woods surrounding us made me feel like we were in a void. Nothing existed but us. I looked at Enzo, waiting. I needed to hear him say it. I needed to know that I wasn't making something out of nothing, misunderstanding the situation.

"Well?"

"Come on, Hawthorn," he said.

I frowned. "You know, you can be a real coward sometimes."

I started back toward my car, pushing past him, close enough for our arms to brush.

Then Enzo's hand was on my shoulder, and he was spinning me around, and the next thing I knew, his lips were on mine, pressing hard, hungry. It was a better answer to my question than I'd hoped for.

My body relaxed. He pulled me closer, held me tight against his body, the two of us radiating heat in the cold October night.

I had kissed boys before, but not like that. I'd never been on autopilot, my body doing things without checking with my brain first to see if it was OK. My entire body was buzzing, and I was sure Enzo could feel it, an electric current passing from me to him. The tension had been building up, and finally, there was a release. We were melting into each other.

Enzo suddenly pulled back, leaving me cold and vulnerable where he'd been pressed up against me.

"Goddammit, Hawthorn." He ran his hands through his hair and looked up at the sky. "This is fucked up. What are people going to say?"

"Since when do you care what people say?"

He reached into his pocket and pulled out his tobacco and rolling papers. After a moment, he spoke. "Maybe you should take me home."

So I did. When we got to his apartment, he climbed out of his car and told me good night as if nothing unusual had happened. Neither of us mentioned the kiss or what it meant. But I knew we were both thinking about it.

It wasn't something we could erase. We couldn't pretend the kiss hadn't happened—nor did I want to. As I drove home, my heart rate still hadn't returned to its normal speed. I ached to kiss Enzo again. I wanted to live in our moment in the woods forever.

CHAPTER 28

TERRIBLE EVERYTHING

I needed to tell someone. I needed to find someone I could be a hundred percent honest with, someone who would listen to the whole story—from the day I met Enzo in the diner until the previous night's kiss. But I was pretty short on friends.

I spent all of Saturday wandering aimlessly. I picked up the phone to call Emily, then realized how absurd I was being, because Emily and I weren't friends anymore. So I hung up and walked to the backyard to see Sundog, since he'd listen to anything I had to tell him. But talking to him about werewolves was one thing. I couldn't gush to him about a kiss and what it might mean. Our relationship wasn't *that* personal. I wished I could tell my mom or even Rush, but I'd never even talked about my crushes with them, and it seemed weird to suddenly start. So I stayed quiet and shrugged when anyone asked me why I was acting so weird.

I didn't call Enzo, and he didn't call me. I wondered if he was sitting in his crappy little apartment, thinking of me and our kiss. I wanted to know if he'd replayed it in his head about eight billion times like I had. I felt weak when I thought about it, like those girls in Victorian novels who are always swooning. One kiss had turned me into a stereotype I'd always despised. I was losing my mind.

I hung Enzo's painting on the wall next to my bed. He'd put so much work into it. He'd spent hours fixated on the painting and nothing else. Which meant he'd spent those hours thinking of me. The same way he'd once spent hours painting a picture of Lizzie. She was gone though, and maybe she wasn't coming back. Now I was Enzo's muse. Maybe I wasn't as beautiful or charming as Lizzie, but Enzo wanted me. I affected him so deeply that he had to put his emotions on canvas, and that made me feel as if I'd drift away if I didn't tether myself to the earth.

There was a knock on my door Saturday evening. I was lying in bed, looking at Enzo's painting, wishing I was scheduled to work so I could babble to Christa.

"What?" I shouted.

Rush swung open the door without waiting for me to say it was OK. "Mom wants to know if you're eating dinner here."

"What's she making?"

"I don't know. Some sort of Tofurky wraps or something."

"Gross."

"I know."

Rush looked around my room, not meeting my eyes, like he wanted to say something but didn't know where to start.

"What's your problem?" I asked.

"No problem. I was just thinking—" He cut off his sentence when he saw the painting. "What's that?"

"Surely, you've seen paintings before. You know, often found in museums or as decorations in homes?"

Rush ignored my sarcasm and walked into the room, uninvited, to get a closer look. "Where'd it come from?"

"Enzo did it."

My brother's jaw tightened.

"It's good, isn't it?" I asked.

"I guess so. It's weird."

"It's supposed to be weird."

"You don't need to get upset."

"I'm not."

Rush shrugged, then sat down on my bed, again uninvited.

"What?" I asked.

"I know you probably don't want to hear this, but Enzo isn't the only guy out there, you know. He's not the best you can do."

"What's that supposed to mean?"

"The guy's a loser, Hawthorn. And you've got your whole life ahead of you."

"You're three years older than me, Rush. Since when does that make you the expert on relationships and life?"

"I'm just telling you how I see it."

I scowled. "Well, no one asked for your opinion. You don't know anything about the situation."

"Maybe you should tell me then."

"So, what, we're going to start having heart-to-hearts now? Why don't you tell me about your life? Who's the new mystery girl?"

"Mystery girl?"

"I'm not stupid," I said. "You slink out of here at odd hours and never say where you're going. You're so eager to comment on my love life, but you're keeping your own a secret."

Rush didn't say anything for a long time, so long that I expected him to get up and leave the room. Instead, he cleared his throat. "She has a kid. She doesn't want him to know that we're dating until we're sure it's serious."

"Oh," I said, certain I wasn't hiding my surprise well. Surprise that Rush was dating someone with a child *and* that he'd admitted it to me.

"Her kid is in the football league I coach. That's how I met Shawna. We only see each other after her son is asleep or when he's at his dad's house. And to tell you the truth, I don't know how Mom and Dad would feel about the whole thing. So for now, it's easier to keep it to myself."

I felt closer to my brother than I had in years. "That's, you know, very cool of you. To stick with her even though it's complicated."

"Well, she's really great. Down to earth. Even you'll like her."

I felt like I had to share my story after that, which was probably the whole point of Rush's confession. Except Rush wasn't the sneaky or malicious type, so maybe not. "Enzo and I aren't dating, so you know. But I kind of like him. I think he likes me too."

Rush leaned over and ruffled my hair, which he hadn't done since I was about ten. "Just be careful, OK?"

"Does this mean I have your approval or whatever?"

He hesitated. "I'm not going to say I approve. But I want you to be happy."

"Enzo makes me happy."

"Good." Rush gave Enzo's painting another long look before heading for the door. "So should I tell Mom you're eating here?"

"Sure."

He hesitated in the doorway.

"What?" I asked.

"There's no good way to ask this."

"That's a terrible way to start into a question."

"It's just… Do you really think you like Enzo, or are you just trying to one-up Lizzie?"

I stared at my brother, trying to decide if I was angry or insulted or if I even cared at all. But before I could figure it out, Mom called to us from the kitchen, wanting to know if we were eating or not.

✹✹✹

My dad grimaced every time he took a bite.

"Honestly, James," my mom said. "It tastes like turkey."

"I don't understand why we can't have the real thing. You want to buy organic, fine. We'll spend the extra money. That doesn't mean we need to be vegan."

"CJ eats raw," I said. "Just be happy Mom hasn't gone that far."

"Who's CJ?" my dad asked.

"One of the hippies. The one with the long hair who thinks he's Jesus."

"That could be any of them," my dad said.

My mom sighed. "You could try to get to know them. The kids have."

The truth was my mom was right about dinner. You almost couldn't tell that we were eating tofu or whatever it was. But I wasn't going to side with her and leave my dad hanging. Instead, I listened to them bicker and eventually zoned out.

I thought about the conversation I'd just had with Rush and how it was sort of obnoxious but also sort of nice. I entertained the idea of confiding in him. I could pull him aside after dinner, tell him about how Enzo had kissed me, and blurt out everything that kiss made me think and feel. Rush would make jokes, and he might even say upsetting things about how he didn't like Enzo. But he would listen. He would care. And that might make all the other stuff worth it.

"Hawthorn? Are you with us?"

"Huh? Sorry."

"I asked how work is," my dad said.

"Fine. Boring. But better than working at a fast-food place, I guess."

"Have you taken your car to the mechanic?" he asked.

"Not yet."

"Wasn't that the point of you getting the job?"

I shrugged. "I'll get to it. I've been busy."

My dad frowned but switched his attention to Rush. They talked about football for a while, and I zoned out again until someone said Lizzie Lovett's name.

"What about Lizzie?" I asked.

Rush rolled his eyes.

"There was an article in the paper today," my mom said. "An interview with the police chief talking about not giving up on cold cases."

"They're wasting their time. She's long gone, one way or another," Rush said.

"You don't know that," I said.

"I know as much about it as anyone else."

"Bullshit."

My parents exchanged a glance, and just like that, their argument over tofu was forgotten, and they were united against Rush and me, alert and ready to prevent a fight at the dinner table.

"What's wrong with you?" I asked. "Do you remember what a huge idiot you acted like when Lizzie first went missing? And now you don't even care."

"I got over it."

My mom opened her mouth to speak, but I beat her to it.

"Got over it? Like it's that easy? One day, you're shuffling around the house as if the world's ended, and the next day, it's like nothing happened. Seriously, you were acting like *you* were the one dating her."

"I guess someone needed to, since her actual boyfriend doesn't seem to give a shit about her."

"He's not her boyfriend anymore!" I slammed my hands down on the table. An extremely uncomfortable silence fell over the room, and I realized how loud I'd shouted.

"That's enough from both of you," my mom said quietly.

Rush and I glared at each other across the table. I said "Rush is dating some chick with a kid. He's hiding it from you 'cause he thinks you'll judge him."

Then I got up and walked out of the room.

I was pretty sure I was a terrible sister. And daughter. And friend. And girlfriend, if that was a title I could even claim. I was a terrible everything. I paced back and forth for what felt like hours, not wanting to leave the safety of my room. Finally, I decided to suck it up and do the right thing.

I caught Rush as he was leaving the house, on his way to see his girlfriend probably.

"Hey, wait," I said, following him out onto the porch.

It was cold outside. I hadn't put on shoes or socks. I crossed my arms in front of me and tried to hold in the warmth.

"I'm sorry. I wish I could take back what I said."

Rush stuck his hands in his pockets. "Let's forget it, OK? I'm sorry too. I didn't mean to antagonize you."

I raised my eyebrows. "You accepted my apology unusually fast."

Rush mimicked my expression. "How would you know? I'm not sure you've ever apologized before."

"Well, not without being forced to anyway," I said. Rush laughed, but I hadn't entirely been joking. I really wasn't a very good sister to him. "I hope Mom and Dad weren't too weirded out. About your girlfriend, I mean."

"They had to find out sometime."

"Well. Sorry again. I'm glad we're OK."

Rush ruffled my hair for the second time that night. "Later, Hawthorn."

Then he bounded down the porch steps and across the yard toward his car. I went back into the house where it was warm. I pulled the afghan from the back of the couch, wrapped myself in it, and curled up in an armchair.

Mostly, I thought about how maybe, probably, when everyone you know tells you the same thing, it's a good idea to at least listen to what they're saying, no matter what you think is right. But I thought of other things too, like how there were other people who still believed that Lizzie could come back, and how I always ended up being awful to the people I cared about. And I thought of Enzo too, of course. He's what I was thinking about when I fell asleep.

CHAPTER 29

A STRANGE NEW PLACE

✳ ✳

The longer I kept the kiss to myself, the bigger it grew. It started to feel like the most important thing that ever happened in the history of the universe. I needed to let out my secret. I needed a friend. I almost wished Lizzie were around, because I could have talked to her, and she probably would have understood my turmoil. Though she might not be thrilled that I was kissing her boyfriend.

Sundog's wisdom about having myself to talk to popped into my head. I figured it wouldn't hurt to give it a shot.

I grabbed my jacket and a notebook and went to the front porch. I tried to draw my feelings. Tried to let everything in my head and heart run out of my body through my hand and reappear on the paper in front of me. It only took about two seconds to realize that wasn't going to work. Enzo was the artist, not me.

I turned to a blank page. I stared at it. Then I started writing.

I never thought I'd be the kind of girl who got kissed that way.

It was a movie kiss.

A fairy-tale kiss.

It was everything I'd ever imagined but didn't think was real.

One moment, we're in the woods, talking. Arguing, almost. The next, Enzo was kissing me passionately.

Do other girls get kissed like that all the time?

Maybe every kiss Lizzie Lovett ever had was just like that one.

Or maybe my kiss with Enzo was special. Not just when measured against the other kisses I've experienced but when measured against all the kisses ever.

Well. Maybe not ever.

Kissing Enzo was fireworks. It was the first day of summer vacation. It was waking up from a nap and finding out the world changed while you were asleep, became a millions times brighter and better.

What if everything that's happened since the morning I found out Lizzie was missing was all to get me to this moment, to this totally strange and awesome new place?

What if—

The sound of tires on gravel interrupted me. Connor's car was pulling into the driveway. I flipped the cover of my notebook closed and set it on the swing.

"Hey, Thorny," he called, making his way across the yard and up the porch steps.

"Rush is out."

"He just texted. He'll be here any minute."

Connor leaned against the porch railing, waiting. I wanted to get back to writing.

"You can wait inside," I offered.

"Trying to get rid of me?"

I shrugged.

"So, I hear you inspired some art."

For a second, I thought he was talking about my writing, and my face went hot. Then I realized how stupid that was. Last time I checked, Connor wasn't psychic.

"Rush told you about the painting?"

This time, Connor was the one who shrugged. We were both silent for a moment. Then he said, "Can I see it?"

That's how Connor ended up in my bedroom, where I was pretty sure he'd never set foot before.

"I imagine Rush didn't give it a good review," I said.

Connor stepped close to the canvas. "It's good, I think. Technically, at least."

"You don't sound very impressed."

He laughed. "I like it just fine. Why are you getting defensive? Don't you like it?"

"Yeah, I like it. I like that Enzo painted it for me. He said it's supposed to represent the way I see the world."

Connor continued to study the painting, which made me feel self-conscious, as if my mind were laid out in front of him.

"Enzo has this painting he did of Lizzie," I said, not knowing why I was sharing but unable to stop myself. "Every time I went to his apartment, I saw the painting and thought about what it must feel like to be her. To be on someone's mind so much that you were his muse."

"And this time, you got to be his inspiration."

"Yeah. I guess."

"Only he didn't paint *you*. At least, not the way he painted Lizzie."

I was going to argue, but a sinking feeling crept into my stomach, the kind you get when you realize something that should have been obvious from the start. "No. I guess he didn't."

Connor was right. My painting was different. It wasn't about seeing me for who I was; it was about *being* me. Enzo wanted to put on Hawthorn-glasses to view the world, because it was better than his own reality.

Connor glanced over at me, and I must have had a weird look on my face. "Hey, don't get upset, Thorny. I was just talking. I don't know anything about art."

I looked at the painting for a long time. Suddenly, I hated its stupid surreal colors and all its little quirks. The painting was juvenile. It was naive. It was cute but not beautiful, not charming, not breathtaking like Lizzie's. I hated the painting.

"I'm an idiot," I said.

"What? Why?"

"When Enzo gave me the painting, I felt special. And it turns out it isn't about me at all."

"Sure it is," Connor said.

"Not like Lizzie's though. I won't ever be her."

"Why would you want to be?"

I turned away from Enzo's painting. I couldn't bear to look at it anymore. "I just wanted to know what it felt like. To be so...I don't know. Lovable, I guess."

Connor chuckled dryly. "Lovable isn't exactly the first word I'd use to describe Lizzie."

"You're just saying that," I mumbled. It was nice of Connor to comfort me, but it didn't change what we both knew was true—no one would ever look at me the way they looked at Lizzie Lovett.

"No, I'm not. Lizzie was...magnetic. But once you started talking to her, you realized there was no substance. She's the kind of person who can be summed up in one sentence. You're strange and complicated and sometimes really frustrating, but that's what makes you interesting, Hawthorn. Doesn't that mean something?"

I wanted to respond, but my mind was racing, and I couldn't get my mouth to form words. No one had ever said anything like that to me before. Connor had listed everything I was insecure about and acted like they were *good* things.

"If I'm so interesting, why did Lizzie have guys lining up to date her?"

Connor shrugged and looked away from me. "Maybe Lizzie put herself out there more. Gave more guys a chance."

I *had* put myself out there with Enzo though. I'd given him a million chances. He was the one who was conflicted. He was the one who pulled back from our kiss, who wasn't available when I needed him, who painted a picture that practically screamed that I'd never be as good as Lizzie in his eyes.

I needed to talk to Enzo right away. I wasn't going to let him dodge my questions anymore. Maybe Lizzie didn't like to analyze feelings, but I needed some answers.

"What are you thinking?" Connor asked, and I realized I'd been lost in my thoughts for a long time.

"I need to find my car keys," I said.

✷✷✷

I got to Enzo's apartment as the sun was setting. I had to knock on the door three times before he answered. His hair was messier than usual, and his clothes were wrinkled.

"Hawthorn. I was sleeping."

"Now? I guess artists don't restrict themselves to schedules, huh?"

"Is something wrong?"

"Can I come in?"

Enzo opened the door and gestured for me to enter. I walked in and tried to keep my gaze off the Lizzie painting. I failed. This time, she didn't look so serene. She looked smug. She was smirking at me because we both knew that Enzo wouldn't ever want me the way he'd wanted her.

"Are you going to tell me what's going on?" Enzo asked.

I turned back to face him. But I had no idea what to say. What was I going to do? Accuse him of liking another girl more than me?

"I want you to see me the way you see her," I blurted.

"You mean Lizzie? Hawthorn, you two are very different people."

"Clearly," I said, stealing another glance at her painting.

"And you're awesome," he said, stepping closer to me. "You know I think you're awesome."

"But you mean awesome like you want to have my perspective on the world. Not awesome like you want to date me."

"Are they exclusive?"

I crossed my arms and stared at him.

"Come on," he said. "It's not like you went into this situation thinking of romance. You just wanted to find a werewolf."

"And what did you want? What *do* you want?"

Enzo sighed. He looked like he wanted to be somewhere else. "You know what I wanted. I wanted to believe Lizzie was alive. That she left on her own and her disappearance had nothing to do with me."

"You used me to make yourself feel better about your missing girlfriend."

"Jesus, Hawthorn. Yeah, I used you, OK? We were using each other."

"And now where are we?"

"Standing here arguing about whether or not I like you as much as you think I should."

At that moment, I hated him. I wanted him to accidentally slam his hand in a car door. I wanted his ice cream to fall off the cone and onto the pavement on a really hot day. I wanted him to read a really great mystery, only to find someone had ripped out the end pages where it was solved.

"Yeah right, Enzo. The starving artist in you is eating this up. You look for conflict so you can have something to be philosophical about. For all I know, people are right, and you actually did kill Lizzie—just so you could let the guilt torment you."

"Not cool, Hawthorn." His expression darkened.

I knew I'd crossed a line but couldn't bring myself to care.

"Yeah, well. There are a lot of uncool things happening right now."

Enzo sighed again and ran a hand through his hair. "This is exactly what I didn't want to happen. I feel like I'm in high school again."

I was angry, but the other emotion slowly creeping up bothered me more. Hurt. I felt like I might cry, and it probably showed on my face, and I resented Enzo even more, because he could see it.

"Hawthorn, you've got it in your head that I'm supposed to, I don't know, be the hero of your story. But I'm not. Life doesn't work like that, OK? You need to let people be who they are, not who you want them to be. Stop making everything so complicated."

"And you must think you're uncomplicated then, is that it?" I asked. "You mope around, acting like no one in the world could possibly understand you. I never know what you're thinking or if you're even thinking at all. Instead of telling me what's happening in your head, it's like you're waiting to be asked, only sometimes, I don't even know there's a question."

"How very poetic," Enzo said dryly.

That's when I should have left. Or before then. Really, I shouldn't have gone to Enzo's apartment in the first place. But it was too late for any of that. We stared at each other for a long time, and I could feel my anger fading, and then I was just left with sadness. My lip trembled. I blinked, trying to push back the tears that were threatening to spill.

The thing about crying is that I didn't do it in front of other people. It would only draw attention to my weaknesses, and I hated making myself that vulnerable. I guess for most girls, it's different. I see them crying in the bathrooms at school all the time, which makes me feel awkward, as if I should say something, but I don't know what. I'd even seen Emily cry when she got a rejection letter for the fancy private school she was trying to get into. But that was different, because Emily was my best friend then, and it only mattered that I was there for her, even if I didn't have the words to fix anything.

So there I was, on the verge of tears, and crying in front of Enzo seemed like a huge defeat. There was no going back and pretending like his feelings for me didn't matter.

"Hey," Enzo said, not sounding angry anymore, "don't get upset."

"I've *been* upset."

"You know what I mean."

I shrugged. I tried to find something to focus on other than him. I found a spot on the carpet where something had spilled a long time ago and directed all of my attention to it.

"Come here," Enzo said, but I didn't move, and he ended up stepping toward me instead. "I'm sorry. I don't want to fight."

He wrapped his arms around me. Stiffly, I let my head rest on his shoulder. I was uncomfortable. I wanted to leave. But I let him hold me for a minute, then I let him put his hand under my chin and tilt it up, and then I let him kiss me. I kissed him back. It wasn't as magical as the first time, but all of the harsh words between us started to melt away. The next thing I knew, he was pushing me back onto the bed and climbing on top. His hands were touching me everywhere at once. When he started to take off my clothes, I let that happen too.

✷✷✷

The thing about sex is that before you have it, people tell you that your first time is going to go one of two ways. The first possibility is that it's going to hurt, a lot. The second is that it'll be mind-blowingly awesome, like all the awesome that's ever existed in the universe crammed into one moment.

For me, it wasn't either. It wasn't good or bad. It just was.

It hurt a little, but in an uncomfortable way, not the way I'd overheard other girls talking about it, like they could feel themselves being ripped open. There was a little blood though, and afterward, when Enzo saw that, he freaked.

"Jesus. You were a virgin," he said, putting his hands over his face.

"I told you I was inexperienced."

"I didn't think you meant you'd never had sex at all."

I thought it was going to turn into some big deal, but he just sighed deeply and started tugging the sheets off the bed. I scooted over to help him. He left the sheets in a pile on the floor, then lay back down and rolled a cigarette.

Another thing that people don't tell you about sex is that it doesn't go the way it does in movies. At least, it didn't for me. In movies, you never see the awkward parts, like how sometimes you can't get a button undone or how it's sort of weird to sit there and pull off your socks while the other person is just waiting. In movies, there's never a terrible silence while the condom wrapper is being torn open, and the girl never seems to panic because she doesn't know whether she should let the guy put it on or if she should do it for him, and if it's the latter, what if you accidentally start to put it on the wrong way? And what about how movie sex always ends with the couple collapsing into bed together and laying close? In real life, the guy gets up to deal with removing the condom while the girl sits in bed feeling very naked and wondering if it would be inappropriate to get dressed.

It turned out that sex was pretty much like everything else in life. Not nearly as magical as you think it's going to be.

"Don't get weird now," Enzo said and took a long drag on his cigarette.

"Me? You're the one being weird."

"I feel like an asshole."

"Because it was my first time?" I asked.

"Because you're just a kid."

"Well, you're not really the most mature person I've ever met."

I wanted to get out of bed and find my clothes and get out of there. Just being in the apartment seemed like too much, as if the walls and ceiling were pressing in on me. I was self-conscious though. I wasn't thinking about her while it was happening, but now that it was over and we were just hanging out, I couldn't get the image of Lizzie out of my mind. The Lizzie from the photo with her shirt unbuttoned, as curvy as an underwear model. How must I look to Enzo after her? Skinny. Boring. Young.

Then I realized it didn't matter. He'd already seen all of me anyway.

I got out of bed and started pulling clothes on as I found them. I could feel Enzo watching me.

"Where are you going?"

"I have some things to do," I said.

"What things?"

"Just things."

Probably sit in my room all night and worry about what all this meant. Which seemed pretty depressing.

I thought about writing in my notebook earlier, describing the kiss. How had everything changed so quickly? I wanted to rewind, to be that girl again. Now I was just very, very confused.

"It gets better," Enzo said. "Just so you know."

"It's not that. It was fine."

"I don't just mean because you were a virgin. People need to get used to each other's bodies. Find the right rhythm or whatever."

"That's not why I'm leaving," I said. "I have stuff going on tonight."

"You're a terrible liar, kid."

I finished tying my shoes and stood up.

"Can I ask you something? And will you give me an honest answer?"

"Sure."

"Did you ever really think Lizzie was a werewolf?"

Enzo seemed startled by the question. He looked at me for a long time. Then he crushed out his cigarette in the ashtray on his nightstand and took a deep breath. "I wanted to believe that she was. I wanted to believe everything you did."

"But you didn't."

"No."

"Then why pretend?"

Enzo sighed. "Because I wanted to stop thinking about what probably happened."

"So I guess it was convenient that I showed up with all of my crazy theories."

Enzo started to roll another cigarette. "I didn't lie to you."

"That's exactly what you did. I'm just a distraction for you."

"That's not true." Enzo stood up, naked. He pulled one of the bloody sheets off the floor and wrapped it around his waist. "I promise, that's not true."

My eyes stung with tears again. The night was getting more mortifying by the second.

Enzo leaned down and kissed me softly. Then he looked me in the eyes.

"Here's the truth. I thought there was a small chance you were right. Not that she was a werewolf, but she was so into wolves that she might have run off because she *thought* she was a werewolf. We read about that, remember? Clinical lycanthropy? When we were searching the woods, I really thought we might find her. Doing research and taking notes seemed useful for understanding what she was going through. And yes, maybe I wanted to listen to you talk about all your magic and folktales because it made all the real stuff easier to handle. But that's not the only reason I stuck around. Spending time with you is great."

"Well. OK then," I said.

"Are you upset?"

"I don't know."

"Do you still want to go home?"

"Yes."

After helping me hunt down my keys, which had somehow ended up under the bed, Enzo walked me to the door. He kissed me good-bye, like he was suddenly my boyfriend, like that was something we always did. He leaned against his open door and watched as I made my way out of the building.

"Hey, Hawthorn," he called.

I turned.

"Do *you* really think Lizzie's a werewolf?"

I thought about it. "I don't know. I guess I don't know much of anything tonight."

Enzo nodded as if it was the answer he expected, and I made my way to my car, where at least I'd be alone with my thoughts.

✹ ✹ ✹

What happened next is what my dad would call "learning a lesson" and my mom would call "karma."

I got in my car, super glad Enzo wasn't looking at me anymore so I could start to sort out my feelings. I figured I'd drive around for a bit, maybe find a place to get some coffee. I didn't want to be at Enzo's, but I didn't want to be at my house either.

I put the key in the ignition and turned it. Nothing happened.

Nothing at all. The car didn't even *try* to start. No clicks, no rumbling. Just silence. I tried again. More of the same.

I could just imagine how smug my parents were going to be. They'd remind me of how many times they'd told me to take my car to the mechanic.

I groaned and rested my forehead on the steering wheel. Of all the times for this to happen. Of all the places. I was going to have to drag myself back to Enzo's apartment and ask if I could use the phone. Then someone, probably my dad, would drive all the way out to Layton, grumbling the whole way, to pick me up. I didn't want to spend the next half hour waiting awkwardly in Enzo's apartment. I didn't want my dad to see where I'd been spending so much of my time. He'd think the apartment was in a bad area and think less of Enzo than he already did. He'd probably instinctively know I'd had sex for the first time and lecture me or—even worse—want to have a heart-to-heart, and it would be unbearably embarrassing.

I tried to start the car again, hoping something had changed. It hadn't. I wished I had my cell phone on me so I could call someone without having to deal with Enzo. I wished I had someone to call besides my parents. But I didn't, and I had to do something.

So that's how I ended up walking home.

✳✳✳

It was a long walk, so there was a lot of time to think.

About how I was no longer a virgin, how I had reached a milestone in my life, how I would always remember the first time that I had sex. Was I happy it had been with Enzo?

I thought about what would happen with me and Enzo. And if I really wanted anything more to happen. I was pretty sure that Enzo didn't understand me as much as I pretended he did and would never be as into me as I wanted him to be. And it wasn't because of Lizzie. For once, it didn't all come back to Lizzie Lovett. It was just who I was and who he was.

I trudged through town, shivering the whole time. I was glad it wasn't snowing yet. We'd had a warm fall. And walking wasn't as terrible as I thought it would be and certainly not as terrible as pacing in Enzo's apartment while I waited for my dad to show.

Cars passed me without slowing down, and I wondered how I looked to the people inside of them. Did I seem different now that I'd lost my virginity? I knew I was supposed to *feel* different, but I still felt like me. Only more confused than ever.

I wondered how old Enzo had been the first time he had sex and how he'd felt afterward. I wished we were the same age, had experienced all our *firsts* together. Maybe our relationship would have been different if it wasn't so unbalanced from the very start.

If I'd met Enzo when he was in high school, back when he had his notebook of bizarre events, maybe he wouldn't have been pretending when he said he believed in werewolves. Maybe our search would have been real.

Or maybe not. I pondered the last thing Enzo said to me. Did I believe Lizzie was a werewolf? Had I ever *really* believed it? Out of all the things on my mind, that was maybe the most important question of all.

CHAPTER 30

DAY SEVENTY-NINE

I hated my first period algebra II class even more than usual. That was because I hadn't gotten home until three in the morning. I'd stumbled up the stairs, exhausted and freezing but thankful my parents hadn't waited up for me. I hadn't anticipated my mom waking me up a full *hour* before I had to get ready for school because the absence of my car in the driveway freaked her out.

Which made it difficult to concentrate on the problems Mr. Bennett was writing on the board without nodding off. I wished my mom had a job. Then my house would be empty all day, and I could sneak home to sleep. But no, Mom would be in the kitchen, baking vegan desserts and hanging out with her hippie friends.

That morning, when I'd been woken up after two hours of sleep, I explained about the car not starting. Surprisingly, my mom didn't gloat or say, "I told you so." She was too distracted by her rage. Rage that I walked from Layton to Griffin Mills in the middle of the night. Alone.

"What were you thinking?" she shouted before telling me I

could have been hit by a car or mauled by a wild animal or murdered by a serial killer.

"At least we know where I get my overactive imagination from," I'd told her. For a second, I really thought she might slap me.

At breakfast, after my mom cooled down, she said I needed to have my car towed to the mechanic's after school. That meant I'd have to go to Enzo's apartment, which didn't exactly thrill me. Maybe I could just leave the car there forever, buy a new car.

Which was what I was *actually* thinking about in math instead of math problems. To stay awake, I started doodling in my notebook. Spirals and squiggles and stars. A crescent moon. A heart. A broken heart. A sad face.

My eyes were stinging, and there was an uncomfortable pressure in my head, and every part of my body ached. I didn't feel like I could possibly make it through the day. And it was only first period.

"Hawthorn?" Mr. Bennett said. "Why don't you do the next one?"

"Huh? The next what?"

People laughed. Of course they did. It's easy to laugh when your car isn't stranded at the home of the person you just lost your virginity to, you've had enough sleep, you didn't spend the whole night walking, and you don't have a teacher and a whole classroom of people staring at you as if you were a gigantic idiot.

I wished that every single person who laughed at me had to say the numbers out loud whenever they were doing math, even if it was just figuring out how much to tip at a restaurant. I wished their favorite clothes would shrink in the dryer. I wished they'd always get stuck behind drivers going five miles under the speed limit.

"The next problem." Mr. Bennett gestured to the whiteboard. A row of problems were written there, all of them completed by a different hand, except for the last one, which wasn't solved yet.

"Oh. Right."

Everyone stared at me. My face burned. I would have struggled with this even on a good day.

"Can I pass?"

Snickers surrounded me. Mr. Bennett frowned. So I sighed and made my way up to the board.

Being called to the front of the class makes me panic. I was sweaty and flustered, and my throat went dry. The whole class watched me, waiting for me to fail. What if I tried to do the math and forgot everything I'd ever known? What if I'd started my period, and that's what all the whispers were about? What if, on cue, everyone pulled out their lunch bags and started launching apples and peanut butter sandwiches at me while Mr. Bennett laughed manically?

I picked up the marker and took a deep breath. Suddenly, it was way too quiet. I closed my eyes for a second and pretended I was in a room by myself, no one watching me, just working on a math problem. An easy math problem.

Then I opened my eyes and got started. It actually *was* OK. There were some parts I was unsure of, but pretty much everything Mr. Bennett taught us came back to me, and my fear was replaced by the euphoria you can only get when you've slept for less than two hours.

I finished right as the bell rang. The classroom filled with noise while kids gathered their textbooks and started conversations.

"Good job, Hawthorn," Mr. Bennett said.

"Thanks."

I grabbed my backpack and made my way to the next class, relieved and happy at my accomplishment, even if it was one of the day's minor challenges compared to dealing with my car and Enzo.

★★★

Most of the day passed without me paying attention. I sleepwalked through school. At lunch, I dozed off on the steps behind the gym, where I now ate alone. I woke up when the bell rang and scrambled to gather my stuff and get to fourth period.

I was about to walk into the classroom when someone called my name.

"Hey, Hawthorn?"

Mychelle Adler. She'd been off my radar for the last couple weeks, blending into the regular annoyances of school. But her standing there in the hall with such a smug look on her face brought back all of my hatred.

"What?"

Mychelle waved a spiral notebook in the air. "Recognize this?"

"It's a notebook. That was easy. Give me another question."

"Not just a notebook. *Your* notebook. You left it on your desk in first period."

I thought back to how I'd run out of the room. "How nice of you to return it."

I grabbed for the notebook, but Mychelle pulled it back, out of my reach. "You should be more careful where you leave your personal things."

"Personal?" I laughed. "It's math homework."

"Oh, is that all?" Mychelle smiled at me, baring shark teeth behind lips that were stretched too wide. She had gossip. Or at least she thought she did. Something I wouldn't like. But it was just a math notebook.

Then I got it.

I pictured myself, less then twenty-four hours before, sitting on my front porch, writing down my feelings about Enzo. Then Connor showed up, and the notebook got shoved in my backpack. Until I took it out in algebra.

It wasn't a mistake I normally would have made, leaving those pages in my notebook and bringing it to school. But going over to a guy's house to confront him about how the picture he painted for you was an insult, having sex for the first time, and spending most of the night walking home could really mess with your head.

"OK," I said. "What do you want?"

"I want to congratulate you, Hawthorn. Your first kiss with Lizzie Lovett's boyfriend. I believe you called it *passionate.* That sort of thing never happens to lonely, pathetic girls like you, does it?"

Shit. I'd written a lot of other embarrassing things.

"Just stop, Mychelle."

"Stop? But you were so *excited* about it. Your very first big-girl kiss."

I shook my head. "God. Why are you such a bitch?"

"Me? What about you? Lizzie Lovett is missing, and you hook up with her boyfriend? I guess taking advantage of someone who's grieving is the only way you can get a guy to pay attention to you."

"Give me my notebook back," I snapped.

"Sure." Mychelle handed over the notebook. "Your diary entry isn't in there though."

I didn't figure I'd be so lucky. "What did you do with it? Photocopy it and pass it out all over the school?"

"Something like that." Mychelle's smile widened. "I told you not to mess with me, Hawthorn."

"You think a little embarrassment is going to ruin me? You'll have to try harder than that." I was bluffing though, and Mychelle probably knew it.

"Don't worry. I'm not finished yet."

Then Mychelle sauntered away, her hips swaying, oozing confidence with every step.

❈❈❈

I wished Mychelle's hair would get tangled in her homecoming queen tiara. I wished a strap on one of her high-heeled sandals would break. I wished she would always weigh two pounds more than she wanted to. I wished her mascara would dry out after she'd only done one eye.

I had stupidly thought that because I hadn't been thinking of Mychelle for the last few days, she wasn't thinking of me either. But of course, she was. What else did she have to think about? I was probably the only person in her life who wasn't doing exactly what she expected, and that made her furious.

It turned out Mychelle hadn't made photocopies. She'd scanned the notebook page and posted it on her blog. Only a few kids made mocking kissy faces at me, but there was a lot of whispering. People kept looking up from their phones and smirking at me.

Ronna Barnes, whose pregnant belly was starting to swell, came into the bathroom where I was hiding between classes. "Sorry about your diary. Thanks for giving me a break though."

"I wish I could say I was glad to be of service." I glanced down at Ronna's stomach. "How's the pregnancy thing going?"

Her eyes widened in surprise, and I wondered if I'd said something wrong.

"Was I not supposed to mention it?" I asked.

"You're just the first person who's asked how I'm doing." She rested her hands on her stomach and frowned. "To tell you the truth, I've never been so scared in my life."

Instead of mumbling something incoherent and scurrying out of the bathroom like I normally would, I boldly said, "Well, I don't have, you know, firsthand experience or anything. But if you ever need someone to talk to, let me know."

Maybe it was just pregnancy hormones, but Ronna looked like she might cry.

My next encounter was far less pleasant. The jock who sits next to Mychelle in math stopped me in the hall and said, "You want some more fireworks and passion? Meet me in the locker room in five minutes." The guys who were with him, other football players, laughed.

"You wish," I muttered. Only he didn't wish that at all, which was part of the joke.

Emily caught me as I was walking into fifth period. "You want to talk?"

She looked nervous, like I might tell her to get lost. Instead, I barely resisted the urge to fling myself at her, sobbing and begging her to be my friend again.

"You'll be late to class," I said.

Emily shrugged. "My GPA can handle an occasional tardy."

We wandered to a hallway that was mostly empty, and I slumped against the wall.

"It's not that bad," Emily said.

"Are you sure?"

"It was a kiss. We're seventeen, not seven."

"It's not about the kiss," I said. "It's the way I described it that's mortifying."

"No one really cares. The only reason anyone's acting interested is because Mychelle Adler told them to."

"I guess you're right." Emily had always been the voice of reason in my life, something I'd seriously been lacking since we stopped hanging out. It was a relief to have her back, even if only for a few minutes between classes.

"Remember when the hippie caravan showed up? You thought everyone was going to make fun of you for forever. Or when you got drunk at the party. Or freshman year when that thing happened with Amy."

"Are you trying to remind me of all my worst moments?"

"No. Sorry. It's just that nothing is as big of a deal as it seems at the time."

I took a deep breath. She was right. Why should I be ashamed of a kiss? Why should I be ashamed that I wrote about it?

"We should get to class," Emily said.

I nodded.

"And about you and Enzo...well, congratulations, I guess."

"Thanks, I guess."

We smiled at each other and went to class. It wasn't like the old days when we spent hours dissecting a situation, looking at it from every angle. But our brief talk in the hall was definitely better than drunkenly screaming at each other in public. It was progress.

✖ ✖ ✖

I was pretty sure I'd never been so happy to have a day end. Until I remembered that I either needed to walk home or take the school bus. Which meant I was walking.

I sighed, shifted the weight of my backpack, then started heading in the direction of home.

"Hawthorn!"

I looked up to find Enzo hurrying toward me. Enzo. At my school. For a second, I thought that I was seeing things, that I'd fallen asleep in my last period class and was having some sort of very realistic dream.

Before I could ask what he was doing here, Enzo's hands were on my shoulders, holding me too tight. "Is everything OK?"

"Yeah, why wouldn't it be?" I twisted away from his grip.

"Why wouldn't it be? Are you serious? I go outside, and your car is sitting in front of my apartment, and you aren't with it."

Oh. That.

"It wouldn't start last night," I explained.

"Do you think you could have let me know?"

"I thought you'd figure it out."

The worry on Enzo's face had morphed into relief but was starting to become anger. "Well, when your last girlfriend disappears, it's not really comforting to see your new girlfriend's car abandoned in a parking lot."

For a second, the entire world tilted. I tried to care about how annoyed Enzo was, but I could only concentrate on that one word. *Girlfriend.*

I swallowed hard and did my best to speak levelly, to not let on how much a stupid word had affected me. "So I'm your girlfriend now?"

"I don't know what you are. That's not the point."

It was for me. He'd said it so casually, as if the title didn't mean anything at all. As if it was a simple transition to make. One second, someone is your friend; the next, they're your *girlfriend.*

"Sorry I freaked you out."

"Just think before you do something like that again." Enzo reached into his pocket and pulled out his tobacco, so it seemed OK to move the conversation in a different direction.

"I need to get my car towed. I was gonna call from home and have one of my parents drive me over to unlock the car and stuff. But I could just go there with you now."

"Yeah, that's fine," Enzo said. He put his cigarette between his lips and flicked his lighter to life.

"OK then."

"I rode the bus here," he said with his cigarette dangling from his mouth.

"I figured."

So we turned in the opposite direction and walked toward the bus stop together, which was pretty lame but not nearly as lame as the school bus would have been. At least I wasn't alone.

We didn't talk much on the way to Enzo's apartment. But in my mind, I was asking him if he really thought of me as his girl-friend. And then I asked myself if that was something I wanted.

✖ ✖ ✖

The guy who answered the phone at the towing company said it would be at least an hour before he arrived. So I settled myself on Enzo's bed, prepared for the long wait.

"How will you get home?"

I shrugged. "One of my parents. Or I can get a lift to the mechanic's from the tow truck guy. The auto shop's not far from my house."

"I can't believe you walked home last night."

"It was pretty stupid," I admitted, my mom's list of worst-case scenarios still fresh in my mind.

"It was."

I lay back on the bed and crossed my arms behind my head. The night before, I'd had sex right there. The sheets were back on, so I guess Enzo had washed them.

He hesitated, then lay down next to me, mirroring my posi-tion but still distant. He made sure not to get close enough that we would touch. There was no risk of one of us breathing too deeply and our skin briefly coming into contact.

"Should we talk about things?" Enzo asked.

"Which things?"

"Us. Last night. All of it."

"No," I said. I rolled onto my side, facing Enzo. He looked over at me. "There's nothing to say. Let's just, I don't know, *be*."

"Yeah, OK. We can do that."

And then we were good. Enzo rolled onto his side too, and we stayed like that, talking for a long time about stuff that didn't matter, like the cartoons we loved the most when we were kids and the best flavor of ice cream and if there was any chance of astrology being real.

I relaxed. It made me think of when we went to the abandoned house in the woods and how, for a little while, we were just hanging out, making up a story, and nothing else mattered. Maybe that's what it would be like if Enzo and I actually dated. Not all of the angst or unhappiness. Just us enjoying each other's company, being friends.

"Tell me something fascinating," I said when there was a lull in conversation.

"About what?"

"Anything."

I watched Enzo think. He had that faraway look in his eyes that he got when he was concentrating. He hadn't cut his hair since I'd met him. I wanted to reach over and run my fingers through it. When he spoke, I let my eyes drift to his mouth, watched his lips form the words.

"There was this psychologist in the sixties who thought he could cure people with delusions by making them confront paradoxes. So he found these three guys who all believed they were Jesus Christ and had them meet, thinking it would snap them out of it."

"What happened?" I wasn't thinking of Enzo's lips anymore. When he told one of his stories, it was impossible to think of anything else.

"They each came up with complex explanations for how the other guys couldn't be the real Jesus. The psychologist wrote a book about it, documenting the whole experiment. But in the end, none of the men had been cured. They held on to their beliefs."

"Good for them," I said. "Tell me another one."

Enzo laughed. "I'm not an encyclopedia, you know."

I opened my mouth to respond, but Enzo's phone rang. He groaned.

"Let it ring," I said. "No, never mind. Get it. It might be the towing place."

Enzo got out of bed and crossed to the kitchen. I immediately wanted him to come back. The bed was cold without him in it.

I rolled onto my back and closed my eyes, listening to Enzo in the background saying hello and yes, it was Lorenzo Calvetti. It wasn't anyone calling about my car. They would have asked for me. I couldn't really hear the rest of what he was saying, but it was weird. In all the time I'd spent at Enzo's apartment, he hadn't gotten any other calls.

Faintly, I heard him put his phone back on the counter, his feet on the floor as he made his way back to me. I opened my eyes.

Enzo stood at the edge of the bed. Something was wrong. His face was an unnatural shade of whitish green that made him look like wax. His eyes seemed too small and too dark. His mouth was open, as if it had come unhinged and he'd forgotten how to close it.

I sat up. "What's wrong?"

For a second, he didn't speak. "It's Lizzie. They found her."

CHAPTER 31

THE LOST GIRL

✶ ✶ ✶ ✶ ✶ ✶ ✶ ✶ ✶ ✶ ✶ ✶ ✶ ✶ ✶ ✶ ✶ ✶ ✶ ✶

Lizzie Lovett did not go into the woods to turn into a werewolf. She went into the woods to die.

There was no shape-shifting involved. Hers was a much simpler story than that. Afterward, everyone nodded and said of course, of course, as if they'd known what happened all along. But they didn't. How could they have known? Their guesses were as good as mine. Girls like Lizzie are not supposed to die.

I couldn't make the news more real, no matter how many times I repeated it to myself. Lizzie Lovett was dead. Lizzie Lovett was dead. Lizzie was dead, dead, dead.

She was not a werewolf. She wasn't hunting or stalking or pouncing. She wasn't developing a taste for blood or raw flesh. She wasn't using her powerful wolf jaw to crack bones. Lizzie wasn't howling at the full moon. She wasn't searching for a pack. She wasn't lost or scared or trying to come to terms with her new identity. Lizzie was dead. That's it. The end. Move along, nothing to see here. Certainly no werewolves. Just another dead girl.

When Enzo first told me what happened, I didn't understand. I kept asking what he was talking about until he grabbed my shoulders and shook me and shouted, "She's dead. Don't you get it?"

I still didn't. Death wasn't familiar to me. It wasn't part of my life. People don't just die, especially when they're young and beautiful and have a boyfriend who paints pictures of them.

I asked Enzo how. I asked him why. But he didn't answer. He sat on the edge of the bed and didn't move. He didn't even roll a cigarette.

Everything was wrong, and nothing made sense. Lizzie Lovett was dead. Five minutes ago, Enzo and I had been talking about her in present tense. One phone call, and she became past tense. One phone call changed everything.

That's when all the details started to blend together. The tow truck showed up, and Enzo had to go down to the police station, and at some point, I must have called my dad, but I didn't remember it. The afternoon was a whirl of motion and lights, and I kept wondering if I had been the one who'd died, because nothing seemed real anymore.

The next thing I remember, I was at home, lying in bed, and people kept trying to talk to me. I saw their faces, but none of them mattered. My mom said I should eat something, that I had to eat, but I didn't want food, not even when she brought me fast food, hamburgers and fries and a soda, which weren't usually allowed in the house. My dad tried to talk to me as if everything were normal. He'd picked up my car from the shop. It was fixed. I could pay him later—or not. He didn't get that someone was dead. My car didn't matter.

Even Sundog came to see me at some point. He'd never been inside our house before. My family was all making exceptions for me, breaking all the rules, but Lizzie was the one who was dead. Why weren't they thinking of her?

When I started crying, I didn't know if it was for me or Lizzie or just tears that had to come out. My eyes burned. Snot leaked from my nose. I thought, *Lizzie will never cry again*, and that made me cry harder.

Days passed. I only got up to go to the bathroom. That's something they don't tell you about grief and depression. In movies and books, the depressed person doesn't ever leave bed. In real life, you have to get up to pee. You have to eat some of the food your mom brings you. You have to accept the box of tissues your brother sets on the bed.

"Rush, wait," I said before he could leave.

He came back and sat down on the edge of my bed. My brother had never seemed so willing to listen to me before. What was happening to the world?

"Where did they find her?"

He hesitated and glanced at my open bedroom door. "Maybe I should get Mom."

"I want *you* to tell me."

"She was in a ravine," he said, sighing. "I guess the woods are pretty thick around there."

"How far from the campsite?"

"A few hours."

I sat up. "A few *hours*? How did the search parties miss her?"

"They couldn't check every inch of the forest, Hawthorn."

But they should have. They should have uprooted trees if they had to.

"Will they catch him?" I asked.

"Who?"

"The person who killed her."

Rush got a weird look on his face. "I thought you knew."

Did I know? Did I know something I was forgetting? "Tell me."

"There's no one to catch," he said carefully.

"So she got lost."

"Hawthorn, Lizzie killed herself."

Time stopped. The air in my room went still. For a fleeting moment, I thought my brother was joking. "What? No. That has to be a mistake."

"I don't think so," he said.

"How do they know?"

"I don't think we should talk about this right now." He reached out to hold my hand.

I pulled back.

"How, Rush?"

He sighed. "They found her hanging from a tree."

My mind raced. "But...no. Someone could have made it look like—"

"They have ways to tell, Hawthorn. I didn't want to believe it either, but they're sure."

I lay back in bed and stared at the ceiling. Lizzie Lovett went into the woods to commit suicide. She was not a werewolf. She was dead, and she was never coming back, and it was because that's the way she'd wanted it.

I kept returning to that night with Lizzie and Enzo in their tent. They whisper and laugh and talk about the future as if it's still going to happen. He falls asleep. But she's awake. She watches him. She knows she won't see him again. Had she known from the start, when they planned their camping trip? Or was it a spur of the moment decision? How could she do it? How could she get up and walk out of the tent and leave *everything* behind?

"You'll never know the answers, Hawthorn," Sundog said later that night. He'd pulled my desk chair next to my bed and was sitting there as if he was keeping vigil over me, as if I were in a hospital, as if I were the one dying.

"She had *everything*, Sundog. How could she walk away?"

"You only know the part of the story people want you to see."

But it still didn't make sense. Nothing did. This was Lizzie Lovett. People loved her. She was a cheerleader. Cheerleaders didn't kill themselves. At least they didn't in the world I used to live in. Now, all the rules were reversed. Nothing was off limits.

On the day of the funeral, my mom tried to get me out of bed.

"You could wear your navy-blue dress with the gold buttons," she suggested. "What do you think?"

"Will they have the coffin open?" I asked.

My mom hesitated on her way to my closet. "She was in the woods a long time, honey."

"Was she just a skeleton then?"

"I don't know. Probably not."

"How tall was the tree that she hanged herself from? Could the animals on the ground get her?"

"I don't think you should think about that, Hawthorn."

"Why?" I asked, getting annoyed. It wasn't my mom's job to police my thoughts.

"It's not respectful."

"I'm pretty sure Lizzie's past the point of being offended."

My mom crossed the room and sat on the chair next to my bed. "I am being patient with you. I know this is a shock. I'm allowing you to stay in bed and miss a few days of school. But I won't put up with that attitude. Understood?"

"Yeah," I said.

"Now, are you wearing the navy dress or something else?"

"I'm not going to the funeral."

"You're not? Don't you think you should?"

"No." I rolled onto my side, away from her. I stared at the wall.

"Funerals help people get closure. Going could help you move on."

I didn't want closure though. Moving on was the last thing I wanted to do. I wanted to close my eyes and pretend I lived in a world where Lizzie Lovett still existed.

✶ ✶ ✶

Except, you know, I couldn't spend the rest of my life in bed. I had to get up eventually. The day after the funeral, before anyone else was awake, I went to the end of the driveway and got the newspaper.

Lizzie's funeral was on the front page. With pictures. The coffin was closed, but a huge photo of Lizzie sat on top of it. Flowers were everywhere. Enzo was pictured in a suit, the same suit he was supposed to wear to take me to the homecoming dance. He was standing next to Lizzie's mom, part of the family. Not the killer some people had suspected.

I read the article a few times. It talked about the night Lizzie went missing. It talked about how she was found by two hikers, which was nothing more than luck. Like Rush had told me, her body wasn't far from where the search parties had trampled through the woods. Lizzie's mom had been interviewed. She said Lizzie was a happy girl, and there was no reason to suspect she'd been contemplating suicide. The end of the article shared a list of suicidal warning signs, even though Lizzie apparently hadn't had any. It gave a number to call if you or anyone you knew was having suicidal thoughts.

Lizzie went into the woods with a rope in her bag, knowing that rope would be the last thing she ever felt. Lizzie made the choice to leave her life. Was she scared? Did she hesitate? At any moment, did she wish to take the whole thing back?

I put the newspaper down on the kitchen table. I stood there, in the middle of the kitchen, trying to figure out what came next. Everything I'd done in the past few months was about Lizzie. About finding a werewolf. But Lizzie was dead. So now what? I didn't know what to do. I didn't even know what to think about.

I crossed the kitchen and picked up the phone. It was early, but what did it matter anymore?

Enzo answered on the second ring. He sounded alert. He wasn't sleeping either.

"It's me."

"Hawthorn. Hey."

"Sorry I didn't call sooner." But even as I was saying it, I realized he hadn't called me either.

"Don't worry about it. I've been pretty busy."

"Look," I said, "maybe we weren't completely wrong."

"About what?"

"Do you know about warging? Say Lizzie wanted to throw us

off her trail, right? So she kills herself, but a second before she dies, she throws her spirit into the body of a wolf or some other animal that's nearby. You see?"

There was a long silence, expanding the distance between us. Then Enzo sighed deeply. "Don't."

"Don't what?"

"We can't do this anymore, kid."

"It doesn't need to be over," I said, hating the desperation in my voice.

"Yes, it does."

I could have tried to convince him. I could have told him he was wrong, that life was a wheel, not a straight line. It kept going and going, and nothing was ever really over. I could have told him that Lizzie was dead, but *we* weren't. But I didn't. I knew the harder I tried to convince him, the worse the sick feeling inside of me would get. It was hurt and hate and sorrow and every other bad emotion rolled into one terrible mass that churned in my stomach.

So I didn't say anything at all. I took the phone away from my ear and placed it gently on the receiver, all the while thinking, *So this is how my and Enzo's story ends.*

CHAPTER 32

ANOTHER GOOD-BYE

❋ ❋ ❋ ❋ ❋ ❋ ❋ ❋ ❋ ❋ ❋ ❋ ❋ ❋ ❋ ❋ ❋ ❋ ❋ ❋

After a tragedy, you're expected to go back to normal life. I found that out pretty fast after Lizzie's funeral. Everyone went from treating me really carefully to not being so patient. It was apparently time for me to *move on*. To *get over it*. To *let it go*. So I pretended to.

I thought my first day back to school would be pretty bad, what with everyone talking about Lizzie. But no one was. I was surprised, and then I remembered I'd been out sick for almost a week. The other kids had already talked about it. They had already *moved on*.

No one was awful to me, which was somewhat surprising. No one made jokes or said anything about how there were no werewolves after all. The only comment anyone made was when Mychelle Adler turned around in first period and asked, "How's your boyfriend taking Lizzie's death?"

I ignored her.

"I noticed you weren't with him at the funeral. Is he sick of you already?"

I pretended that I couldn't hear her. I pretended she was speaking some foreign language that I couldn't understand. I pretended that I didn't care what she was saying.

"Maybe he decided being alone was better than being with you."

Maybe he had.

I sat on the back steps during lunch but didn't eat. Food wasn't really interesting anymore, not even junk food. My mom kept telling me I was so skinny, I couldn't afford to lose weight. But I sort of liked that idea. Maybe I would waste away a little more every day until I disappeared entirely.

When the gym door opened and Emily stepped out, I didn't react. My senses were dulled. I felt medicated.

"Hey," Emily said.

"Hi."

She sat down in her old place, like we'd gone back in time.

"How are you doing?"

"I've been better."

"I know it must have been a shock to you."

"One I deserved, right? I spent months running around and talking about werewolves while Lizzie was rotting in the woods."

"You didn't know," Emily said.

"But I should have taken it more seriously. I should have known that someone going missing isn't a game. That's how I treated it. You know, like Lizzie went missing just for my amusement."

"You're being too hard on yourself," Emily said quietly.

I shrugged.

"Look, Hawthorn. I know things have been a little off between us. But we've been friends our whole lives. A couple weeks of not hanging out doesn't change that. If you want to talk, I'm here for you."

"There's nothing to talk about."

"Maybe we could still hang out. We could go to a movie. Or maybe watch them light the town Christmas tree in a couple weeks. Remember how we used to do that?"

"Maybe."

"Think about it at least."

I told her I would. But I didn't want to think about anything.

✭✭✭

My parents didn't want me to work at the Sunshine Café anymore, but I wasn't ready to quit. I couldn't sever that connection with Lizzie quite yet.

Christa talked about Lizzie a lot, and I listened but didn't give much of a response. I'd already caused enough trouble by making speculations about Lizzie's life. One night, when Christa was saying how she just couldn't believe Lizzie was dead, how she never figured Lizzie was the kind of girl who'd kill herself, Vernon looked up and said, "Doncha know Lizzie's a woof?"

I was startled and almost started to cry. Vernon had been paying attention to me after all. Even though it seemed like a silly thing to get so emotional about, I was grateful. "No, Vernon. I only thought she was. Thanks for listening though."

I watched the door a lot during my shifts. Part of me thought it would swing open, and the little bell would jingle, and Enzo would be standing there in his leather jacket, asking me what time I got off work, if I could leave early. But he never showed up. I knew I needed to stop waiting for him. Life wasn't a fairy tale. Enzo wasn't my prince. It was time for me to *get it together*. I had to *deal with it* and *get a grip*. So I tried to keep my heart from racing when I heard the bell ring. I tried to pretend I was just another waitress doing her job.

✖ ✖ ✖

It was a Tuesday in the middle of November when I pulled into my driveway after school and saw that the caravan was on the move. Tents were wrapped up and being carried from the back-yard. One of the more capable hippie guys was checking the oil in the cars.

I walked up to Sundog, who was supervising.

"You're leaving," I said.

"There's snow predicted this weekend."

"But…" I didn't have any way to finish the thought. There were no buts. Their camping gear wasn't meant for the cold. So instead, I settled for the truth. "I don't want you to go."

Sundog smiled. "Young Hawthorn, when we first pulled into town, the *only* thing you wanted was for us to leave."

"Things change."

"I know. I hope that's a lesson to you."

"Can I talk to you alone?" I asked, suddenly feeling exposed on the front lawn, the rest of the caravan milling around us.

We went around the side of the house where it was quieter and no one was watching us.

"Give me a name," I said.

"A name?"

"A spirit name. Like you gave my mom when she was my age."

Sundog laughed, and that dark twisting started in my gut again.

"What's so funny?" I asked. "I'm not as special as one of the members of your commune?"

"Hawthorn, you already have your name. You got your spirit name at birth. Most people aren't so lucky."

"So Hawthorn is my spirit name," I said flatly. "After a tree my parents had sex under."

"Do you know about the hawthorn tree? They're tough, sturdy. They can outlast storms. Hawthorn trees provide food and shelter for animals and insects. They nourish the world around them. It's a name anyone would be honored to have."

"Take me with you," I said suddenly. "Please."

If Sundog was surprised, he didn't show it. Instead, he seemed to consider it seriously. I wanted him to say yes. I wanted him to take me to the desert, where the sun would dry my tears. I wanted him to whisk me away to some magical land where we would travel and have adventures, and everything would be OK.

But of course, it didn't happen like that. Fairy tales aren't real.

"Hawthorn, running from your demons only gives them more power."

"Yeah," I said and sighed. "Got it."

I started to walk toward the back door, but he put his hand on my shoulder to stop me. "Your werewolf girl—she ran. You're meant for more than that."

I turned away so he wouldn't see my eyes fill with tears. I'd never believed in the mystical healing stuff the hippies went on about, but I did know Sundog had the power to make me feel good about myself. I knew how lonely I'd be with him gone.

Back in the front yard, I found Timothy Leary sitting patiently near a stack of luggage, as if she knew it was time to leave. I picked her up and nuzzled her. I thought about asking if I could keep her, but Sundog would probably say something about how animals couldn't be kept.

I helped the hippies load up the last of their belongings, then hugged Journey and Calliope and CJ good-bye. When Sundog bowed to me, I bowed back.

Then my mom and I stood on the lawn and watched the caravan pull away from the curb. My mom waved to them. I wiped at my eyes and hoped she didn't notice. Before rounding the corner and leaving my life, Sundog honked the horn of the big old bus.

I sniffed. Mom put her arm around me and said, "I'm going to miss them too."

When the last car in the caravan was out of sight, I walked around the house to the backyard. The grass was trampled flat where the tents had been set up. The remains of the last bonfire were still there, cold now. A long scarf lay forgotten on the ground. The yard looked lonely.

I lay down on the cold, matted grass and closed my eyes. I was surprised how quickly endings came. One day, the yard is filled with talking and laughter; the next, it's abandoned. One day, a young girl is full of life; the next, she's dead.

Why did Lizzie want to die? That's what I didn't get. How could someone like Lizzie, someone who had all the best things in life handed to her, want to kill herself? And if Lizzie Lovett couldn't find a reason why life was worth living, what hope did the rest of us have? What hope did *I* have?

CHAPTER 33

HANGED

❋ ❋

By Thanksgiving, it seemed like no one cared about Lizzie anymore. Not my family. Not the kids at school. Not the police or reporters. The mystery of her disappearance had been solved, and no one was interested in the mystery of her suicide.

Except for me. And, I assumed, Lizzie's family. And probably Enzo. I thought about calling him to ask. I wanted to connect with someone else who was desperate for answers. She hadn't left a suicide note. Did that mean her decision was spontaneous? Or did she just feel like she had nothing to say? In Lizzie's mind, had she already tied up loose ends?

That's what I thought about while the rest of my family enjoyed Thanksgiving dinner. My mom made a real turkey, which was how I knew she was still really worried about me. I wasn't hungry though. I pushed my food around on my plate while everyone else acted as if everything were normal.

"I really appreciate you inviting me over," Connor said to my mom.

"We wouldn't have you eating Thanksgiving dinner on your own," my mom said, making it clear that she disapproved of Connor's parents going out of town without him. Despite her aversion to social conventions, my mom was really big on family holidays.

The rest of the conversation was boring. My dad kept saying how great everything tasted, and Rush shoveled turkey in his mouth like he thought my mom might snatch it away, shout, "Just kidding," and run to get the Tofurky.

The whole holiday made me feel hateful. I wanted to throw my plate across the room just to get their attention. I wanted them to remember that Lizzie was dead, and turkey and forced conversation wouldn't change that.

I couldn't stop thinking about how Lizzie would have looked hanging in the woods. Did she even look like Lizzie anymore? I wanted to track down the hikers who found her so I could ask them exactly what it had been like to find her, but their names weren't in the news. Probably so they wouldn't have to talk to people like me.

"How's your car been running?" my dad asked, trying to pull me into conversation.

"Fine."

"No more issues?"

"Not really."

I didn't want to talk about my car. I wanted to talk about something that mattered, like why Lizzie chose to hang herself. It was supposed to be a really painful way to die. Since they'd found her, I'd done a lot of reading online. Had she done research too?

I couldn't shake the idea that she could have changed her mind—but she didn't. She made a decision and stuck with it. I guess she knew that if she could get through a bit more pain, then all the pain would end forever.

What if someone had stopped her? What if Enzo had woken up that night and followed her? Maybe Lizzie would have only put her suicide off until a later date. On the other hand, maybe he would have convinced her how much she had to live for. Not that Enzo was particularly great at dealing with tense situations.

What if *I* had been there? If I had just ten minutes with Lizzie, I could have told her how loved she was. That whatever she was going through would pass. That there was help out there, if only she was willing to ask for it. Lizzie would have probably looked at me and said, "Little Creely, you should take your own advice."

"Why don't we all say what we're thankful for this year?" my mom suggested.

That pulled me out of my thoughts and made the rest of the table go silent.

"No one really wants to do that, Mom," Rush said.

"Don't be silly. It'll be good for all of us."

"What if we're not thankful for anything?" I asked.

"Come on, Thorny," Connor said, "It's not *all* bad."

"Lizzie Lovett is dead."

"You hardly even knew her," he replied.

I could feel my family go still, probably because they'd all been thinking it but hadn't dared to say so.

"I wanted to know her though."

"No, you didn't," Connor said. "You wanted to know the werewolf version of her."

I looked around the table at my family. "I guess I'm thankful that someone I know will actually be blunt with me."

"Is that what you want?" my mom asked.

It wasn't about what I wanted. It was about what I deserved. But I didn't know how to say that, so I went back to poking at my turkey and listening to my dad talk about how he was thankful for his family and that we were safe and healthy and happy—for the most part.

✖ ✖ ✖

I'd thought doing research on suicide would make me feel better. That I'd find some answers or at least gain an understanding of what Lizzie was going through. But I'd read everything I could find about death by hanging and didn't feel any closer to the truth. All I'd managed to do was fill my head with enough gruesome information to last a lifetime.

The worst thing I read was that when a person hangs themselves, they're making a statement. It's not fast or painless. It's not a cry for help. They're trying to punish themselves or the person who finds them.

I didn't know if that was true, but it made me shudder. Why would Lizzie have wanted to punish herself? Why did she choose to end her life in such an agonizing way?

After Thanksgiving dinner, while my family and Connor were downstairs eating pumpkin pie, I hid in my room and thought about what it must be like to die, to make the decision to die, to know the exact time it was going to happen, to feel as if the pain of death didn't compare to the pain of living.

A colorful scarf was sitting on my desk, the scarf left behind by one of the hippies. I picked it up and tied a slip knot, another thing I'd learned while researching. I walked to the mirror and looked at myself. Pale, plain, dark circles under my eyes. I looked as dead as Lizzie. I put the scarf around my neck.

I reached behind me and tightened the noose, just to enough to be uncomfortable. Then I pulled it tighter. It surprised me that I could still breathe just fine. I expected to feel my throat closing, pushing all the air out of my body, but it wasn't like that at all. Instead, my head started to throb, pulsing in tune with my heartbeat. A warm tingly sensation started behind my eyes, and I got dizzy.

Then my door opened, and Rush leaned in, saying, "Hey, Mom wants to know if—what the fuck are you doing?"

I tore the scarf from my neck, and there was a sudden jolt in my head. "Nothing. Keep your voice down."

He strode into my room. "Are you out of your fucking mind?"

"I wasn't trying to *do* anything. I just wanted to see what it was like." I rubbed at my neck. It felt sore, and I hoped I hadn't held the scarf tight enough to leave a mark.

Rush's voice still seemed very loud. "This isn't a game."

"I know. I was just curious. Please don't say anything to Mom and Dad."

I could feel a headache starting. Was it from the scarf or the stress of my brother walking in at the worst possible moment?

"Promise me you weren't trying to hurt yourself."

"I promise. I just…" I started to tear up. "I just wanted to know what it was like for Lizzie at the end. I don't want to kill myself. I swear."

Rush sighed.

"Honest, Rush."

He held out his hand. "Give me the scarf."

"It's mine," I said, holding it to my chest. My last piece of the hippie caravan. But Rush continued to hold his hand out until I grudgingly passed the scarf to him.

"I never want to see anything like this again," he said.

"You won't."

He looked at me for a long time, like he still wasn't sure if he believed me. "You take everything too far, Hawthorn."

That was probably an accurate assessment of my character. Before I could tell him so, my mom appeared in the doorway.

"What are you two doing?" she asked. Then to Rush, "Did you ask Hawthorn if she wants to play Monopoly with us?"

"I did." Rush gave me a look. "She said she'd love to."

CHAPTER 34
WEAK, SELFISH, BROKEN

✳ ✳

The day they found Lizzie's body was the worst day. But the day after Thanksgiving came pretty close to beating it.

Christa and I were both working. Even Mr. Walczak was there to oversee the diner. He seemed to be expecting a big lunch rush, like people would be craving scrambled eggs from the Sunshine Café after they finished their Black Friday shopping. That didn't exactly happen, but to his credit, we were busier than usual.

In between waiting tables, Christa told me all about her family's Thanksgiving. Her younger sister got into a huge fight with her fiancé about the wedding cookie table, and their grandfather got drunk and kept saying the food was overcooked, which made her mom cry, and her youngest cousin announced that she was dropping out of school and moving to New York to become an actress. It seemed chaotic in a totally normal, comforting way.

"And then," she said, as we passed each other in the kitchen doorway, "my sister said maybe she should call off the entire wedding, which made my mom just about lose it."

I laughed and carried food to an elderly couple in the dining room. As I was asking if there was anything else they needed, the bell on the door jingled. I turned to greet the new customers, and for a second, it was as if the whole world stopped.

Mychelle Adler walked into the café, her shark smile on her face. And two feet behind her, sheepish, hands in his pockets, was Enzo.

From the corner of my eye, I could see Christa come out of the kitchen, tray in hand. She stopped too, her mouth an O of surprise. Even Vernon seemed alert in his place at the counter, waiting to see what would happen next.

Then the world rushed back to life. There was movement and sound, and I knew Christa was starting to tell me she'd handle it, but it was too late. My feet were already moving in their direction.

"Mychelle," I said, sounding calmer than I felt. "I didn't think you ate at this sort of place."

"I make exceptions sometimes. And I know Lorenzo enjoys eating here." She reached behind her and grabbed Enzo's arm, pulling him next to her.

"How nice of you to look out for *Lorenzo's* feelings."

"We shouldn't have come," Enzo mumbled, and I didn't know if he was talking to me or Mychelle.

"Nonsense," Mychelle said. "I'm sure Hawthorn's been dying to see you."

Enzo shifted his gaze to me, and I looked back. I wasn't about to duck my head or scamper away.

"How have you been?" I asked.

"OK. You?"

"OK."

And that was it. After everything that had happened between us, that was all we had to say to each other. I was sad in a way I'd never felt before, like part of myself was being torn away violently.

For the past few months, I'd spent almost all my free time with Enzo. I'd told him everything I was thinking and feeling and obsessively looked for clues about what was happening in his mind. Enzo made me happy and angry and relaxed and frustrated and every other emotion that one person could make another person feel. Sometimes, I hated him, and sometimes, I thought I could love him. He gave me the only perfect-fireworks-movie kiss I'd ever had. I gave him my virginity. And now he was standing in front of me with my nemesis hanging on his arm and acting as if he never knew me at all.

"I guess we'll seat ourselves," Mychelle said.

Enzo pulled his arm out of her grip. "We should go."

"But I'm hungry."

"I'm not," Enzo said. "I'll wait in the car. Later, Hawthorn."

He walked out the door, already pulling his tobacco out of his pocket.

"Well," I said to Mychelle after the bell jingled again. "Did you accomplish what you wanted to?"

"I guess I did." Mychelle grinned at me, and for the first time in my life, I had to restrain myself from throwing a punch.

"So someone upsets you, and you steal their boyfriend to get back at them. I guess the joke is on you. Enzo and I weren't dating."

Mychelle laughed. "That much is clear. It seems to me Lorenzo was done with you after you bled all over his sheets. Figures you were a virgin."

I bit down on the inside of my cheek and willed myself not to react. Because the only thing worse than Mychelle's comment would be her knowing how much it stung.

"Isn't that a lot of effort just to mess with me?"

"I don't think of it that way. There are rules, Hawthorn. You forgot them. I'm just reminding you of your place."

"Which is where exactly?"

"Wherever I want it to be."

I managed to laugh at that one, but only because I knew it would make Mychelle angry. "You know, I can't wait until we're out of high school and no one cares about you anymore. It must suck to know that your life is never going to be better than it is right now."

I saw the flash of anger in Mychelle's eye.

"Don't worry," she said, her grin pulling her skin too tight. "I have no intentions of turning into Lizzie Lovett."

She turned and left the diner. For a moment, everyone was silent, and I realized how loud we must have been. We'd caused a scene. Then Vernon said, "An' good riddance to ya!"

There were laughs all over the diner, and everyone went back to eating. Knives scraped plates, coffee mugs were picked up then set down, and bags rustled as people looked at what they'd purchased.

Christa came over to me. "Are you OK?"

"I don't think so," I said.

"Maybe you should go home."

I thought that was an excellent idea.

✭✭✭

At first, I was fine. I turned on the radio as loud as I could stand and focused on the road. I tried to keep my mind blank.

But I wasn't even halfway home when I started crying, and once I started, I couldn't stop. The road blurred, and I had to pull over. I leaned against my steering wheel and sobbed. I didn't care if people in other cars could see me, didn't care if everyone else in the entire world knew that it felt like someone was ripping my insides in half. Everyone except for Mychelle Adler, that was. And Enzo. Weak, selfish Enzo Calvetti. The two of them deserved each other.

After a while, I calmed down enough to drive, though I sniffled the whole way home. I was pretty sure I'd cried more in the past two weeks than I had in my entire life up to then. I couldn't help it though. Enzo had taken my heart out of my body and was slowly crushing it under his shoe, the way he put out a cigarette. Had he crushed Lizzie's heart like that too? Did that have anything to do with why she walked into the woods and never came out?

There wasn't anyone at my house. For once, I wished for

family. I didn't want to be alone. I imagined Mychelle would be smug about it. "See," she'd say, "even Hawthorn's family doesn't want to be around her."

Enzo, Sundog, even Lizzie in a way. Everyone was leaving me. I felt as alone as a guy in a zombie movie who goes outside to discover his city is ravaged and he's the only survivor.

Except not *everyone* was lost to me.

I went to my room and found my phone, which still had a tiny bit of charge left. Emily picked up on the first ring.

"Can we talk?" I asked.

She told me she'd be right over.

★★★

I spent a lot of time crying, and Emily spent a lot of time trying to make me feel better.

Eventually, my sobs turned into gasps and hiccups, and I was able to start talking. So I told her everything.

"God," Emily said, "Mychelle is such a bitch."

"I hate her."

"If it makes you feel any better, I don't think she was after revenge. I think she was jealous."

I wondered if Emily was feeling OK, because she sure wasn't having coherent thoughts. "You think Mychelle Adler was jealous of *me*?"

"That kiss. The way you described it. I think it got to her."

"Why?"

"How many kisses like that do you think Mychelle has had?" Emily asked.

"Like, a million?"

"Yeah, right. Guys kiss Mychelle for one reason, and it has nothing to do with romance."

It was a little crazy to think about. That while you were envying other people, they could be envying you too. It reminded me of something Connor had said, about life looking different depending on where you were standing.

"What about *him*?" I asked. "What's Enzo doing with her?"

"I doubt Enzo could even answer that. He's so broken, Hawthorn."

Emily and I sat on my bed and talked and talked, and it was no different from every time we'd ever hung out, every sleepover we'd ever had. Except I'd never been so miserable before.

"You can say 'I told you so' if you want," I said.

But she didn't. Instead, she talked about how everything was going to be OK. Some of what she said was probably true, and some was probably to calm me down, but I appreciated it either way.

"I feel so stupid," I said. "She was dead the whole time, Emily. From the very start."

And then I cried again.

"Look, you made a mistake. Yeah, you should have known better. But it happened, and it's over, and there's nothing you can do about it now. You just have to move forward."

"I can't. I can't deal with all of this."

"You can," Emily said. "You will."

"Lizzie couldn't. She gave up."

"You're stronger than Lizzie."

That seemed absurd. How could I be more *anything* than Lizzie? Lizzie was perfect. Lizzie had everything. She *was* everything.

"Why do you think she did it?" I asked quietly.

Emily shrugged. "I don't know. I don't think we'll ever know."

"It's weird. After all this time searching for her and trying to understand her life, I *still* don't feel like I know her. Everyone I talked to saw her as a totally different person. And I thought it was intentional. Like Lizzie changed personalities depending on who she was with. But now, I don't know."

Emily thought about it for a moment. "Maybe people saw her the way they wanted to see her. Maybe that's how it always is."

If that was the case, I wondered how people saw me. How many different versions of Hawthorn Creely were out there in the world, living in people's heads? How close were any of them to the actual me?

"If that's true, then no one ever really knows anyone else. Not completely."

"Maybe that's OK," Emily said.

Maybe. But maybe if someone had known Lizzie, really understood her, maybe she could have been saved.

"It's so sad," I said. "Lizzie had, like, a billion people who loved her and wanted to be around her. But in the end, she was as alone as the rest of us."

Emily laughed. "Hawthorn, you're not alone."

I looked at Emily. As always, she was right. When I needed her, all I had to do was pick up the phone and call. Emily didn't share all of my interests or condone all of my actions, but that didn't make her any less of a friend.

"Thanks," I said.

"For what?"

"For being here." I paused, thinking of what Emily had said to me during our fight. "How have *you* been, Em?"

She tilted her head and gazed at me like I'd asked her a trick question. "I've been good," she said cautiously.

"What's been going on with you? I want to know everything I missed."

"Even the stuff about Logan?" she asked, raising her eyebrows.

"*Especially* the stuff about Logan." I grinned. "Has he talked you into any tattoos yet?"

Emily laughed and threw a pillow at me.

"Come on," I said. "Certainly something fascinating has happened in the past few weeks."

"Are you sure you want to talk about this right now?"

"Positive," I said.

"Well," Emily started, still a little hesitant, "I told you about the music program."

I nodded and settled myself more comfortably on the bed. I couldn't bring Lizzie back to life. I couldn't make Mychelle less horrible or make Enzo into the person I wanted him to be.

But my friendship with Emily was something I had control over. I could be there for her, the same way she was there for me. For once, I could shut up and listen.

CHAPTER 35

IN THE WOODS, AGAIN

✻ ✻

I waited until the first big snow to return to the woods. It was way later than usual. We'd had flurries, but none of it stuck. Fall seemed to last forever, the trees barren except for the few leaves still managing to hold on, poised in some terrible in-between.

But one morning, I woke up to snow falling and collecting on the ground. I was ready for it. I grabbed my bag and left the house, careful not to wake my family.

I went to Lizzie and Enzo's campsite first. I still thought of it that way, as belonging to them, even though I'd been there more with Enzo than Lizzie had. We had talked there and plotted there and fought there and kissed there. But it was the last place Lizzie and Enzo were together before she died, and that overrode all of the time he and I had spent there.

I unzipped my bag, took out a map, and spread it on the flat rock where Enzo and I used to sit and talk. I was just stalling. I didn't need the map. I'd already traced the path a thousand times. I knew where to go and how to get there. It was pretty much impossible to not know.

That's the thing about high school. Even social outcasts can't help but overhear gossip. Like how kids were already daring each other to go out in the woods in the middle of the night, to the place where Lizzie killed herself. It was turning into another site on the Griffin Mills haunted tour. First stop, the Griffin Mansion; next up, the Lizzie Lovett suicide grove. With an extra reputation boost for anyone brave enough to stay there all night.

Pretty soon, it would be like Lizzie had never been a real person at all.

If Enzo were there, I could have told him it scared me how Lizzie was already becoming irrelevant. He would have understood. He would have turned my feelings into a painting, allowing me to distance myself from them.

Or maybe he would have made everything more complicated.

I folded the map and set off.

When Lizzie had walked through the woods, there hadn't been a path. But with so many people trampling through during the past month, a trail was starting to form.

I wished I had been the first to follow her. But my feet stepped in the same places hers had, and my clothes got snagged on the same underbrush. I tried to see the woods the way she would have on the night she died.

What had she been thinking when she walked through the trees? Was she scared? Was she sad? Was she happy that she was making her escape?

When I found out about Lizzie, it was the first time I considered that I was eventually going to die. I was going to die, and so were my parents and my brother and my friends and everyone in the world. Death is the only thing in life that's for sure going to happen. Didn't someone famous say that once? It's true. One day, we'll all die.

It was the mystery of death that I found most awful. Will it be fast or slow? Will you be young or old? Will it be easy or painful? There were so many ways to die. Accidents and sicknesses and even more terrible ways, like murder. Leaving your house is dangerous. Staying inside is dangerous. The odds are against everyone, and it seemed like dumb luck so many people stuck around for eighty or so years. And that bothered me.

I was going to die. But I didn't know when.

What if Lizzie thought the same thing? What if that was part of why she killed herself? Maybe she hated being out of control, knowing that someone or something else was dictating her fate. Because it's really not fair. A drunk driver runs a red light, and you end up dead. A guy in a movie theater coughs on you, and you catch some rare, fatal disease. You sit in class minding your own business, and there's the kid from sixth period holding a gun in his hand. Why should other people be in control? Why should someone else get to choose when you die?

Maybe Lizzie decided the world was crazy, and it was always going to be crazy, and there was nothing she could do about it. But her death? That was another story. That was something she could control. She could beat everyone to it, do it her way.

On the other hand, I'd learned from Enzo's stories that sometimes it's better not knowing the ending. The most magical part of life is the mystery. When she killed herself, Lizzie gave that up.

The path I was on was hard to navigate, and when Lizzie walked there at the end of summer, it would have been even more overgrown. And she did it in the dark. Did she have a spot already picked out? Or did she just walk until she was too tired to go any farther? How did she manage to take step after step, knowing what waited for her at the end?

I heard a noise behind me, something like a twig snapping. I scanned the woods. Nothing was there. Unless it was Lizzie's ghost.

What about ghosts? And what about heaven? Did Lizzie believe in it? Most religions consider suicide a sin, so Lizzie probably wasn't religious. But did that mean she didn't believe in the afterlife at all?

I wasn't too sure about the afterlife either. My dad always said that he didn't know one way or another, but he wasn't going to worry about it while he was still alive. My mom would say people have different beliefs about where we go when we die, and maybe everyone is right in their own way. I wished I knew what Lizzie believed. I wished I'd asked Enzo. But why would I have? I thought we were chasing a werewolf, not a dead girl.

It crossed my mind that I might not know the spot when I got there. Maybe I would walk past it and go deeper and deeper into the woods until I was hopelessly lost, more lost than Lizzie. But I didn't need to worry. After hiking down a steep ravine—where I was very aware of the danger of slipping and breaking a leg—I saw a piece of crime scene tape still tied to a tree.

I froze and sucked in my breath. I'd sought out the site of Lizzie's death, but I hadn't anticipated how much it would hurt to actually *be* there. It was like being punched in the stomach.

The woods around me weren't special. There was nothing to indicate why Lizzie had chosen that spot for her last moments. I looked around for anything she might have left behind—an earring that had fallen out, a shoe that had been kicked off. But there was nothing. I wasn't even sure which tree was The Tree.

The woods had swallowed Lizzie's secrets. She had lived, and she had died, and now, there was no trace of her. Elizabeth Lovett was just a name in a newspaper article, a statistic, someone people used to know.

Another *crack* came from behind me. It sounded like a bone snapping, something crawling out of a grave. I spun around, part of me expecting to see Lizzie, purple skin and ligature marks around her neck, asking me why I was disturbing her.

But it wasn't Lizzie. It was my brother.

"Rush? What are you doing here?"

"I'd like to know the same thing about you."

For a moment, we stared at each other, the snow falling softly around us. Rush was the one who spoke first.

"I heard you sneaking around the house. So I followed you."

"Why?"

He shifted back and forth, for once looking as awkward as I usually felt. "I've been worried. Ever since Thanksgiving. With the scarf."

"You think I came here to kill myself?" I asked, surprised. Though after a moment of consideration, I realized my behavior *had* been pretty suspicious.

Rush shrugged.

"I'm not suicidal," I assured him.

"So what are you doing out here?"

"I needed to see the tree. You know. The one she hanged from."

"That's morbid."

It was my turn to shrug. "I guess it is. I just needed some closure."

"So which tree is it?"

"I don't know. I thought I'd be able to tell."

Rush sat down in the dirt and leaves and snow. I sat next to him. We looked at the trees together in silence, trying to pick out the same one as Lizzie, the tree that was special enough to die beneath.

"I wanted to be close to her for a little while," I said. "And the snow...maybe it seems stupid, but snow makes everything feel safe and clean."

"Snow is a symbol for purity, if you can trust my community college English lit professor anyway."

We both laughed at that, louder than we should have, because it wasn't really that funny. But it was like being scared of the dark. With a little light, the shadows disappeared, and your surroundings weren't so frightening.

"I brought these," I said. I reached into my backpack and took out a stack of photos. The photos Enzo wanted to turn into art.

Rush flipped through the pictures. "Where'd you get these?"

"I took them from Enzo's."

"Don't you think he might want them? Especially now?"

"Enzo doesn't deserve them. I want to leave them here. Like a memorial."

So Rush helped me arrange the photos in an arc on the ground. I knew the snow would ruin them and the wind would scatter them. By next summer, by the anniversary of Lizzie's death, the photos would be unrecognizable. That was OK though. The place where Lizzie died now held a small glimmer of her life, and that was enough. A moment is all any of us has, really.

"Why do you think she did it?" I asked Rush.

"I don't know. Maybe there wasn't some big reason. Maybe she was just unhappy."

"She didn't seem like an unhappy person."

"I saw her crying once," Rush said. "I'd left the locker room after everyone else, and Lizzie was in the hallway crying. She must have thought no one was around."

"People cry all the time. That doesn't mean they're suicidal."

"It wasn't that. When she saw me, she just stopped. Like, from sobbing to perfectly OK in two seconds. I asked her what was wrong, and she told me it was nothing, that she was just being dumb. Then we left for a party, and she seemed happy for the rest of the night. But I always wondered, if she could turn her feelings off like a switch, how much was she hiding from us? It made her seem mysterious. Which is stupid. She wasn't mysterious; she was depressed."

Could the answer be as easy as that? The person I'd admired and hated and envied and compared myself to for years was depressed. I looked down at the pictures of Lizzie. One of the versions of Lizzie anyway. I'd assumed she switched personalities to put on fronts for other people, but maybe she'd actually been lying to *herself*. Hoping that if she reinvented herself enough times, one day, she'd become a Lizzie Lovett who wasn't deeply unhappy.

"I shouldn't have believed her," Rush said. "I should have made her talk to me. Maybe things would be different now."

"I doubt there was anything you could have done."

"I guess we'll never know." He looked at the pictures of Lizzie for a little while, then back at me. "Everyone's worried about you, you know."

"By everyone, you mean Mom and Dad?"

"And me. Don't I count?"

I shrugged.

"Connor keeps asking about you," Rush said.

"He does?"

"Half the time, I think he uses me as an excuse to see you."

I raised my eyebrows at that unexpected bit of information.

"You need to let go of this thing with Lizzie," Rush said. "Stop obsessing over her. Stop wishing you had her life. Even Lizzie didn't want to be Lizzie."

A month ago, I wouldn't have believed him. I thought Lizzie had been born with some magical luck that I missed out on. I wasn't so sure of that anymore. Maybe the luckiest people are the ones who know that no matter how bad things seem, there's always something to live for.

"Do you think I'm horrible?" I asked.

"What? Why?"

"For the whole werewolf thing."

"No," Rush said. "You're not horrible."

He put his arm around me and pulled me close, the way he used to when we were little kids and he thought it was his job to protect me from the rest of the world.

I felt safe. Out there in the woods, where a girl had killed herself, during the first snow of the season, sitting next to my big brother, who was doing his best to look out for me, I felt safe and content. For the first time in a long time, I felt like maybe, probably, everything was going to be OK.

CHAPTER 36

AND LIFE WENT ON

L izzie was dead, but life went on. That's what I found out
that winter.

Sometimes, it felt like Lizzie sucked all the magic out of the
world when she died. Out of my world, at least. And sometimes,
that made me think there wasn't any point to anything. On those
days, I would curl up in bed until one of my parents or Rush
dragged me out. But even then, even on those bad days, I had no
desire to join Lizzie. I was sad but not ready to give up.

Life went on at school, and life went on out of school. I
studied for midterms and went Christmas shopping and wiped
down tables at the café before I closed up. I did most of that stuff
by myself, but that was OK. I was alone, but for once, I didn't
feel lonely.

My brother spent a lot of time trying to entertain me that
winter. Every few days, he'd stick his head in my room and ask
"What about seeing a movie tonight?" or "Some people are going
sledding. You want to come?" When school let out for winter

break, I finally told him he didn't need to babysit me. He said he wasn't—he just wanted to hang out. I didn't know if he was telling the truth, but it made me feel good.

I tried not to care about Lizzie, but no one in the history of the world has ever gotten over Lizzie Lovett easily. Sometimes, late at night, I would look out the window at the icy road and bare trees and imagine Lizzie's ghost walking into my yard. She'd be pale and wearing white, and her hair would blend in with the snow. She would stop under my window and look up at me and smile that knowing half smile, the one that looked haunted even when she was alive. And I would run outside to her, and I'd be shivering from the cold, and she wouldn't be, and I would say, "Just tell me why."

I only wanted one conversation. One hour. I wanted to ask why she did it, what about the world seemed so terrible that she had to leave it. I wanted to tell her there were so many people who would have tried to save her if she would have let them. I wanted to tell her how much I'd hated her and loved her, even though I never knew her at all—but that I would have done whatever I could to help her.

But Lizzie wasn't ever coming back. I knew I had to learn to be OK with that.

I thought about Enzo sometimes too. Even if I wanted to forget him, Mychelle wouldn't let me. All through first period, I had to listen to what they'd done the night before. One morning, she even slipped a photo of them kissing into my locker. It was a sloppy photo, way too close, with tongues and spit. My first instinct was to tear it up, but I submitted it for the year-book instead.

Mychelle slowly started talking about Enzo less and less, until she stopped mentioning him at all. Then, the day of midterms, I saw her making out in the cafeteria with Noah Ridgeway, the freshman quarterback. I waited for her at her locker after school.

"A freshman, huh?" I said by way of greeting. "It's only midterm, and you've already exhausted your options in the senior, junior, *and* sophomore classes?"

Mychelle brushed past me and opened her locker. "I don't know what you're talking about."

"I guess Enzo was way too old for you. What is he, ten years older than Noah?"

Mychelle stopped rooting through her locker and looked at me coldly. "What do you want?"

"I want to know what it feels like."

"What *what* feels like?"

"You gave yourself to Enzo to mess with me. You didn't actually like him, right? How many people have you slept with just to get what you want? And how do you think those guys feel about you when they realize what a manipulative bitch you are?"

Mychelle slammed her locker shut and started to walk away.

"That's what I wanted to know," I called after her, not caring about the crowd that was starting to form. "What's it feel like to be a regret?"

She didn't answer, of course. But as I was leaving school, Ronna Barnes, who looked ready to go into labor at any second, told me she'd seen Mychelle crying in the bathroom, and that everyone was talking about what I'd said. It was the sort of thing you think will make you feel awesome but instead leaves you empty and as awful as the person you're putting down.

That's why I figured it was time for me to stop thinking about Mychelle Adler. Which I was mostly successful at. It wasn't so easy with Enzo though. I felt sort of bad for him, even though the thing with Mychelle was his own fault. And for all I knew, he'd been the one to break it off with her, not the other way around. Maybe after Lizzie, Mychelle, and me, he'd had his share of crazy girls.

Either way, life went on.

But it didn't go on for everyone. Christa called me two days after Christmas and told me about the obituary. I went to the computer and looked up the Layton newspaper. It was there, just like she said. Vernon Miles, age eighty-one, passed away from health complications.

I cried because he had died, and because the obituary mentioned how much he enjoyed doing puzzles, and because up until that point, I hadn't even known his last name.

I thought for sure that by the day of his funeral, my tears would have all dried up, but they hadn't. The service was in the little chapel adjacent to the cemetery, and only about a dozen people attended. Christa and I stood together, and she passed me tissues from a seemingly never-ending supply in her purse.

I cried for Vernon, but I also cried for Lizzie. I cried because I had been too weak and scared to go to her funeral, even though I'd really wanted to. I cried because I knew there had been a hundred people saying good-bye to Lizzie, but Vernon, someone who lived such a long life, barely had ten. And two of those people were waitresses from a diner he hung out at.

An elderly woman, Vernon's sister, hugged Christa and me before we left and said, "It would have meant so much to him that you came."

I guess that's just the way it is. Sometimes, there are things that are really hard to do, and it sucks the whole time you're doing them. But you also know it's the right thing, and you might be making a huge difference for someone else.

While we were walking to our cars, Christa asked me if I wanted to get some coffee. "It'd be nice to drink coffee with you instead of serving it to other people."

"Yeah," I said. "That would be nice."

So we went across the street to a little café. As we sipped our drinks, I thought about how normal it was. The sun was shining, and the coffee was steaming, and Christa and I were talking and laughing. It was simple. It was easy. It was perfect.

And life went on.

CHAPTER 37

THE LAST THING

✳ ✳

The last thing that happened was a walk in the snow. Which doesn't seem like a big deal, not after everything else, but it was actually totally interesting. The walk made me realize that in real life, there isn't actually a *last thing*. Nothing ends; it just turns into a different story.

But I'm probably getting ahead of myself and skipping all over the place, which I'm trying to stop.

So the end, which wasn't really an end at all, happened like this:

Sundog had a PO box in Texas. That's where I sent the letters I wrote him. I'd started putting all my feelings on paper, just like he'd told me to. I knew the letters would stack up before Sundog was in Texas and got them. I wasn't sure he'd even read them. But in a way, that made it easier for me to be honest.

I was in the middle of writing one of those letters, writing about how Emily had started eating lunch with me again sometimes, and how one day, Ronna Barnes even joined us, when there was a knock on the front door.

"Rush isn't home," I told Connor.

"I actually came to see you."

I was pretty sure I did a terrible job hiding my surprise.

"Are you busy?" he asked.

I shook my head. Sundog could wait.

Connor looked sort of bashful, which was not an expression I was used to seeing on his all-American-boy face. He pulled a tiny, black key chain and a small box with a button on it from his pocket.

"I did this final project for my electronics class. We had to make something that helped people in their day-to-day lives. And, well, there were a few times I was over here, and you couldn't find your keys. That gave me the idea. See, you attach this piece to your key chain. This other part has a button, and when you press it…" He pressed the button, and the key chain piece started beeping.

"That's totally awesome. Can I look at it?" I asked, holding out a hand.

"Actually, it's for you. You inspired me to make it, so I figured you should have it."

"Really?"

Connor nodded and handed me the device.

"Now I need to make sure I don't lose *this*," I said, holding up the box with the button.

"You know, I didn't really think about that."

We both laughed, then Connor said, "You want to take a walk or something?"

"It's freezing."

"Oh, come on. Like walking in the snow is the craziest thing you've ever done."

He had a point. I got my jacket.

We talked about regular things while we walked, like what we'd gotten for Christmas, and what classes he was taking next semester, and how I still didn't know what I wanted to do after high school, but I wasn't filled with dread at the thought of the future. I was surprised at how normal the whole thing felt.

"There was an article in the paper the other day about a bridge in New Philadelphia," Connor said. "It's supposed to be haunted. Made me think of you."

"I don't believe in ghosts," I told him.

"Since when?"

I thought about saying *since I stopped believing in werewolves*, but I just shrugged.

"Thorny, we both know you're lying."

"I'm not."

"So you've never had a single ghostly encounter?"

I knew Connor was teasing me, but it wasn't mean. It wasn't in the brotherly way Rush teased me either.

"I guess maybe one time," I said, and it made Connor laugh.

I told him about the house in the woods, the one where Enzo and I'd heard noises in the basement.

"You ever think of going back there? Finding out what it was?" he asked.

"Are you offering to go with me?"

"Sure. Why not?"

I thought about it for a minute. We could get in the car and go to the house and find out if there was really someone or something there. Maybe it was a monster. Maybe it was a serial killer. But maybe it was a bum, or a raccoon, or nothing at all.

"Nah," I said finally. "It's better if it's a mystery."

As long as something was a mystery, there was still the potential for amazement. Maybe that's where I went wrong before. Some riddles weren't meant be solved.

"Do you think there's magic?" I asked Connor.

"Sure. I mean, not like wizards and crystal balls or anything. But I think there are things in the world that shouldn't be able to happen but happen anyway."

"Good."

Connor grinned at me. I smiled back. He was my older brother's friend. I was just a kid to him. Or maybe not.

We walked down the snowy street, sometimes talking and sometimes being quiet. Sometimes, our hands bumped together by accident, but neither of us moved away.

It was January, the beginning of a new year, and it felt like a fresh start. My life was changing, but for once, that was a good thing. I felt like I was seeing the world more clearly. I knew that even though someone seemed perfect, it didn't mean they weren't hurting inside. And that our lives are only as good as we make them. And that there probably weren't any werewolves.

But it didn't take a girl turning into a wolf to make the world magical. If I kept looking, I'd always find new and fascinating adventures.

And in the future, I wouldn't jump to conclusions or share far-fetched theories without having supporting evidence. I'd think before I spoke. I'd look for magic but wouldn't invent it. I would be smart. I would be logical. I would act like an adult.

At least, I would try to.

I'd give it a really good attempt.

Maybe. Probably.

ACKNOWLEDGMENTS

Sometimes I wish I could be a hermit writer and live in a cabin in the woods with zero human contact. But the truth is, this book wouldn't exist if it weren't for the help of so many amazing people.

This is the part where I get to gush about them.

Before I started querying, I had a list of "dream agents." Suzie Townsend was at the top of it. Suzie, the reality of working with you is even better than I'd imagined. Thank you for your passion, your hard work, and for being my champion through every stage of this process. In addition, thank you to all the wonderful people at New Leaf Literary, with a special shout-out to Sara Stricker, Kathleen Ortiz, Mia Roman, Chris McEwen, Pouya Shahbazian, and Hilary Pecheone.

The brilliant insights of my editor, Annette Pollert-Morgan, have both improved this book and, as a whole, made me a better writer. Thank you for falling in love with Hawthorn and for being as excited to share her story as I am. And a huge thanks to the entire Sourcebooks team. I'm so grateful for the opportunity to work with such a warm, dedicated, enthusiastic group of people.

My local critique group, especially Aileen, Becky, Bill, Carlos, Chris H., Chris M., Elizabeth, JJ, Mary, Mandy, Paul, Rachel, and Raz. Not only have you helped me grow as a writer, you inspire me with your own stories every week. Thank you for Monday nights filled with shape-shifting starfish, human remains in bowling bags, singing cockroaches, and all sorts of other awesome weirdness.

The r/YAwriters crew: Alexa, Anna, Caitie, Greg, Jason, Jess, Jo, Josh, Katelyn, Katie, Kristine, Leann, Morgan, Phil, and Rachel. Thank you for feedback, for advice, for support, for laughter, for cogs, for The Line. I'd be lost without all of you.

Thank you to the Swanky Seventeen debut group. This publishing journey is so wonderfully bizarre, and I'm lucky to be on it with such kind, encouraging, and talented writers.

Joanna Farrow, a.k.a. the ghost in my attic, a.k.a. the first person not related to me who read this book. Thank you for your wisdom, for knowing when I need cookies, and for being so much more than just a critique partner.

Thank you to Dan O'Sullivan for spending hours talking writing with me and for reading and critiquing an early draft of this book. And for, along with Bobby Hicks, inadvertently giving me the idea for Hawthorn's curses.

There's a card from Anna Priemaza taped to my fridge that says,

"You can do it!" Anna, thank you for reminding me of this a billion times and for regularly pushing me outside my comfort zone.

Thank you to Evan Sedoti for making this one of the three books he's willingly read; Susan Schoonover-Arguelles, who after a lifetime of friendship, has put up with more crazy scheming from me than Emily has from Hawthorn; Lucy Sanchez for insights into high school life and hippie wisdom; my dad for giving me his dark sense of humor; my entire extended family for always being ridiculously supportive; and Steve Conger for getting excited about this book when it was only a vague idea (also, for werewolf hunting with me).

For years my mom told me I should write a novel. Thank you for encouraging such an impossible-seeming dream, and for raising me to believe I could become anything I wanted to be. The pride I hear in your voice when you tell people about this book means everything to me.

My incredible husband, Steve Phillips, contributed more to this novel than I could possibly list here. Thank you for believing in me when I didn't believe in myself, for understanding when I ignored the real world for a make-believe one, and, on all those occasions I wanted to throw this book in the trash, for telling me to stop being melodramatic and keep writing.

Lastly, thank you to Joanna Bruzzese. When we were little kids, she was the first person to read my stories. She always insisted I'd be a "real" writer one day. More than anything, I wish she was here so I could hand her this book and say, "Look, Jo, you were right. I did it."

ABOUT THE AUTHOR

Chelsea Sedoti fell in love with writing at a young age after discovering that making up stories was more fun than doing her schoolwork. (Her teachers didn't always appreciate this.) In an effort to avoid getting a "real" job, Chelsea explored careers as a balloon twister, filmmaker, and paranormal investigator. Eventually she realized that her true passion is writing about flawed teenagers who are also afraid of growing up. When she's not at the computer, Chelsea spends her time exploring abandoned buildings, eating junk food at roadside diners, and trying to befriend every animal in the world. She lives in Las Vegas, Nevada, where she avoids casinos but loves roaming the Mojave Desert. To read more about her adventures, visit chelseasedoti.com.